Sword of the Voivode

T. G. JOYE

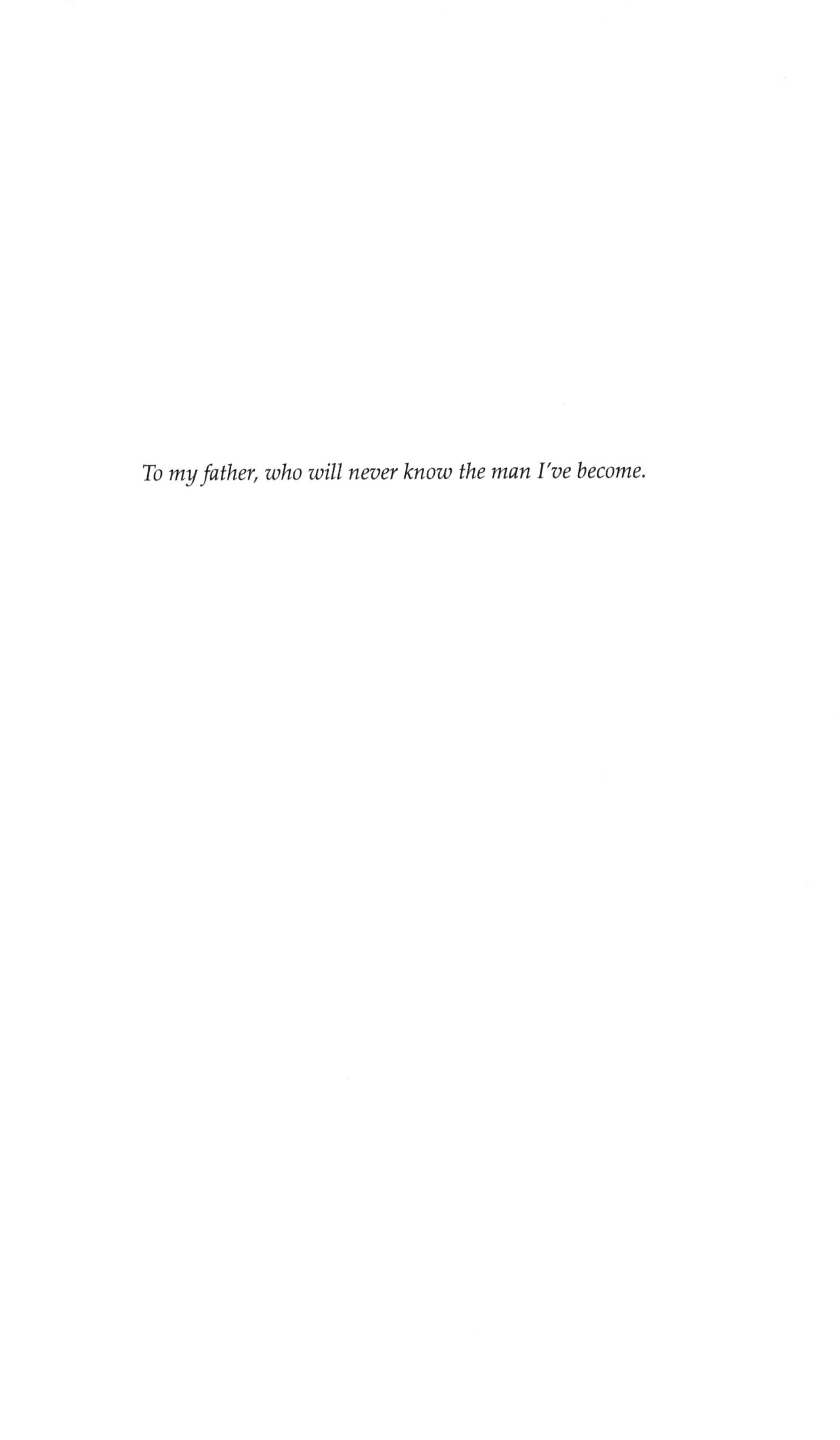

To my father, who will never know the man I've become.

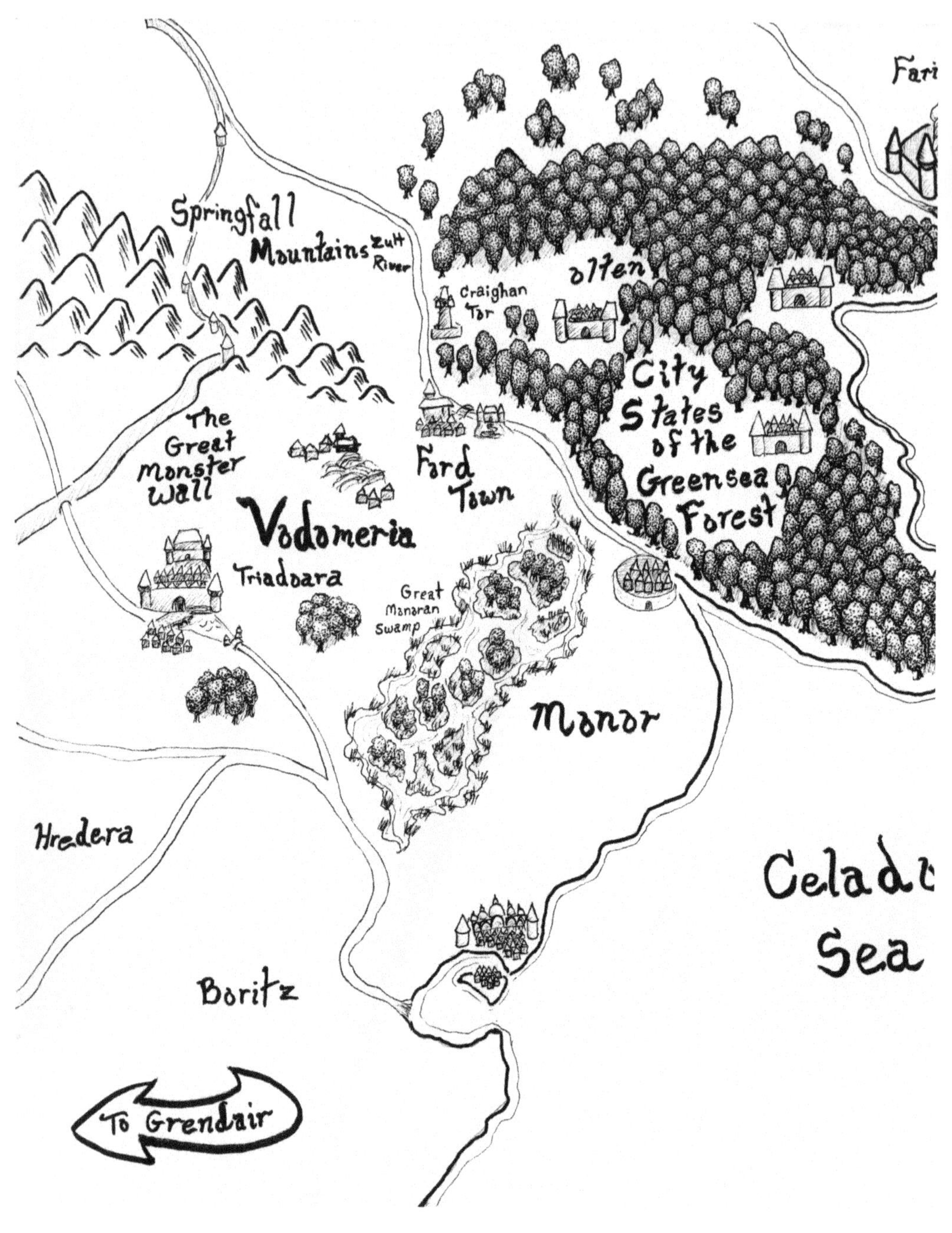

Fari
Springfall
Mountains
Zuft River
Craighan Tor
Olten
City States of the Greensea Forest
The Great monster Wall
Vodomeria
Triadoara
Fard Town
Great Manaran Swamp
Hredera
Manor
Celad
Sea
Boritz
To Grendair

zhniv
Farizhniya
Great Khanate
Grasslands
Thornback Mountains
Vuretsiv
Dry Plains
Shining Sultanate
n

Glossary

Animalis: Animal-like people only found within the borders of the former Finndrigairian Empire. Animalis come in three distinct types: Cat-bodied Felis, Bear-bodied Ursus, and Wolf-bodied Lupines. Outside of their animal characteristics, the Animalis are just as intelligent as humans and ogres.

Boyar: Landed aristocracy.

Inferni: Insect-like metallic monsters that plague the Great Monster Wall Region. While they come in several forms, Devil Ants are the most common type sighted around the Great Monster Wall and the surrounding area.

Tsar/Tsardom/Tsarevich: The modern translation for Tsar is Grand Duke. A Tsardom is a country ruled by a Tsar. A Tsarevich is the son of a Tsar.

Voivode/Voivodate: The modern translation is 'Duke'. A Voivodate is a country ruled by a Voivode.

One

"LOOKING FORWARD TO THE SUMMER MARKET?" Dan asked as he idly polished Cyril's prized possessions to a high shine.

"I'll be too busy to enjoy the bulk of it." Cyril shrugged, distracted by his thoughts as they wandered to other business.

Ford Town's Summer Market lasted two months and it coincided with the Feast of Saint Vodomor, patron saint of Vodomeria. The combined market and festival crowds made it the busiest two months of the year for Keepers of the Peace like Cyril. He'd mediate disagreements and help merchants resolve disputes so the town Guard could keep travelers safe from bandits and handle other violent crimes around the Novadi fief. As hectic and frustrating as the work could be, Cyril found bringing people together to settle their differences with words rather than fists personally gratifying.

It was a sight better than his old job as a sword for hire, at least. While he worked as a mercenary, it took him places he'd only ever dreamed he'd visit. However, it wasn't a business where one could form strong bonds with other people. Cyril forced his attention back to the task at hand. Dan finished polishing his old blade and deftly placed it back into its scabbard, along with the matching dagger.

"These are fine enough blades," Dan said, and handed them back to Cyril, "But they've seen a lot of combat. Why not replace them? You could get the finest steel the Tsardom—or even the Sultanate—has to offer right here in Ford Town."

Cyril frowned at Dan's question. "They're a family heirloom," he half-lied. "I can't just get rid of them!"

Dan flinched a little at Cyril's sharp response. "I didn't mean to offend, friend. I should have known they were special to you with the way you care for them." He held aloft a worn hammer for Cyril to inspect. "This is the first hammer I ever made. It's not perfect, but it's special to me." He chuckled and tucked the little hammer back into his belt. "If you ever need to replace your blade, I hope you'll speak with me first so I can point you to a fine blade smith!"

Cyril thanked Dan, paid him for his work, took his leave and left the smithy.

The blades had once belonged to Cyril's father, and while Cyril wasn't overly fond of his sire, he still treasured them. He'd been fascinated by the stories tied to them as a child, and he felt honored to have been given the blades, even if he'd received them under unusual circumstances. He simply wasn't yet ready to part with these old weapons. They were the sole material connection Cyril had to his old life, outside of his uncanny resemblance to his father.

A man with Cyril's looks would have no trouble finding a wife, if it was a wife he wanted. A bit shorter than the average man, he had a strong body and a muscular build from long years honing his craft as a swordsman and former hired blade. Cyril's long, dark, deep red hair and matching goatee attracted the most attention from admirers. Though braids helped keep it out of his face, the hot wind blew his hair about, and it stuck to his forehead while he walked to the market grounds.

He began his rounds through the already bustling market, scanning the crowds for any disturbances. Merchants didn't often result to throwing fists when they argued, but their hired help sometimes did. The summer heat swelled and arrived with the Market traders. The sun baked the crowds, making them irritable. Despite this, the overall mood around the market remained calm so far. Cyril smiled and greeted some friendly faces while he walked through the grounds.

He'd made Ford Town his home for about five summers now but found himself familiar as anyone born on this side of the Zult River. It was a pleasant change after long years on the road living a hired blade's nomadic lifestyle.

Boyar Petru Novadi's best men worked hard alongside the merchants while they erected temporary shop fronts and brought goods to the market grounds. Petru Novadi wasn't an exceptionally rich boyar and he didn't have the largest fief in Vodomeria. But he did pride himself on fair governance and strived for efficiency. Tax men collected fees, secretaries recorded the names and types of merchants present, and Keepers of the Peace helped direct traffic. Along with Vodomerian merchants, many more people would arrive from outside Vodomeria to buy and trade large quantities of rarer and more exotic goods more readily available from the numerous City-States across the river and from the Tsardom of Farizhniya to the east. Some goods would be taken deeper into Vodomeria—and possibly to the bordering Voivodates of Hredera, Boritz, and Monor.

The Market kept Cyril busy other ways besides work. His current lover—a large, handsome ogre named Daumantas—would stay in town for the entire Market before setting out across Vodomeria the rest of his summer. A silk merchant and tailor by trade, Cyril longed to feel the big man's arms wrapped around him. Daumantas' presence also meant the ogre's sister, Svetlana, would also come to visit. She often traveled to Ford Town from Farizhniya to visit both her twin brother and Cyril during the feast of Saint Vodomor. While it could be a hassle, the months-long Summer Market, with the feast day of Saint Vodomor right at its heart, was truly the most joyous time for Cyril. It brought many of his friends and good company to town.

A large hand clapped him on the back and brought Cyril forcefully to the present. "Old friend! How I've missed you!" Bohden exclaimed and hugged Cyril to his big shoulder.

The warm greeting made Cyril smile wide. "Bohden! Do you

escort a caravan to the Summer Market every year now?" He laughed and embraced the larger man.

Bohden, a childhood friend and a former casual lover, laughed at Cyril's remark. "Someone has to keep an eye on you!"

They both chuckled and walked along the path, dodging crowds as the throngs moved hither and thither on missions of varying importance.

"I want to talk to you tonight," Cyril said, gripping Bohden's shoulder. "Will you meet me at our usual tavern this evening?"

Bohden frowned. "Is everything alright?" He gazed down at Cyril with concern.

"Everything is fine! Better than fine!" Cyril's words came out in a nervous rush. "I just…it's a little embarrassing is all."

Bohden nodded and smiled mischievously. "I can't wait to hear what you think is so embarrassing!" He gave a big laugh.

Cyril felt his face redden. Thankfully, no one nearby reacted to his crimson cheeks. Bohden bid him goodbye and left to finish business with the caravan he'd traveled with. He still worked as a sword for hire, though he limited travel to between the City States and Vodomeria these days. Bohden's presence inevitably brought along bittersweet memories of Cyril's childhood along with the urge to cross the Zult River and run away from Vodomeria once again. Cyril had fled Vodomeria years ago as a youth, and old anxieties persisted about his past well into adulthood.

The town boasted quite a few inns and taverns for its size, and The Drunken Whale was widely considered Ford Town's best. Once he finished with his rounds for the day, Cyril headed right for the Whale. The sun set and the crowds poured in for cold beer and good food after a long, hard day. Bohden sat at a booth, and he enthusiastically waved Cyril over as he waded through the throngs of patrons.

Iuliana also spotted Cyril as he walked across the crowded room and followed him to the table where Bohden waited. A well-endowed woman with generous hips and soft breasts, she was widely regarded as the most desirable prostitute in town. She put her elbows on the table and gave an exaggerated pout. "Cyril! You haven't been to see me in ages! What happened?"

Bohden choked on his ale behind him while he slid into the booth.

"My apologies," Cyril crooned, took Iuliana's hand and kissed it. "I've been preoccupied."

"With someone else!" Iuliana huffed but allowed him to dote on her. "Well, would you like some food and a drink?" She drummed the fingers of her other hand on the tabletop as she spoke. "If I'm not on my back, I have to earn my keep other ways."

Cyril barked a short laugh and handed her too much coin for his meal. "This big crowd and not a soul you fancy to take upstairs?" he asked, arching an eyebrow, though he wasn't surprised. Iuliana also had a reputation for being very picky about what clients she took.

She shook her head and waggled her hips suggestively as she walked away. "No one half as interesting as you!" Iuliana disappeared into the crowd and ignored the men desperate for her attention.

Cyril scratched his bearded chin. If his heart wasn't taken by another, Iuliana would be a nice person to bed for the rest of his life. He wasn't forbidden from warming his bed with another person while he and Daumantas were apart, but Cyril felt guilty at the thought and simply hadn't bothered. Cyril had employed Iuliana when he first arrived in Ford Town. Since that time, she'd continued to bed him whenever he asked and refused to take his coin. Cyril assumed it to be out of pity at first, but Iuliana genuinely enjoyed his company.

"You and a *woman*?" Bohden scoffed, his mug making a wooden thunk as he set it down on the table.

"I like women, too!" Cyril shot back. Admittedly, though, not as much as he liked men.

"Is that the embarrassing thing you wanted to tell me?" Bohden asked as he took a bite out of a crispy potato wedge.

"If I was embarrassed by the people I like to fuck, I'd be embarrassed as hell of you!" Cyril exclaimed, and he shoved—or, rather, *tried* to shove—Bohden in response.

The much larger man yielded ever so slightly and laughed at the attempt.

Cyril cleared his throat and tried to be serious. "Do you remember Daumantas?" he asked, just as Iuliana returned with his food and ale.

"Oh, is that who you've been busy with?" She slid into the conversation as if she'd never left. "He's very sweet." Iuliana smiled, and Cyril knew exactly how red his face turned from the heat on his cheeks. She sat across from them and waited for Cyril to continue his story.

Bohden went to pick up his mug and stopped. "Daumantas? The tailor? Are you serious?" he laughed.

"Bohden, please!" Cyril begged.

His friend struggled to stop chuckling. "Okay, okay! I'll be serious." He took a moment to calm himself, but the smile remained plastered on his face.

Cyril swallowed the lump in his throat. "I'm in love with him."

Both Iuliana and Bohden leaned close.

"You're what?" Bohden asked. His eyes widened, stunned by the proclamation.

"In love?!" Iuliana exclaimed and leaned across the table.

Cyril tipped his mug and took a big swig to fortify himself. "Yes! I'm in love!" he half shouted over the din of the crowd. "I..." He swallowed hard. "I want to settle down. Really settle! Be with one person. No more being fickle with my partners." He stared at the table.

Iuliana and Bohden gave Cyril a combined embrace.

"That's wonderful, love!" Iuliana kissed him on the cheek before she returned to her work. She smiled, waved, and disappeared into the crowded tavern once more.

Bohden held Cyril close for a few moments before letting him go. "That's...big! You're in love" He chuckled and shook his head. "I, ah...actually, there's a reason I keep turning up in town myself…" Bohden spoke sheepishly into his mug as Dan, the black-smith, slid onto the bench across from them.

"This seat taken?" Dan asked a bit gruffly while he made himself comfortable.

Broad, dark haired, thickly muscled, and scarred from the forge, Dan cut an intimidating figure. He could be a rough and blunt-speaking man, but he was honest, and Cyril wouldn't trust his sword with any other smith in town. Bohden greeted him warmly, and he and Dan smoothly fell into conversation. In that moment, Cyril knew exactly why Bohden returned yearly to Ford Town. They ate and drank together and enjoyed one another's company well into the evening.

The hour grew late, and Cyril could tell his companions would rather be elsewhere. He sleepily dismissed himself and shuffled out of the Drunken Whale. Bohden and Dan's affection for one another gave him hope that he, too, could find happiness here in Ford Town. He felt light and a bit giddy as he made his way back to the Keeper's barracks. Cyril had admitted aloud to his friends that he was in love. He'd never allowed himself to feel so strongly about any of his lovers before. Cyril went to bed, he felt warm and anxious for Daumantas' arrival.

The following days saw the numbers at the market grounds swell dramatically. Carts, people, and goods streamed steadily to and from Ford Town. From the guard towers, the long caravans were reminiscent of multiple lines of busy ants as they converged on the town—both bringing goods and people to and taking them from town in steady streams.

While Daumantas lived and worked primarily in Olten, a town a few days journey northeast across the Zult River, he traveled the Voivodates during the summer and into the fall to ply his trade. Daumantas wasn't keen to discuss his other destinations elsewhere with Cyril, who dismissed it as the ogre being worried about boring him with the tedium of business.

Delayed this year, the artisans from Olten began to arrive with their wares a full week after the Summer Market opened. Cyril ran to the bridge as soon as he received word their caravan had reached the river crossing. Weary merchants swayed tiredly in their wagon seats. He bounced on his heels while they rolled by. carts and wagons kicked up dust as they crossed the bridge and hit the hard dirt road into Ford Town. Daumantas and his large, brightly painted traveling van were at the very end of the line. Cyril took a running leap and climbed into the seat beside the ogre as he crossed the bridge.

Ogres and humans weren't very different in shape and size; the only obvious differences were an ogre's distinctive horns and pointed ears. Some people around the Voiovodats feared ogres as wicked sorcerers because ogres were legendary for their magical aptitude, but Cyril had only ever known them to be nice and pleasant. It probably helped, though, that he'd met some. Ogres are most common to the east of Vodomeria and to the northeast of the Principalities, from the deep forests of the City-States and the Tsardom of Farizhniya to the rolling vast plains and dazzling cities of the Khanate further east beyond the Thornback Mountains. He assumed the people who held such nonsense ideas about their "wickedness" had never been to any of those places before.

Thankfully, ogres were a normal sight around Ford Town, and Daumantas had become as familiar in town as Cyril himself. Meeting at the bridge became a ritual for Cyril and Daumantas. Cyril would climb into the wagon, and Daumantas would feign surprise.

"Oh, a rogue!" Daumantas laughed softly at his own poor acting. "Whatever shall I do?" he added, as he leaned dramatically away from Cyril.

Cyril grinned and he leaned close to Daumantas, their knees brushed together with every movement of the wagon. "You know you have to pay me to stay in my territory." He puffed out his chest and did his best overwrought brigand impression.

Daumantas chuckled and wrapped a large hand around Cyril's thigh. "Is it really 'payment' if I enjoy it?"

Cyril moved closer to Daumantas, and they leaned against one another, chuckling together as they acted through their playful farce.

"I missed you," Cyril said, and he felt the full weight of his longing.

Daumantas moved his hand from Cyril's thigh to his waist and pulled him nearer. They rode silently to the market grounds, bodies pressed close to one another despite the uncomfortable warmth.

Two

WARM SUMMER DAYS ARRIVED, and they filled Ruslan with an all too familiar restlessness. He hiked alone into the wilderness between the Zhupensken stronghold and the Wall, eager for some peace and quiet. The Great Monster Wall loomed nearby, it caught the light from the rising sun and the strange energy barrier shimmered like a mirage. A much more mundane stone and mortar fortification wound through the hills in the foreground, a battered reminder of how much the world changed over the centuries.

Ruslan became accustomed to the sight of the Wall after years of living within the Zhupensken fief. The Zhupensken holdings ran the Wall's length from the Springfall mountains to the north all the way to the border with Hredera to the south. The fief was long and thin, and it was sparsely populated even before the rebellion years prior. The remaining inhabitants lived close to the borders of other fiefs, and many avoided the Wall and anyone loyal to Boyar Hadeon Zhupensken.

Ruslan's shadow danced ahead of him as he sauntered through the tree dotted hills and surveyed the area for anything of interest. A tall man with a muscular build and dark blonde hair, his skin sun kissed from hours outside, Ruslan never wanted for intimate company. He was the Monster Wall made flesh- handsomely built, rugged and hard with an air of ever-present danger.

The sparse structures close to the Wall itself were castles and watchtowers built by the Knights of Saint Dragos the Mad. Ruslan had briefly thought about joining the order, and he'd served along the Knights at the Wall for a time, but there was no money to be made doing such work.

Instead, he'd taken to plumbing Finndriairian ruins within the fief for treasure and taught himself to break apart Devil Bugs. The iron that made up most of the metallic monster's bodies wasn't worth much, but there was gold and silver at every Inferni's core. Once Ruslan's operation proved lucrative, Boyar Hadeon Zhupensken accepted him into his meager retinue. The fief used to be prosperous serving traders headed to and from Grendair. The hot tempered Hadeon impoverished himself and ravaged his own fief, attempting to crush a Sorcerer King worshiping cult in what was now known as the Heretic War.

The noise of battle from the direction of the Wall brought Ruslan out of his thoughts and back to the present. A faded weakening in the ephemeral Wall and steel on steel echoed across the hills, heralding Bugs being beaten back by the Knights. He trotted towards the disturbance to survey the spoils he'd be taking.

A dozen Devil Ants climbed over the stone fortification. Their sharp legs dug into its surface, scoring the stone. The knights fired on the Ants with hand cannons, forming a defensive line to inter-cept the survivors. The remaining Ants moved methodically over the wall, unfazed by the knights firing upon them.

Shaped roughly like their insect counterparts, a Devil Ant's body was constructed of gears and iron plate which shifted as it moved. Twice the size of a large horse, their scissor mouths and sharp appendages made them formidable opponents. For unknown reasons, the Inferni never attacked wild or domesticated animals. However, they would race to kill any sentient beings they came across.

Successive volleys of hand cannon fire destroyed most of the Ants scaling down the wall. A lone survivor made it to the ground and lashed out at the knights, catching one with a knife-leg and piercing their breastplate clean through. The knights rallied and knocked the Ant over with a concentrated volley of hand cannon fire. The line of knights then moved in, their war hammers and maces clanging and crunching as they attacked the Ant's joints and the enchanted crystal that served as its heart.

Swords were of virtually no use against these steely creatures. The Knights of Dragos the Mad spent the last 700 years perfecting techniques to battle the Devil Bugs. The sight of the creatures no longer bothered Ruslan as he'd fought and defeated more than a few himself in the last decade or so.

"Would you like me to have my men come out here and clean this up?" Ruslan strode towards a Knight Captain who scowled at his approach.

The stern-faced Grendairan man frowned but nodded. "May as well. I'm not thrilled with how you invest your spoils, but I'm happier there are less dead Bugs cluttering the area." Ruslan turned to go when the captain cleared his throat. "There's something else, if you're willing to pay some alms to a poor soldier..."

Ruslan's eyebrows raised—but only a little. He didn't want to seem too eager.

Money exchanged hands, and the captain leaned close. "Someone saw what they thought may be cultists in the woods a little ways north of here. I suspect they're probably just poor souls looking to put bread on their tables by looting the ruins." He paused, pointing towards the craggy remains of Finndrigairian buildings jutting out above the tree line not far to the north. "I think it would be best if someone more level-headed investigated before Hadeon jumps to any conclusions and starts burning villages."

Ruslan agreed to the knight's request and began the walk back to Hadeon's citadel. The aging castle, once a grand structure, now stood half empty as it slowly decayed. Hadeon Zhupensken was the last of his line and the state of the castle resembled its current master in many respects. The once bustling town that surrounded the castle also stood half empty. A full fourth of it was now dominated by Ruslan's workshops, where they broke the Devil Bugs apart. Promises of steady pay working for Ruslan had brought some life back to the town, and he capitalized on the common folk's distrust of his current master.

A felis man with pitch black fur trotted towards Ruslan. The feline-faced man gave Ruslan a military-like salute. "Good morning, sir! Anything of note along the wall today?"

"There was an incursion north of here," Ruslan told him. "We'll need to send a dozen wagons and the fastest chopping crew we've got."

The felis man nodded, trotting back towards the smelting works to gather the teams and collect their cargo.

Ruslan continued to the castle, walking into the barracks. More than a few of the soldiers attempted to make themselves appear busier than they were when Ruslan entered.

"I need a handful of trustworthy men to go into the ruins north of here with me," he said. "There's extra coin for anyone who's interested."

A handful of gruff individuals stepped forward.

Ruslan nodded. "Get armed and meet me in the courtyard in ten minutes."

He turned on his heel and entered the keep, making for his private chambers. The state of the keep's interior made him frown. Sparsely furnished and drafty, he found it barely habitable. Ruslan had to have the roof repaired over his own personal chamber before he could move in years before.

"Ruslan, my boy! Where are you off to?" Hadeon's voice cut across the great hall, and Ruslan reluctantly stopped to greet his Boyar.

"Just retrieving some Bugs from the Wall," Ruslan said. "Nothing to worry about." He didn't enjoy discussing business with the old man.

Hadeon held out a letter. "Tymor Valentin wrote me. Says he wants to talk and try to mend our relationship." He spat into the dust on the floor. "Like I don't want to see his head on a spike!"

Ruslan took the letter, examined its contents, and shrugged off Hadeon's reaction. Their mutual distrust of Voivode Tymor had brought Ruslan to the Zhupensken fief, but Hadeon wore his grudge with the Voivode like a badge of honor. It grated on Ruslan's nerves.

He shoved the letter into Hadeon's chest. "Talk to him or don't, but you know full well this spat keeps me from doing regular business with the neighboring boyars!"

"Don't you dare blame me!" The old man grabbed Ruslan and waved the stump where his left hand used to be at his face. "His bitch daughter—"

Ruslan forcefully shoved Hadeon away. "Don't talk about her like that."

The boyar stumbled backward, landing on his rump with a grunt.

"You did that to yourself when you challenged her." Ruslan loomed over him. "Don't blame other people for your mistakes!"

Tired of Hadeon, he turned on his heel and marched away. His quarters could wait. Now eager to be out of the castle, he took servant's passages to the courtyard to avoid further conversation. Bitter memories crept up on him, and it took all of Ruslan's will to force them away. His parting from the princess of Vodomeria had been a contentious one, and he didn't want to get distracted by those memories now.

The volunteers he'd sought earlier awaited him in the courtyard. With a whistle and a wave, Ruslan bid them to follow without breaking stride, and they hiked out to the ruins in grim silence.

Outside of the Wall, very little of the Finndrigairian Empire remained intact. Though now reduced to ruins, the area north of the Zhupensken citadel was once a fair-sized Finndrigairian town. The most valuable and useful items had been stripped from the crumbling buildings long ago, but the sprawling and overgrown ruins still yielded secrets from time to time.

"What are we looking for?" one of the men asked quietly as they entered the long-abandoned town. Neatly laid boulevards stretched out before them, their surfaces broken apart by tree roots and time.

"We're looking for looters," Ruslan half-lied. He didn't want anyone acting too rashly here.

The ruins weren't much more dangerous than any place else within the Zhupensken fief. Despite Ruslan's and the Knight's best efforts, gangs of thieves favored the ruins, and Devil Ants sometimes found their way into the area from passages hidden underground. The negative association was enough to keep most people away. Ruslan spotted a small knot of Knights standing at the corner of one half ruined building. One of their number waved his party over.

"You must be Ruslan. The captain told me to expect you." The big bear-bodied ursus Knight kept his deep voice low while talking. "We saw them enter this building earlier, but the captain told us not to follow."

Ruslan nodded. "My team and I will take a look. Can you spare some time to aid us if needed?"

"We'll stay close by." The Ursus knight gave him a salute and a nod before turning back to his own companions.

Ruslan turned to his men. "I want to handle this as peaceably as possible. Don't draw your weapons unless I tell you, understood?"

The group nodded as one man. Ruslan took a few moments to light a torch and lead his team into the remains of the building. He scanned the floor for clues as to where the squatters may have traveled through or camped within its walls.

The dirt and debris on the floor harbored signs of recent disturbance. Ruslan led the party through the gloomy passageways, treading quietly lest he startle their potential quarry. More obvious signs of habitation lay deeper within the ruined building: A recently extinguished campfire along with stacks of firewood and food scrap dumped in a corner.

Movement and light nearby caught Ruslan's attention, and he motioned for his men to move forward. The light from Ruslan's own torch betrayed his position and the quarry's source of illumination retreated deeper into the derelict building. The party crept along the corridor and down a flight of stairs, allowing the squatters to retreat out of sight ahead of them. Now underground, there were much more obvious signs of habitation within the ruined building. Markings had been painted recently on several walls, and empty crates and barrels lined the underground room Ruslan and his crew now found themselves in.

Ruslan lost track of the light they'd followed into the chamber and examined the floor for any possible sign of his quarry's path through the space. A sword hissed out of its scabbard, and he whipped around to admonish his men. "I told you not to—"

Slowly, it dawned on him that the unsheathed blades were intended to keep him where he was. This group hadn't needed much convincing to make the journey to the ruins. Ruslan raised his arms over his head.

"If you spare me, I won't breathe a word to Hadeon," he promised.

A grizzled older fellow stepped forward to speak for the group. "We don't mean you any harm, but we can't have you running off. Please, surrender your weapons and we'll lead you to our master."

Ruslan frowned but did as he was told. His captors took his weapons and deftly led him through the labyrinth beneath the building. Adjoining underground structures were linked by fresh tunnels, some of which were simply lined with roughly hewed wood. A significant part of the journey took them through what must have been an impressive sewer system at one time. Ruslan's companions kept their weapons in hand as they walked along.

The underground maze bled together the further they walked. Ruslan barely noted their ascension until they stepped into a sunny corridor above ground. The building was ancient and needed repair, but it was no less beautiful for it. The walls were once brightly painted plaster and were covered in swirling floral designs popular with the ancient Finndrigairians. The floor was made of worn but still equally beautiful floral tile work. A shimmering barrier not unlike the Great Monster Wall gave the windows an ethereal appearance.

Ruslan caught sight of the Wall itself looming in the distance through the windows, and it nearly made his heart stop. He stumbled, startling his captors. They'd taken him to the other side of the barrier.

"Why in the name of the Saints would you journey out here?" Despite his best efforts to remain calm, panic rose inside him.

The gruff man leading the party sheathed his weapon and held up his hands in a disarming manner. "Please remain calm. This place is safe. It's where we lived before journeying beyond the Wall."

Curiosity quelled Ruslan's most pressing fears. "So, the rumors are true? People do live on this side of the Wall?"

The other members of the party followed their leader's example by sheathing their weapons as the man said, "I don't have time to explain, but yes. There are people on this side of the Great Monster Wall. Our ancestors became trapped here when the barrier was erected more than seven hundred years ago."

The gruff old man motioned for Ruslan to follow. As they walked down the hall, the other members of the party quietly melted away. Ruslan allowed himself to be led through the building and into a richly furnished seating room.

"I'll return your weapons once we're back on the other side of the Wall." The gruff old man turned to leave the room. "Please wait here for the master. He'll be with you shortly."

The door closed, leaving Ruslan the chamber's sole occupant. Whoever this 'master' was, they'd better have a good reason for kidnapping him. He made himself comfortable in a plush chair to wait.

After a short while, the door opened and admitted an impossibly beautiful man. "I apologize for the nature of this meeting." The man sat down, his raven-dark hair spilled over slim shoulders in gentle waves. "There's no easy way for my people to get around without catching the attention of the Knights."

Ruslan temporarily became lost in the stranger's deeply blue eyes, and it took him a moment to respond. "I'd have preferred an invitation, rather than a kidnapping," he let out a sharp breath, the weight of the situation crushing him. "What do you want with me?"

"I have a business proposal for you." A slight smile appeared on his alabaster face. "I'm hoping we can reach an agreement that's mutually beneficial."

"Alright, what did you have in mind?" Ruslan leaned back in his chair and crossed his arms over his chest.

"We both want access to the other side of the Great Monster Wall," the strange man said. "My people need supplies, and you want more valuable artifacts." He leaned back, folding his hands neatly in his lap. "Hadeon is no great leader, and I'd like him replaced with someone more agreeable."

Ruslan rubbed his chin, deep in thought. "Why just Hadeon? If we could put someone pliable in the seat of the Voivode, you could have potential access to all of Vodomeria."

The raven-haired man smiled. "Ah! I do like that idea, though it's a bit ambitious." He leaned forward, offering his hand to Rulsan. "They call me Laurent."

Ruslan took Laurent's hand, frowning slightly. "You're named after the Mad Sorcerer King?"

"Mmmmm...sort of, yes."

Three

ONCE HE ERECTED his trading stall, put the oxen out to pasture, and prepared his campsite, Daumantas met with Cyril, and they made their way back into town. The lovers reached The Drunken Whale as the sun dipped below the hills. The tavern bustled with activity, thanks to a felis bard who sat and sang songs at the bar. Dark gray fur covered his body and his sleek feline features. He wore very fine clothes for a traveling minstrel, and his singing talent certainly paid for the fine cloth.

At first, Cyril couldn't make out the words the bard warbled over the noise inside the tavern. Once he caught the tune, though, his hair stood on end. He recognized the melody: "The Ballad of the Dueling Princess." Just as quickly as he'd walked in, Cyril spun on his heel and marched out. He nearly collided with Daumantas, who'd been following closely behind him.

Cyril continued briskly down the dusty lane towards another—*any other*—establishment in town. Daumantas struggled to keep up as he rushed away. He caught Cyril's arm and tugged gently to slow him.

"What's got you so upset?" he asked.

"Let go of me, Daumantas."

Cyril's whole body stiffened when Daumantas seized him; he was used to the other man's gentleness. Daumantas loosened his grip, and Cyril's arm slid free from his hand.

"It was that *stupid* song!" Cyril snarled between clenched teeth. His stomach churned. He rubbed his hot face with his hands. *"I hate that fucking song."*

"Why?" Daumantas asked gently, confused at his companion's sudden outburst.

Cyril's face screwed up into a scowl. "Because it's about *me.*"

They ate quietly that evening at the Golden Oak. Cyril liked to come here when the Drunken Whale was too busy for him to enjoy. Daumantas stuck to polite conversation through dinner. Cyril tried to perk up, but his mood had fallen hard upon hearing the Ballad, and he was struggling to recover. The last thing Cyril wanted was to remember his past, and the damned song pushed uncomfortable memories to the front of his mind.

"Would you like to stay with me tonight?" Daumantas asked quietly as they strolled leisurely through the streets back towards the edge of town.

Cyril took Daumantas' hand and squeezed it in response. They made their way away from town to where the trees met the clearings at the far end of the market grounds. Many traders and artisans camped within the meadows near the river during the Summer Market to save coin.

After a lengthy walk, the pair reached Daumantas' wagon. Stepping inside, Daumantas lit a single hanging lamp. Its light warmed the cheery interior and bathed it with a welcoming glow. The pair gently kissed one another as they took turns undressing, but Cyril was distracted. He felt years of doubt crushing him all at once. Discomfort from his past pushed in on him as memories of his youth played out in the back of his mind. He grimaced and pushed the memories away.

The teachings of Saint Vuretz said that his body was his own and to reshape. It was a sacred rite the saint bestowed upon those whose hearts and minds didn't match their bodies. Cyril had strong faith in those teachings. It didn't matter what he had once been—*who* he had once been. What mattered was what he was now.

Besides, Daumantas' hungry eyes, mouth, and groping hands favored men's bodies over all others, and the attention was enough in this moment to banish Cyril's self-doubt.

Once they were fully naked, Cyril sank to his knees in front of Daumantas. He wanted to taste him, to lose himself in the simple task of giving another pleasure. He loved the way Daumantas ran his hands though his long hair as he sucked on his erection. With a shuddering gasp and a long lusty groan, his partner's bittersweet climax filled his mouth.

Cyril stood, and they began to kiss again. Daumantas gently laid Cyril down in the soft bed built into the traveling wagon. His hands traced Cyril's jaw, lingering on his thick goatee. His fingertips glided along Cyril's neck and to the middle of his chest. He gently followed the scars on Cyril's chest, the marks left behind when Vuretzian monks reshaped Cyril's flesh.

In most respects, Cyril's body was virtually indistinguishable from someone born a man. He'd worked hard to build a lean, muscular body for himself through years of exercise and martial training, and his chest was now flat as it always should've been. But while the monks could have crafted him a penis, Cyril had chosen not to take on that difficult reshaping. He liked what was between his legs, and he didn't feel any less of a man for keeping it as it was.

Cyril used to believe he couldn't go on living before traveling to Vuretsiv. Being in this moment, here with Daumantas, made him thrilled to be alive and in good health. His lover bent over him, nipping at Cyril's chest. His muscles twitched, and Daumantas chuckled. He kissed along Cyril's muscular trunk before moving himself between his legs. He gently pushed Cyril's thighs apart and placed his mouth on the wetness between them. Cyril grabbed Daumantas' horns and gently rocked against his face as his lover lapped at him. His own climax came swiftly, and he let out a shuddering groan.

Too tired to do any more, the pair lay together and simply held one another. Cyril happily fell asleep in Daumantas' thickly muscled arms.

Warm sunlight woke Cyril in the morning. He could not feel Daumantas in the bed, but the sounds of him preparing a meal outside the wagon wafted through the open window. He laid still, enjoying the softness of the mattress until Daumantas came in bearing breakfast. Cyril kept quiet as his companion carefully laid out the meal before turning to wake him.

"Ah, you're already awake!" Daumantas beamed when he saw Cyril's sleepy gaze following him. "I brought some food. Nothing fancy, mind you."

The ogre made himself comfortable on the edge of the bed as Cyril sat up. There were slices of bread, along with apples and some cheese on a long tin plate for the two of them to share. Beside it were two ceramic cups filled with a hot beverage. The warm aroma radiating from them was unmistakable.

"You brewed coffee?" Cyril asked with a grin.

He hadn't had a cup of coffee in a long time. It came all the way from the Sultanate, and Ford Town was much too far from any port to get the beans often.

A smile spread across Daumantas' face as he handed Cyril one of the cups. "I'm glad to see your mood is better this morning," he said as he drank his coffee.

Cyril smiled back, sipping delicately at the hot beverage. "Mmmm. Well, I have good company."

They chatted casually as they ate breakfast. Daumantas consciously avoided talking about last night, and Cyril was happy he didn't have to explain himself. Despite knowing his presence would be missed if he didn't return to the barracks, he lingered anyway, taking his time. The two reluctantly parted only after all that was left of their shared meal was the thick grounds at the bottom of their coffee cups.

Cyril walked to the river and took a quick dip before fully dressing himself. He combed his waist-length, rose red hair with his fingers as he walked back into town.

Dimitru, Boyar Petru's son and the head of the Keepers of the

Peace, met Cyril on the street outside the barracks. "I was beginning to think you'd gotten bored and left town." Dimitru yawned, trying to hide his fatigue behind his hand as he did so.

Cyril shrugged, and they fell in step beside one another as they entered the barracks. Dimitru followed as Cyril walked all the way into his personal room.

"You missed and exciting night last night!" his superior wearily exclaimed as Cyril grabbed his sword from where he'd left it hanging the night before, belting it to his waist. "There was a ten-man brawl at The Thirsty Otter. It was a mess."

Cyril nodded, only half listening.

"I need you to go to the Central Market and talk to some people," Dimitru continued. "A child's been stealing food from the vendors there. No one can catch them, though"

Cyril scoffed and rolled his eyes. "You know how I feel about children."

Dimitru smirked at Cyril's reluctance. "I do," he replied, "And I also know you wouldn't let a little child go hungry, either. There are some monks from the abbey of Saint Vodomor in town. They'll take the child in if you can catch our little thief."

As much as he didn't want to spend his day hunting children, he took the task Dimitru gave him because his superior was right. Cyril hated that this world had so much wealth and abundance to offer, yet people found themselves lacking food and shelter. Many people suffering through lean times took to being permanent pilgrims. Their numbers were often absorbed by the various religious orders formed around the veneration of the numerous saints of the Great Monster Wall region. Others became bandits. Cyril wanted to understand why some people chose one path over the other, though he had yet to find an answer.

Clean, armed, and ready to go, Cyril made his way out of the barracks towards Central Market. It was much more permanent than the Summer Market and situated at the geographical center of Ford Town. Here, the streets were properly cobbled, and the brightly painted brick and stucco shops surrounded a square peppered with sturdy wooden vendor stalls. A large church dedicated to Saint Vodomor dominated one full side and its façade loomed over the square.

Cyril drifted around the food stalls, chatting with vendors and casually browsing wares until he spotted the little thief. The child crept along the edge of a baker's stall, trying to reach some bread without being detected. Cyril waved his hand and shook his head to stop the vendor from sounding the alarm as the child snatched a loaf.

The child tried to make off with their take when Cyril came from behind the stall next door and scooped them off the ground without breaking stride. The bread nearly tumbled to the ground, and Cyril barely managed to catch it as his quarry thrashed in his arms. It took a few moments to fully subdue his diminutive thief.

"Please! You aren't in trouble!" Cyril begged for the child's cooperation. "Aren't you tired of stealing food?" They nodded shyly as they nibbled.

Cyril placed their feet back on the ground and let the child chew on the pilfered loaf. He tossed a few coins to the baker while keeping hold of the child. "Do you have more food?" the child asked around a mouthful of bread.

"I don't, but they do." Cyril pointed at the monks anxiously waiting by the church on the other side of the square as he guided the child towards them.

Saint Vodomor embodied defense of the weak and helpless, and the monks who dedicated their lives to the saint lived by those ideals. Cyril wasn't a devotee of Saint Vodomor himself, but he trusted the monks to keep the child safe and give them shelter.

"They have clean clothes and a nice place for you to stay, too," he added.

The child gazed over their shoulder at Cyril as the two monks led them into the church. Cyril gave them a smile and pulled his medal of Saint Vuretz out from under his tunic. He kissed it and said a silent prayer for the child as they disappeared.

Cyril had sacrificed his ability to have children when he became as he is now. While he didn't regret his choice, he still wondered about parenthood. Pressure to bear children had put him off the idea for years. Now he felt guilty for his desire to become a parent at this time in his life. The conflicting feelings swirled inside him until another Keeper flagged him down for aid, and he tucked the thought away for another time.

As the day wore on and the crowds swelled, Cyril found himself called to all corners of Ford Town. A brawl broke out in one of the cheaper drinking establishments. Later, a heated argument sparked fruit vendors to lob rotten produce at one another. Far too many arguments came to blows as the heat and press of bodies wore on the throngs of marketgoers.

The day passed swiftly, and Cyril found himself aching for a proper bath. Ford Town had a simple stone public bath house situated between the town and the nearby citadel. The evenings tended to be quieter than mornings, and Cyril enjoyed bathing in relative silence. He was settling into a cool pool to relax when a certain bard walked up to where he lounged at the side of the bath.

"Mind if I join you?" The felis bard's whiskers twitched as he talked.

Cyril thought about it for a moment and grudgingly gestured for the bard to take a seat beside him. The felis bard murmured his thanks as he lowered himself into the water beside Cyril. They both regarded one another with suspicion.

"You didn't like my song the other night?" the bard asked with surprising ease. His eyes closed, and his large triangular ears faced forward. His countenance betrayed no concern with what Cyril might say.

Cyril shrugged, twirling stray hairs around his finger from the long braid wound around the top of his head. "I just don't care for 'The Ballad of the Dueling Princess.'"

He took a few moments to study the bard relaxing beside him. The felis man's face didn't betray any emotion. His eyes opened under Cyril's scrutiny, just enough so that Cyril could tell the golden orbs were locked on him.

"I'll speak plainly," the bard said. "Your father sent me. I didn't think I'd actually find you." His eyes opened fully as Cyril scoffed and climbed out of the bath. "Your father has expressed many regrets concerning your upbringing, and he wants only to speak with you."

The bard was talking loud enough for the few others present to overhear, and the words did what they were intended to do: they stopped Cyril from walking off.

He turned back and knelt beside the bath, leaning close to the bard. "He only cares for people who suit his needs, and he doesn't reciprocate the love shown to him," Cyril hissed in response.

The bard nodded, nonplussed by Cyril's assessment.

"How long have you been observing me?" Cyril demanded.

"Oh…about a week or so now?" His golden eyes blinked slowly. "Your father's description of you was…painfully outdated. I'm not fully certain he knows what a New Man is, either. He'd heard rumors you were living here, though those sorts of rumors fly from people's lips on the regular around Vodomeria. I only became certain of your identity when I saw you still bear weapons with your family crest."

Tymor, the Voivode of Vodomeria, had given the sword and matching dagger to Cyril the night he fled, an inexplicable act of kindness that Cyril still hadn't deciphered. The man could have stopped him or otherwise made his life hell in that moment. Instead, Tymor had angrily thrust his own sword and matching dagger into Cyril's hands, and Cyril left Triadoara that night without incident. It took several days for the call for Cyril's capture to be raised within the Voivodate.

Cyril tried to bring his focus back to the present. He stood but didn't immediately leave, murmuring, "I just want to be left alone. Please don't bother me with this again."

The felis bard peered up at him, ears twitching. "My name is Octavius, by the way. I have a letter he intended for you. You'll see it sitting on my instrument over there. Please take it and read it at the very least." Octavius turned away and spoke no more.

The conversation stirred unpleasant feelings in Cyril. He dressed himself angrily and glanced towards where Octavius had placed his belongings. Curiosity beat back his anger, and Cyril snatched the parchment from between the strings of Octavius's lute.

He walked slowly towards Daumantas' wagon. He'd been promised a nice dinner cooked by the fire tonight. Turning the letter over and over in his hands, he debated reading its contents. His legs walked by instinct back to Daumantas' camp.

As he stood to greet him, Daumantas' expression changed from joy to worry when he saw Cyril's face. "Did your day not go well?" he asked, his brows knitted together as he handed Cyril a wooden bowl full of what smelled like venison stew.

Cyril shook his head as he sat, prodding his stew with his spoon. "That bard who sang at the Drunken Whale the other night was sent here by my *father*." He pulled the letter from his belt and angrily tossed it to the ground.

"Oh." Daumantas glanced at the letter and stared into his bowl for a moment. "He didn't...he didn't threaten you, did he?"

Did Cyril detect a hint of anger in Daumantas' voice?

"Thankfully, no," Cyril responded. "My father supposedly wants to speak with me, though I doubt that's true."

He gingerly helped himself to a spoonful of Daumantas' piping hot cooking. His companion let out a long breath as he relaxed.

Cyril chewed a moment, weighing his response, "I don't know why the bard's request irritates me so much."

It was all very perplexing. Until recently, Cyril hadn't traveled through or near Vodomeria in a very long time. He'd lived his entire adult life up to this point outside the Voivodates and far away from the Great Monster Wall region. Cyril knew living in Ford Town presented a risk since it lay within Vodomeria's borders, but five summers came and went with only weak rumors of his heritage following him around.

Why would his father contact him now? Had Voivode Tymor concocted some scheme that involved him? Cyril didn't wish to dwell on it. The Summer Market was his time to spend with Daumantas and he intended to use that time well.

He tried to forget about everything as they ate, and later that evening, Cyril put the letter in a drawer where he kept a few personal effects in the wagon. He and Daumantas spent the rest of the night lost between the bed sheets. The feeling of Daumantas fiercely driving himself between Cyril's thighs chased away all his remaining thoughts that night.

When morning came, the ritual of waking alone repeated. Daumantas rose early by habit, and it was something Cyril was slowly growing used to. Today, the other man worked through martial arts forms outside the wagon, and Cyril peeked out the window to watch him.

Cyril observed his lover with rapt fascination. Daumantas moved confidently against an invisible enemy, as if he was dancing through a series of kicks, blocks, and punches. Bare chested and glistening from sweat, he was a feast for Cyril's eyes. The ogre often joked about his soft middle, but Daumantas' thick arms and defined chest gave away the strong body he usually hid under his fine clothes.

Coming to a rest, Daumantas turned to meet Cyril's gaze with a smile. He walked over, and they shared a kiss through the window.

"How did you sleep?" Daumantas asked, panting lightly from his workout.

Cyril gently toyed with some of Daumantas' straight, blue-black hair which had fallen across his face. "I'm a bit sore this morning," he answered with a smirk, "but I slept very well."

Daumantas tried to hide a self-satisfied smile. "Would you like to spar with me a little? It might help loosen you up a bit."

A wicked smile slowly spread across Cyril's face. "What did you have in mind?"

As Daumantas caught his implied meaning, his face reddened dramatically. "Not *that* kind of sparring!"

They both shared a laugh. Cyril extracted himself from the bed and put on his loose trousers. He went through the door and hopped down off the wagon's steps into the grass.

"I haven't sparred in a bit." Cyril stretched as he talked. "I'll admit I'm not as good at hand-to-hand combat as you are."

Daumantas chuckled at Cyril's assessment of his martial prowess. "I could always teach you what I know," he said earnestly.

Daumantas kept a close eye on Cyril as the two circled one

another. Cyril lashed out with his fists, but Daumantas casually batted them away.

"I much prefer the other 'dancing' we do," Cyril said.

He tried to land another punch, but Daumantas grabbed his arm, pulled him off balance, and pushed him off his feet. He landed in the grass with a soft thud. Daumantas casually pinned him there, smiling.

"Is this more your speed this morning?" he asked, leaning close for a kiss.

Cyril laughed and sat up to meet him. "You just wanted an excuse to have me on my back again," Cyril mumbled against Daumantas' lips.

He could feel the other man smiling before he pulled away.

Four

BACK IN THE WAGON, Cyril and Daumantas lay together after they enjoyed one another's company more intimately. The morning's sparring "match" had aroused them both too much to deny one another. Cyril draped himself across Daumantas' chest, listening to the other man's deep breaths.

"We can't make love all day, though I do wish we could." Daumantas heaved a dramatic sigh.

Cyril sat up, but his partner didn't follow. "I'm not sure how I'm going to be on my feet all day, but I'll manage."

He rubbed his legs and stretched them out on the bed. His thighs felt weak in the most satisfying way. He and his lover gazed at each other, enjoying the afterglow of their lovemaking.

Daumantas smiled, putting a hand on Cyril's chest. "I'm so lucky to have a man like you."

Cyril gave a short laugh. "How do you mean?"

As Daumantas mulled over his response, he brought his hand up and laid it gently on Cyril's cheek. "You aren't intimidated by me. Or anyone, really. You're so sure of yourself." He sat up. "Many men aren't as confident in themselves as you."

Cyril laughed at his lover's remark. "You mean to tell me

natural born men aren't secure in their manhood?" He rolled his eyes for dramatic effect. "Do tell me something I don't already know, love."

"You've never called me 'love' before." Daumantas leaned forward and kissed Cyril on the cheek.

As nice as it felt, Cyril's stomach fluttered with embarrassment. He hadn't meant to say that; it'd simply slipped out.

Daumantas pulled Cyril close and whispered into his ear, his soft breath hot on Cyril's cheek. "Do you love me?"

The question held a great deal of weight for both men. This relationship was supposed to be casual. While they could bed other people when separated by Daumantas' work, both men simply waited to be with one another instead.

Come on, Cyril thought to himself. *Say the words, you fool!*

"I think I want to go back with you to Olten when summer ends." Not quite "I love you," but they were the words Cyril could produce.

Daumantas' shoulders slumped. "Hm. That was an odd dodge. But not a 'no.' I suppose it'll have to do for today." He stood and sullenly began to dress. The mood in the wagon cooled considerably.

"I'm sorry. I'm not…ready yet to say if…" Cyril stumbled over his words. *To say that I love you.* The thought made Cyril's heart ache.

"It's alright. I didn't say it either," Daumantas murmured. He leaned over the bed, and they shared one more kiss. Daumantas smiled, though its usual warmth was subdued by sadness. "You should get dressed before Dimitru finds you here naked and alone."

The two parted with a heavy silence hanging between them.

———

Several weeks passed. The summer days grew long and sweltering. Joy over the warmer weather wore thin, and the inevitable grumbling about the hot weather began.

The two lovers found their way into one another's arms as often as possible. The question, "Do you love me?" hung between them, though both men fastidiously ignored it. The question would have to wait for calmer days and cooler nights to answer. The feast of Saint Vodomor fast approached, and the festival brought the thickest crowds Ford Town would see all year.

The days leading up to the festival became incredibly busy for both Cyril and Daumantas. Cyril spent most days mediating all sorts of petty disagreements, and Daumantas' cloth stall was mobbed by throngs of people trying to buy his finest wares before the crowds picked his stall clean. The two lovers saw very little of one another during those days. They were often too tired for anything other than their own beds.

Thunderous church bells tolled at first light and heralded the arrival of the feast day. Cyril dressed and headed downstairs to the main hall where his fellow Keepers of the Peace laughed and enjoyed a fine breakfast.

Dimitru hailed him and clapped him on the back when he crossed into the room. "Happy feast day, my friend!" he exclaimed, smiling from ear to ear.

Cyril couldn't help but do the same. "A happy feast day to you!" He greeted Dimitru as they walked together to the feasting table.

The other Keepers chatted and had a leisurely morning. Marcus, a dark-skinned man originally from Grendair, waved Cyril over. He handed him a plate heaped with eggs, sliced tomato, and thick bread spread with creamy butter.

"Do you see this ridiculous meal Dimitru provided?" Marcus laughed.

"I humbly accept this bounty." Cyril recited the ritual phrase customary for the feast of Saint Vodomor before seating himself. He grinned while Marcus playfully sampled everything on the table, the other Keepers of the Peace making merry all around.

Sharing food was an important part of the festival and sharing the morning with his fellow Keepers made Cyril's spirit light. They were all good-natured souls, and he was glad to work with them.

Only a small handful of the town's Keepers would be working

the crowds today. The festival would be busy, but most people set aside their grievances to enjoy the day. Dimitru and his father, Petru, would be highly visible among the masses crowding Ford Town, and the sight of the Boyar and his son always lightened people's moods.

Boyar Petru took great pride in his small trading post turned bustling hub. Their family had built the stone bridge across the Zult river and made travel to and from the City-States much easier. The swift flowing Zult River had very few ford points, and the next closest one was a full day's travel north of Ford Town.

Full of food and missing Daumantas, Cyril bid his fellow Keepers farewell to seek out his lover. Though it was still early, great crowds bustled about on Ford Town's streets. Most walked their neighborhoods exchanging food, as was customary. Others had set up small stalls to give food to passersby. Yet others simply handed food to people from the ground floor windows of their homes. There was much laughing and chatting with neighbors and out-of-town visitors while children ran and played with wild abandon.

As he passed through, Cyril shared some of the early harvest from the Keeper's garden. Along with an exercise yard for the Keepers to train and stay fit, the barracks had some green space where they communally tended a small gardening plot. Along with fruits and vegetables, Cyril grew medicinal herbs he'd learned about while receiving care from and later working for the monks at Vuretsiv. He'd loaded a basket full and now took time on his walk to distribute herbs to people he knew would benefit from their properties. He received a wealth of fruits, nuts, and sweet buns in return.

Giving away the excess he received, Cyril kept the choicer exchanges for himself. The sweet buns with berries were his favorite, and he saved most of the ones he'd been given. He made his way slowly to the caravan camps by the river. The trader's camps were also lively with folks dancing, playing music, and indulging in the customs of the feast day. Daumantas was sharing coffee by his own campfire with several merchants Cyril vaguely recognized when he walked up. He wasn't sure why, but his lover's companions shifted uncomfortably at Cyril's arrival.

Daumantas, however, gave him a warm smile. "Happy feast day, Cyril! Would you like some coffee?"

Not a native to Vodomeria, Daumantas wasn't a devotee of any of the saints, but he was familiar with the customs of the major feast days. Cyril knew from Svetlana, Daumantas' twin sister, that they worshiped the Great Dragons of the Khanate. Being from Farizhniya, their traditions were often mixed, as the customs of the Khanate and the Voivodates overlapped in the Tsardom and City-States.

Cyril smiled and hefted his full basket as he took the warm cup he was handed. "As you can see, I have plenty of food to share. You can't pass by almost anyone without being handed something today. Are you in town for the festival?" Cyril asked the merchants as he took a seat by the fire.

He recognized the felis woman. She'd been by Daumantas' stall often these past few weeks. She had brilliant green eyes, and her fur was a mottled black and ginger. She smiled and nodded politely at Cyril's question. The other person, an ogre he'd seen but never talked to, ignored him to talk to Daumantas in hushed tones.

The felis woman frowned at her companion's rudeness and said, "It's good to finally have a moment to talk to you, Cyril. I'm Claudia. It's very nice to meet you." She extended her hand to Cyril in a friendly gesture.

"It's very nice to finally be formally introduced," he replied as he took her hand and gave it a gentle kiss.

"My companion and I actually belong to the same guild as Daumantas. Sadly, we aren't staying for the full festival," She sighed and gazed into her cup, "I plan on traveling home later today before the roads get too busy."

"Ah," Cyril said as he sipped his coffee.

He didn't believe either resembled the other tailors he'd met. They both wore fine travel clothes, but otherwise they traveled lightly and, as far as Cyril could tell, without a wagon or goods.

He'd always taken Daumantas at his word about his profession, but occasionally Cyril felt the man hid something from him.

"We should be going. Come, Claudia." The unfamiliar ogre stood, his face a stony mask.

Claudia's brow furrowed, but she didn't argue. "I hope to see you again, Cyril. Enjoy the festival!" She gave Cyril a smile and a friendly pat on the shoulder before she walked away.

Once the pair walked out of earshot, Daumantas mumbled under his breath, though Cyril didn't catch what he said.

"What was that?" Cyril asked.

"My apologies for my friend. He's very leery of strangers." Daumantas frowned at his companions' backs as they left. Cyril offered him one of the sweet buns he'd collected, but the big man politely refused.

"It's alright," Cyril said, "Though his sour ass could probably use the day to relax." He took a big bite out of the bun in his hand.

Daumantas laughed. "I agree. Kanat can be…difficult to work with."

"Claudia seems nice. Do you work with them often?" Cyril asked with a mouth full of sweet bun.

"We have an assignment together. Collecting foreign wares." Daumantas stared in the direction his companions traveled in for a moment. "It's a bit difficult to explain. We have very strict rules about guild business. Have to protect our trade secrets, after all!" He gave a smile Cyril didn't quite believe was genuine, but he let it go. Daumantas had proven to be more trustworthy and reliable than any other man he'd met.

Deciding it was best to mind his own business, Cyril changed the subject. "Are you competing this year?"

"Hm?" The big ogre helped himself to some of the nuts and fruits Cyril brought as he considered the question. Then he swallowed hard and grinned. "I'm going to be in the wrestling tournament!"

"Oh, really?" Cyril smiled. "Showing off?"

"Watching you win the fencing tourney last year lit a fire in me!

I want to push myself to my limit!" Daumantas pulled the sleeve up on his tunic to show off his arm as he flexed.

Cyril chuckled at his boyish antics. "So…showing off?"

"As if you weren't!" Daumantas teased with a smirk.

The two of them shared a laugh, but Cyril couldn't deny Daumantas was right. Last year he'd entered the fencing tourney just to show off his skills.

"You don't have anything to prove, you know." Cyril put a hand on the other man's knee.

"I know, but I'm a bit nostalgic for some physical competition." Daumantas sounded wistful for a faraway time and place. He went to sip his coffee and grimaced when he found only grounds at the bottom of his cup. "I've been a bit eager to put my martial training to the test again."

Wrestling wasn't exactly fighting, but Cyril understood what Daumantas felt. Sometimes Cyril missed the duels. The constant testing of his skills had made him the swordsman he was now. He wouldn't be nearly as skilled if he hadn't spent several rigorous years being pushed to the limit on the regular.

He imagined Daumantas didn't often get opportunities to use his martial arts training. He'd witnessed a time or two when a drunken buffoon or unruly patron would get too physical with the large man. Daumantas balanced his physically large frame with an easy smile and calm demeanor. He wasn't particularly confrontational by nature, in stark contrast to his boisterous twin sister. Sometimes that led crass types to believe he could be bullied. Though never unnecessarily rough, he'd always find a way to restrain the offending party with ease. He could move with a swiftness and a grace one wouldn't expect form a man of his size.

After they cleaned up the remnants of their meal, they headed together towards the festival grounds. The fields had been marked and roped off for various physical competitions, some of which were already under way. Those who won their respective tournaments would be allowed to feast with Boyar Petru Novadi later in the evening. The main virtues embodied by Saint Vodomor were both great strength and kindness, and his feast day was filled with demonstrations of both in equal measure.

Along with the various physical competitions, there were also games and entertainers of every kind. As the two worked their way through the crowd, they stopped to admire jugglers, acrobats, contortionists, and musicians, all trying to outdo one another for the pleasure and coin from the crowds. Among the Vodomerian humans, there were large bear-bodied ursus, lithe cat-like felis, and even reclusive wolf-like lupines mingling in the crowd. Fewer in number were the local ogres, though they were easier to spot today with their ribbon-decorated horns.

Cyril stopped to admire a particularly deft juggler when he noticed Daumantas' eyes following someone in the crowd. He strained to see what had caught the other man's eye, but being so short, his view was blocked by the mass of people. As he was about to ask, a familiar figure broke through the throngs and caught Daumantas in a fierce hug.

"Baby brother!" she cried.

"*Svetlana?*" Cyril and Daumantas practically shouted in unison.

Cyril laughed as Daumantas attempted to extricate himself from his sister's grip. Svetlana looked resplendent in a beautiful dress, rich with delicate embroidery popular in the Tsardom of Farizhniya.

She released her brother, laughing. "I missed you! Mother and father wanted me to check in on you."

Daumantas made a face. "I can take care of myself," he snapped defensively. "I'm not a child."

Svetlana's face fell a little. "I know. But you know father."

It was clear Daumantas regretted his words, as his entire countenance slumped. Before he could apologize, Svetlana turned her attention to Cyril. With a big smile, she lifted him right off his feet with a big hug. Cyril couldn't help but laugh as she squealed and jostled him to and fro.

"Your chest is really soft," Cyril said, he grinned as Svetlana put his feet back on the ground.

Svetlana hoisted her breasts proudly. "Not bad," she said with a smirk, "considering I wasn't born with them."

The comment made Daumantas laugh along with Cyril and Svetlana. "I'm happy to see you, too," he said a bit sheepishly and gave her a reassuring smile. "You know I love you more than anything in the world."

Svetlana let a warm smile spread again across her face. "I don't doubt it for a minute, little brother." She loved calling him 'little brother' despite them being twins. She'd been born a little before him, but that didn't mean she couldn't hold it over his head.

She took Daumantas' hand and squeezed it, and they continued their journey across the festival grounds. Daumantas needed to hurry and join the wrestling tournament. As they approached the wrestling ring, they could hear a facilitator calling for entrants to step forward. Looking nervous at the sight of his competition, Daumantas rushed forward to declare his intent to participate.

Taking their places with the other spectators waiting for the match to begin, Svetlana and Cyril stood holding hands. "Has my brother been good to you?" she asked quietly as other spectators milled about, jockeying for places to stand or sit with a good view of the wrestling ring.

Cyril leaned onto her shoulder, smiling. "You know he is." A happy warmth bloomed in Cyril's chest as he spoke. "Do you even need to ask?"

She giggled at his response and grinned broadly. "No, but I like to make sure!"

People came and went, handing out food and drink to those they passed by. Cyril and Svetlana happily helped themselves to everything they were offered. One stranger insisted Cyril help himself to a great quantity of sweet cakes with berries. Svetlana passed on the sweets, but Cyril casually ate the berry cakes as they watched the tournament. The first several rounds were mixed, and some of the competitors were wildly unevenly matched. A large ursus man and an ogre Cyril didn't recognize put on a better show, heaving and pushing bodily on one another until the ogre shoved his opponent from the ring in an impressive display of physical power.

Finally, Daumantas stepped up for his match. Cyril and Svetlana whooped and waved from where they stood. He nervously waved back at them from the edge of the ring. Cyril swore quietly when he saw Daumantas' opponent. Bohden stepped up to the other side. Scattered cheers went up for him from around the crowd. Being a frequent visitor and a generally decent fellow, Bohden was well liked within Ford Town.

Both competitors were stripped to the waist. They were about the same size, though Bohden clearly had more obvious lean muscle. They met in the middle of the ring and assumed their stances.

Cyril saw Bohden had his long, dark auburn hair tied back and a dangerous glint in his eye. While he hadn't been Bohden's lover in a while, Cyril knew the man had an over-protective streak. He had a hard time imagining his lifelong friend and former lover hadn't engineered this match against Daumantas.

"What in the name of the Saints is that fool up to?" Cyril wondered aloud as the match began.

Cyril held his breath as they clashed, pushing against one another. Bohden would heave and Daumantas would slide or yield a bit, then brace himself and return with equal force. The crowd's attention was concentrated on the men straining against one another in the ring. Cheers of encouragement went up throughout the crowd for both men.

Struck by sudden illness, Cyril turned from the match to seek some relief. His heart thundered in his chest and felt as though he was racing even though he was standing still. While he walked unsteadily away, he lost his balance and found himself staring at everyone's feet. Cyril became confused and frightened, unable to recall the moment he fell to the ground. He tried to stand, only to collapse once more, and he heard someone scream. Darkness pressed in around his field of vision. Fighting to stay conscious, he could feel Svetlana at his side, and the crowd frantically moved around them.

Daumantas' worried face swam before his eyes before everything went dark.

Five

CHAOS SWIRLED around Ruslan while he searched the palace for Voivode Tymor. The celebrations for the feast of Saint Vodomor quickly fell into chaos as revelers within the palace, including the Voivode himself, collapsed suddenly at the feasting table. Laurent had made no guarantee the poisoned parties would die, only that it would act fast and cause a stir. Ruslan wanted to delay any treatment Tymor might receive, and time was short. The healing priests of Saint Nauen had a substantial presence within the city and the head of their order was in attendance, which made it difficult to kill anyone by poison. His personal desires pushed aside his better judgment, and he shouldered his way through the crowd in search of the Voivode.

Hadeon had been more than happy to agree to their plan, once he saw reason. Laurent's appearance at the castle had stirred bitter feelings at first, but Hadeon's desire for revenge and power quickly tempered his hatred for the rebels Laurent led. Ruslan accompanied Hadeon on the trip to Triadoara several weeks prior under the false pretense of answering Voivode Tymor's letter to seek reconciliation.

The poisoning had been easy enough to carry out. Laurent had operatives loyal to himself sneak in cakes baked full of dangerous berries into the kitchens. Ruslan didn't fully understand the particulars of their semi-magical concealment, but the results of their labors were plain to see. He spotted the Voivode being hauled through the palace on a litter, accompanied by the head of the Royal Guard, a priest of Saint Nauen, and the Princess Consort. He rushed forward to stop them, but Laurent caught him and held him with an unnaturally strong grip.

"What are you doing?" Ruslan hissed at his companion, his anger rising fast.

Laurent tightened his grip on Ruslan, giving him a frosty glance. "The Voivode has been displaced. There's no need to do more damage."

"But he has to die for—"

"He only needs to be displaced. Go chasing after him to hinder their efforts, and you'll give us away!"

Laurent turned Ruslan loose once the Voivode and his caregivers moved out of sight. Ruslan remained calm for a moment, then sprinted off to search for the Voivode's teenaged son. He wanted leverage over Voivode Tymor if he survived the attempt on his life.

The panicked crowd kept Laurent from catching Ruslan once more as he dashed to the courtyard. Sure enough, he spotted Symon and the felis bard, Octavius, entering the stables among the throngs of guests now retrieving their own horses and carriages to flee the palace.

In vain, Ruslan shouted at the small knot of Zhupensken soldiers, trying to get them to stop Octavius and his charge. His words were lost in the chaos, and he bounded down the stairs into the courtyard after them. He made a mad attempt to grab the horse the pair rode on, but Octavius gave a primal hiss and lashed out at Ruslan with a dagger. The horse whinnied and reared up, threatening to throw its riders. Ruslan was forced to retreat from the horse's flailing hooves, and the pair galloped through the gate with the rest of the fleeing guests.

Swearing and kicking dust, Ruslan seethed and raged while the courtyard emptied around him. Panting and exhausted, he stood in the darkening yard for several long minutes before he ascended the stairs and headed back into the palace.

Laurent waited at the top of the stairs with his hands on his hips. "Are you quite finished?" He fell in step alongside Ruslan while he trotted back into the palace.

"*Nothing* has gone the way I planned it," Ruslan muttered under his breath.

Laurent scowled. "You keep adding your own flourishes, like the poisoning of the Princess."

"It was necessary." Ruslan grunted. Hadeon's shouted orders echoed off the walls around them while he did his part to secure the palace. "The Steel Rose is a coward. I thought her strong once, but she gave into her own childish whims and ran away a long time ago."

"Yet you still seem to fear her." Laurent threw him a questioning glance. "Why is that?"

"Because I don't know what he's scheming. Why else would he come back to Vodomeria?" Ruslan felt anger burning deep within him. He'd journeyed to Ford Town a week prior and confirmed the identity of the former princess himself.

"He?" Laurent quirked an eyebrow.

"Slip of the tongue! I'm exhausted!"

Ruslan marched away from Laurent, intent on finding a quiet place to clean up and bed down for the night. Laurent's servants should be riding back to the Zhupenksen fief now, and in a day or so, the soldiers assembled there would descend on the capital. He wanted to be well rested to enact the next steps of their plan.

Bathed and in a comfortable bed, Ruslan couldn't find relief for his restless mind. He tossed and turned, unable to rest. The door squeaked open, and he sat upright, clutching a dagger. Ruslan allowed himself to relax when Laurent entered his chamber.

Laurent smiled slightly as he walked towards Ruslan's bed. The slim sorcerer casually shrugged off the plain traveling priest's robes he wore to disguise himself. He slid onto the bed with Ruslan, making no effort to hide his arousal. "You've been wound so tightly since we put this plan into action," he purred, running a hand along

Ruslan's jaw and through his sandy blonde hair. "I hope I can find a way to calm your disposition."

Desire ignited within Ruslan, and he dragged Laurent further into the bed, giving him a rough kiss as he did so. The pair spent the night testing each other's endurance. Ruslan was happy to have a companion he could be rough with, and Laurent seemed inexhaustible. Once spent, the two slept soundly until well into the morning.

Aching but satisfied, Ruslan dragged himself from bed to assess the situation beyond his room. Eerily quiet now, the royal palace was all but abandoned, save for a few older servants and Zhupensken soldiers working to secure the building. Ruslan found Hadeon Zhupensken and his meager inner circle eating breakfast in the grand hall.

"Ruslan! Come join us!" Hadeon enthusiastically slapped the table beside him as he called to the younger man.

Ruslan frowned at the state of the room as he walked towards Hadeon and his men. Uneaten food littered the tables and chairs lay scattered about, upended as last night's guests panicked and fled the palace. The older men sitting with Hadeon regarded Ruslan with varying degrees of suspicion.

Ladislaus, one of Hadeon's oldest attendants, dug into Ruslan before he could settle into his seat. "This plan of yours is going to go to shit if we can't shift suspicion onto someone else."

"Blaming the bard will be easy enough." Ruslan leaned back in his chair and assumed a casual stance. "The fact that he fled with the prince will work to our advantage. We only need to catch him and torture him into confessing to the crime."

Ladislaus snorted. "Awfully confident in yourself, aren't you?"

"We control the palace, don't we?" Ruslan stood, gesturing around him. "We only need to secure the rest of the capital and apply the correct amount of pressure on the other boyars to achieve our goal."

"If you're so concerned, maybe you should fetch the boy and the bard." Hadeon gave Ladislaus a glare that made it clear it wasn't a suggestion. "Gather a detachment and go find them!"

"Now?" Ladislaus sneered. Being Hadeon's right-hand man, he wasn't used to being treated like a common underling. The two were so like-minded, he'd never been in a position where Hadeon didn't agree with him.

Hadeon stood and waved him away dismissively. "You heard me! All you've done is bitch and moan this whole time!" He paced anxiously in front of his chair. "Ruslan has gotten results. It's time for you to pull your weight!"

His jaw slack, Ladislaus rose from his chair and left the room. Several other men around the table stood and walked away with him. The rest of the meager party quietly found other business to attend to, none too eager to lose whatever little favor they had with Hadeon.

The old boyar chuckled to himself as the room emptied. "Can't let them forget who's in charge for one moment, or they go soft." Hadeon glanced over at Ruslan. "Your willfulness annoys me sometimes, but at least you understand."

"I live to serve, sire." Ruslan gave a bow with more respect than he felt for the old man. Hadeon only had to believe in Ruslan's loyalty.

A foot soldier ran into the great hall. "My lord!" He bowed as his eyes landed on Hadeon. "The troops from the fief are here!"

"Already?" Ruslan knew Laurent had some trickery at play to expedite the process, but he had no idea it would be *this* quick.

Hadeon's face went from shocked to thrilled. "Wonderful!" He clapped Ruslan on the shoulder. "The sorcerer has made good on all the things he promised!" The old boyar's face became more serious. "We need to secure the capital as quickly as possible. Take the sorcerer and get to work. No time to waste!"

It took a bit to find Laurent, but Ruslan finally spotted him in the library, casually leafing through the modest collection of books there.

"Your trick worked," Ruslan said, leaning on the door frame. He watched Laurent's slim fingers gently flipping the pages of a delicate tome. "It's time. Are the gates secure?"

Laurent didn't immediately respond, but eventually he said,

"My men have forced most of the city guard out. They're currently holed up in a guard house at the Pauper's Bridge east of Triadoara." He glanced around the room, the expression on his face unreadable. "I'm surprised these primitive people managed to preserve so many Finndrigairian documents."

His mind wandering, Ruslan walked deeper into the room. The Princess spent long hours here reading. The image of her sitting near the windows appeared ghost-like in his mind. He felt a strong urge to rip the books off the shelves and flip the tables. He wanted to tear the palace apart and rebuild it in his own image. He wanted to erase her memory from his mind.

"Ruslan?" Laurent called to him, bringing him back to the present.

"This place harbors a lot of memories for me," Ruslan mumbled, turning to exit the room. "I'm eager to move forward with our plans. Come, it is time to stake our claim."

Laurent pulled his hood up and over his face as they walked through the halls of the palace.

Daumantas' and Svetlana's voices drifted across Cyril's mind as he struggled to regain consciousness. The fear of death brought diffi-cult memories back to Cyril as dreams.

———

"Marriage?" Cyril was furious.

He'd never agreed to marry anyone, but his father had announced his betrothal to the Monoran crown prince during dinner that very evening. Vexed, he'd stomped all the way to his father's private chambers to have a word with him.

There's no way in hell I'm marrying some man I've never met, he thought to himself as he stormed past the guards and into his father's private study.

"Father." Cyril poured all his anger into the word as he pushed through the door.

Voivode Tymor sat behind an impressively carved desk. Two lamps on either side provided the only illumination in the space. Tymor barely glanced up from the parchment he was writing on. His brow furrowed slightly at Cyril's arrival, but otherwise his attention stayed on the document under his quill.

Cyril crossed his arms over his chest. "I'm not marrying the Monoran crown prince. Not without dueling him first."

That was their agreement. He'd wear dresses and play the part of being a princess, but he refused to marry unless the suitor could best him in a duel. His father had agreed, totally unaware the princess he'd sent away as a small child was now quite proficient with a blade. The princess proved to be a sword-wielding marvel, and even after several years Cyril remained undefeated.

Clearly, Tymor grew tired of the spectacle. "No. You will not be dueling this one." He stood and leaned over the desk, his hands pressing into it as if bracing against his child's pleas.

Cyril raked his nails across the material of his dress. The tight cloth felt like a prison. It pushed his chest forward and exaggerated it in a way he hated, and it only enraged him further. He charged the desk, slamming his hands on the surface so hard the oil lamps shook. "But father!"

"But nothing! You will marry the Monoran crown prince!"

Identical sets of gray eyes locked angry gazes, and Cyril's jaw worked silently, mouthing unvoiced protests.

"You should be grateful I found you a man at all," The Voivode continued, walking around his writing desk. "No man in the kingdom would take you with your reputation, and—"

Cyril's fist silenced him as it connected with his jaw with a meaty thwack. Tymor stumbled backward, and Cyril launched himself at his father, though the guards caught and restrained him before he could assault his father further. Thrashing and screaming with rage, Cyril tried to break free of their grip.

Tymor stood a moment, massaging his bruised jaw. His eyes were hard as flint as he regarded his unruly child. "Take the princess to her chambers," he said, rubbing his face. "She can stay there until she sees reason!"

Cyril wailed and fought the guards until they threw him into his private chamber. He lost his fury as he heard the door lock behind him. Collapsing to the floor, he began to sob.

Lilya; his surrogate mother and only attendant, was quietly darning socks when the guards forced Cyril inside. She rushed to him, and he felt her warm hands on his back. Lilya was the mother Cyril never had. She and her husband Orest were tasked with raising Cyril when Voivode Tymor left to quell the rebellion at the Monster Wall to the west, and she'd been his near constant companion through this difficult time in his life.

With a primal wail, Cyril clawed at his uncomfortable dress. His fingers found a weak seam, and he dug into it, ripping the fabric. He stood suddenly, tears obscuring his vision and sobs still wracking his body. He could feel Lilya following his movements, unsure of how to comfort him. Ripping the fabric away, he exposed his chest. The soft breasts felt impossibly large and unsightly to his eyes. He rummaged inside a large wardrobe and found a knife he'd hidden there for protection. Grabbing a handful of his own breast, he placed the knife along the underside where it met his body.

"If I didn't have these things they wouldn't treat me this way!" The knife bit into his flesh, causing blood to flow down his torso.

Lilya's trembling hand pressed on top of his own. "My darling child. My beautiful child, please…" Lilya begged. Her voice cracked and wavered.

With a sob, Cyril released the knife and Lilya took it gently from his hands. He cried into Lilya's shoulder until he felt empty. "I can't do this anymore," he whispered as they stood there, holding one another.

Cyril never really thought of himself as a girl and was devastated when he began to develop a woman's body. Orest had always tolerated his keen interest in boyish pursuits, and allowed him to assume a boy's name, wear a boy's clothes, and continue to learn knightly skills. In return for this privilege, Cyril agreed to spend some time on reading, writing, and womanly pursuits with Lilya.

Being called back to court and the scrutiny of Voivode Tymor at seventeen years of age had upended Cyril's whole existence. His father forced him to give up his boy's name and lifestyle for that of a woman of the royal court. Now he was twenty, and he still hadn't been able to convince his father he was a man. Lilya tried to help him maintain a good disposition, but Cyril had wilted and became despondent during his years in Triadoara.

Only the duels now brought him joy.

"What am I supposed to do?" Cyril's voice was thick with despair.

Lilya gently treated his self-inflicted wound. She pursed her lips, deep in thought. "Perhaps the answers you need are at Vuretsiv."

"Vuretsiv? The Healing City?" Cyril felt like his head was stuffed with cotton from weeping.

Lilya took a breath. "Maybe the healing monks of Saint Vuretz can take this chest from you." She gazed at him with an expression full of love and concern. "You clearly can't stay here. They can help you be the New Man I know you are."

The thought had never occurred to Cyril that he could go to Vuretsiv. It was easily a month's travel from Vodomeria. The monks of Saint Vuretz practiced incredibly potent healing magics—so powerful, in fact, many thought it the stuff of legends. Supposedly, they could heal any wound and cure any illness. But could they really do such a thing? Take away these breasts that had tormented him for so long? And would Cyril's predicament even warrant their treatment?

But Lilya had never steered him wrong before, and Cyril felt hope kindle deep in his chest. "I do wish I could live as a New Man. Do you really think they could help me?"

He allowed Lilya to help him out of his torn dress and into a soft nightgown. She took his face between her soft hands, and they gazed at one another, tears still sparkling in Lilya's eyes.

"My *son*," she said emphasizing the word in a way that warmed Cyril's heart, "I want you to live! If you stay here, trying to live as a woman, I know you will die." The older woman tried to swallow her tears, but they escaped in slow rivulets down her face.

Cyril pulled her close. "I don't want to die, Lilya. Not really."

In truth, he thought about how easy it would be to end his life regularly. He hated how much he wanted to escape this life. He hated that he'd rather die than keep living trapped in an existence he despised so much. But he didn't want to leave Lilya or his friends. And so, he'd hung on.

But how much longer could he hold it together?

Thoughts of escaping to Vuretsiv gave him a hope he hadn't felt since he'd first arrived in Triadoara. Cyril's tired mind conjured images of a new life in a faraway place. Escaping the palace and living how he pleased felt too tantalizing to not at least entertain.

That night, they agreed to a plan of action. Cyril would remain confined to his chambers while Lilya and Orest prepared to secret him out of the royal palace. Lilya agreed to smuggle supplies into Cyril's chambers, then, together, they would work to bundle essentials for travel to Vuretsiv.

Cyril further kept himself occupied by shadow fencing and continued his daily workouts. He'd need to keep his skills sharp for the long journey. It would take weeks to reach Vuretsiv, even if they managed to procure horses. Orest came and stood within view of his bedchamber window. He would notify Cyril when the time came to put their plan into action. He'd signal by shaking or nodding his head slowly. Three days and three slow shakes. The time was not yet right.

On the fourth day, Lilya came bearing a great bundle of laundry so big it obscured her from view. She awkwardly wobbled through the doorway as she pushed past the guards vigilantly monitoring Cyril's chamber. The confusion was plain on his face as Lilya unceremoniously dumped the bundle on the floor. She giggled as she undid the careful concealment: a heap of dresses had been cleverly wound around a central bundle of men's clothing.

A smile slowly teased its way across Cyril's face. He'd refused to put a dress on these past several days, favoring a loose pair of trousers and bindings across his chest. He observed while Lilya assembled a particular outfit from the assorted articles of men's clothes she'd smuggled into the room.

"I need you to try these on," she said. "I want to make sure they fit."

She handed him a wrap tunic made of linen, a brightly colored sash, a baggy pair of trousers favored by swordsmen, and a fine woolen overcoat. Once he was dressed, Cyril looked down at himself and smiled. Usually, he was only able to wear men's clothes when he sneaked out of the palace with his friends.

Lilya fussed over him and smoothed the fabric with her hands for a few moments. "They aren't the finest, but I've been working with the washer women for days to get you proper clothes." She pushed his short rose red hair behind his ears, taking the moment to hold his face. "You look happy."

"Thank you, Lilya." Cyril cupped her hands with his own, pressing them to his cheeks.

"I can't have you going off without proper clothes," Lilya said, obviously trying to remain upbeat. "I'll miss you. I know you're more than capable, but…"

"I'll come back," he promised. "One day."

Cyril swallowed the fear swimming inside him. He was eager to leave, but he knew Voivode Tymor would relentlessly pursue him to the border. He was unsure of his father's reach beyond the Voivodates. The nearest port was in Monor, and he had no doubt that if he went there, they'd cooperate to return the runaway bride-to-be to their crown prince.

Orest planned to head east and cross the Zult River into the City-States of the Greensea Forest. It was a major overland route favored by pilgrims traveling to Vuretsiv. The road curved north around the inland sea and then south along the coast, past the tip of the Thornback mountains and to the Healing City cradled among the hills. Hopefully, it would help him avoid capture.

Cyril opened his window to look for Orest, who stood on the other side of the courtyard. With bated breath, Cyril waited to see what he would do, tamping down a whoop of joy when the man gave a short nod.

It was finally time.

The next morning, Cyril dressed as his father would expect him to and asked the guard very politely if he could speak with the Voivode. After a short consultation, they led him to his father's apartment. Voivode Tymor was inside, servants helping with his final garments when they entered.

"Seen reason, have you?" Tymor's smug tone grated on Cyril's nerves.

He stared at his feet to disguise his disgust and to appear demure. "Yes, father." He tried to sound as pitiable and meek as he could.

The Voivode walked over to Cyril and took him by the chin, tilting his face up in an uncomfortably firm grip. "Not planning anything foolish, are we?" His words twisted Cyril's stomach. "I heard you cut yourself."

"No, father." He breathed again as he relaxed. Any mention of the wound under his breast made it itch.

"Good!" Tymor walked past Cyril towards the door. "Then I'll allow you to have free movement about the palace again. The crown prince of Monor will be here within a few days to formally accept you as his bride-to-be. I expect you to be on your best behavior. I'd hate to have to put you in a cell until he arrives."

Cyril bowed low. "I'm not happy about it, but I'll do as I'm told." He included a little truth to help disguise the lie.

Tymor dismissed the guards and escorted Cyril to the main chambers below.

The rest of the day went by in a blur. Cyril went about monotonous appearances and various court functions. The sun began to dip low, and a feast was set to celebrate the impending wedding. Twilight gave way to darkness, and the night wore on. The drink flowed freely, and merry making began in earnest as the rest of the court relaxed and enjoyed the evening.

Cyril waited until the festivities were beginning to peak before slipping away. He retrieved a bundle Lilya had hidden and snuck down to the latrines to change his clothes. Cyril took his time as he made his way back through the palace, checking to make sure his path was clear.

The one downside to his escape route was that he'd have to pass the main hall on the way to the side gate he planned to leave the palace from. Cyril hurried with his head down as revelers spilled out into the corridor. Some sought to relieve themselves and headed for the latrines; others were feeling their drink and the merriment spill over in other ways. He hoped to pass through the halls unnoticed, and he'd cleared most of the crowd when he ran bodily into a man walking the other direction.

Mumbled apologies were exchanged, and Cyril tried to slip past, but the man grabbed his arm and pulled his hood away from his face. Tymor sputtered a few moments. He was very drunk, but he clearly recognized his own child.

Cyril's heart sank. He'd blown it. Being caught by his father trying to sneak out was the end of his adventure—his future.

He released Cyril's arm, and after some fumbling, he thrust his belt—sword, dagger, and all—into Cyril's chest. "You want to be a man? Fine! When you're done fooling around, you'll do as I say!" The Voivode stumbled off, angry but not acting to stop his wayward child.

Cyril bundled the weapons away and fought the urge to run the rest of the way out of the palace.

Six

CYRIL COULD FEEL himself drifting in and out of consciousness. He occasionally heard things happening around him: frantic arguing over treatment, someone sobbing softly at his side, praying, his own sobbing as he struggled to move and speak. He felt someone's hands on his for a time. These brief moments of consciousness were all that punctured the dark swallowing Cyril's mind for what felt like an eternity.

He wasn't sure how long it gripped him, but the darkness finally receded, and Cyril opened his eyes. The weak light in the room felt blinding to him at first. His body was weak, akin to the deep lethargy one had after a serious illness. His head felt like it was stuffed with cotton, and half-formed thoughts bumped slowly around inside his mind.

Had he died? Is this what death feels like? Cyril had to concede that everything felt too mundane, and his body ached too much for him to be dead and in the afterlife. As his eyes adjusted to the light, he willed his head to move.

The architectural style appeared familiar, but it was much too clean and polished to be a plain Vodomerian building. Cyril couldn't identify anything familiar, so he didn't believe he was in Ford Town. Where was he?

Someone snored somewhere in the room, just beyond his sight. Cyril tried to call out, but his words were only breathy whispers. He wriggled around, searching for another way to rouse whoever was sleeping. Sitting up proved to be a monumental task. He managed to lift himself partway before flopping back into the pillows. Thankfully, the movement was enough to wake the snoring person.

Svetlana came into view as she walked around to Cyril's side. Tears filled her eyes as they met his own.

Cyril smiled and reached for her. "—a…ter. Water." His throat was so dry the discomfort stole his attention.

She dried her eyes, nodded and went to fetch him water to drink. When she returned, she helped him with the cup because he didn't have the strength to hold it himself.

"How are you feeling?" She gripped his hand, and Cyril could feel her trembling.

"I'm weak and tired. Could be worse." He tried to chuckle, but it came out a dry wheeze. "Where are we?" he asked, trying not to sink too deeply into the pillows.

Svetlana looked around, clearly weighing whether to answer his question. "I think I should let Daumantas explain."

She turned to walk away, and Cyril grabbed at her sleeve. "Please don't leave." His voice sounded weak and pathetic, but he couldn't stand the thought of being so helpless and alone.

She took his hand and gently set it back on the bed. "I'll summon him another way."

Svetlana moved to a cord hanging from a device on the wall. She gave it a few tugs before pulling a chair to Cyril's side to wait. She took a few moments to arrange Cyril's hair away from his face as they sat quietly. Cyril worried he may fall asleep again before Daumantas walked through the door.

He looked incredibly fatigued, but his face brightened when he saw Cyril was awake. "Thank the Four Great Dragons." Daumantas relaxed visibly as he walked over to the bed.

"Daumantas, what happened? Where am I?" Cyril asked weakly. He could feel his thoughts starting to flow more freely through his mind.

Daumantas took his hand and gave it a gentle squeeze. "Someone poisoned about a dozen people at the festival." His face screwed up and his shoulders slumped as he relayed the news. "Poisonous nightshade berries baked into cakes. Three children died. I...No one could save them." Daumantas' body shook, and he rubbed his face with a free hand. His jaw clenched as tears escaped his eyes. "You should rest. Svetlana and I will keep watch over you." His voice wobbled as he spoke, then he leaned down and kissed Cyril gently on the lips.

"I love you," Cyril murmured as he drifted back to sleep. Daumantas smiled as his eyes closed.

———

The next few days bled together. Cyril was only awake for short periods of time, long enough to eat, drink, and relieve himself. Daumantas and Svetlana both worked hard to help him regain his strength and attempted to make his recovery as comfortable as possible. By the third or fourth day, Cyril could finally stand and lift things on his own.

For some reason, the two kept declining to answer where exactly they all were, no matter how much he asked. Now that he could comfortably walk on his own and didn't need constant supervision, Cyril decided to venture out and see what lay beyond his room. Curiosity ate at him, and Cyril longed for something outside of the room he'd been in.

The building had smooth stone walls like those found in ancient Finndrigairian structures. It looked to be a fine marble, polished to a high shine. The ceiling was a dark, time-worn wood. Looking at it, he believed the wood to be newer than the stone, despite the stone's pristine appearance compared to the aged wood. Cyril wondered if the smoothness and precision laying of the stone was only possible through some feat of sorcery.

· · ·

Emerging from his room, he found the hallway was built with the same materials. Here and there he observed odd, time-darkened scars on the fine stonework, hinting at some struggle in the building's distant past. A placard hung beside his door with a clip and papers with notes written on them. The papers, written in the local language of the Voivodates, contained his name and a few details about the incident in Ford Town. Cyril understood nothing else written on the papers. He could only assume it was medical information and was there for the benefit of whoever provided his care.

Perhaps he was in a monastery? The reuse of ancient Finndrigairian structures wasn't unheard of; the lost civilization's ruins dotted the countryside across the Great Monster Wall region. The shells of buildings large and sturdy enough were often repurposed into churches and other communal structures. And if he received medical care here—wherever *here* was—it stood to reason that monks were involved.

Windows along one side of the arched hall let in enough light to brighten the interior of the building, enough so the brass lamps dotting the hall were unneeded this time of day. Several dark wooden doors punctured the walls at regular intervals on the other side, though one doorway in the middle of the hall had an elaborate metal gate. The building reminded him of paintings he'd seen of the tall tower houses popular in Grendair. Had he been taken there?

Before he could explore further, a strange click-clacking caught Cyril's attention. His heart pounded, and he nearly collapsed. *Please, for the love of all the Saints, do not let that be some Inferni coming down the hall.*

Cyril had only encountered Finndrigarian monsters a handful of times in his life. Inferni, often called Devil Bugs by locals, were strange, insect-like, metallic creatures spawned in old Finndrigairian ruins with no real explanation as to how. Their presence in Vodomeria often heralded an issue with the Monster Wall or disturbed ruins.

He pressed himself against the wall in fear. But instead of a monster, a diminutive ogress in a walking chair appeared on the landing of a stairwell set at the far end of the hall. Still a little stunned, Cyril stayed awkwardly plastered against the wall, certain he looked more shocked than he'd like.

A familiar face walked into view behind the woman. The lanky Kanat, whom he'd seen conversing with Daumantas days before, appeared on the landing as well. He stopped behind the seated ogress, clearly winded from climbing the stairs.

"Awake, the barbarian is," the ogress in the chair said in the language of the Tsardom.

Cyril found his composure and responded dryly in the same language. "Barbarian, I am not."

Kanat looked unsure of what to do. He bowed low to Cyril, choosing to speak in the language of the Voivodates. "I humbly apologize for my rudeness the other day. I was eager to return home, and the festival crowds had hampered my travel."

Cyril straightened his clothes and assumed a more relaxed stance. "Is this your home, then? It's very impressive." He gestured around at the polished walls.

Kanat looked relieved, though his face stayed pinched with worry. "I'd love to show you the Tor, but—"

"The *Tor*!" Cyril cried. "We're in a Finndrigarian *Tor*?" Another thrill of panic ran through Cyril, though he'd tried to tamp it down.

The ruins of Tors are where Inferni come from! The thought hammered around in Cyril's mind.

Kanat pinched the bridge of his nose. "Please, Mr. Valentin, the Tor is perfectly safe, I assure you."

"I…I'll have to take your word for it," Cyril said as he rushed to join the two ogres at the other end of the hall, still reeling from the revelation.

The seated ogress rolled her eyes and went back down the stairs, disappearing without another word.

Kanat sighed, shaking his head. "I actually came to fetch you. You have a visitor downstairs." He pursed his lips, "He's brought… troubling news."

Though Cyril's mind overflowed with questions, the stairs sapped his strength, and he had to concentrate to maneuver around the long spiral instead of asking them. He followed Kanat down several floors and emerged into a large main hall. Dimitru sat to one side, his gaze fixed on the floor until he heard them approach and turned his attention to their arrival. Daumantas entered the room with a tray of tea as Kanat and Cyril walked across the room to greet Dimitru.

Dimitru closed the gap between them. "I have some grave news." He wrung his traveling gloves with both his hands. "Your father was also poisoned during the festival. Word didn't reach Ford Town until yesterday."

"Did he die?" Cyril asked as he made for a seat. His legs felt unsteady, and his heart fluttered uncomfortably against his ribs.

"Word has it he survived. A priest of Saint Nauen and the Princess Consort managed to save his life, but it sounds like he's struggling." Dimitru paced the room as he talked. "They're both sequestered away in a monastery outside of Triadoara."

Cyril nodded. Tymor was alive for now. Self-entitled boyars were probably scrambling to try and snatch his throne.

"So, the capital is in chaos, I take it?" Cyril's question sounded more like a statement of fact.

Dimitru ran one of his hands through his hair. "Hadeon says he's the rightful Regent because he claims to be favored by your father. Things seem stable now, but it's hard to tell since we're so far from Triadoara."

Cyril gripped his chest. "Even if Tymor succumbs and dies, there will be an election. The council of boyars will decide the new Voivode." Cyril's tone grew bitter. "Hadeon hopes to position himself to make it hard to tell him he can't rule Vodomeria."

Dimitru pursed his lips. "No one knows for sure, but your half-brother seems to be missing as well. Some fear Hadeon is behind it."

This made Cyril's blood run cold. "We have to find him! We need—"

"No." Daumantas finally spoke, his tone firm. "You still need some rest. You should be fine in a few more days, but you can't leave right now."

"My brother—"

Daumantas held up a hand to hold back Cyril's protests. "If you aren't at your best, you won't be any help to anyone." The words stung, but Cyril knew Daumantas was right.

He decided to swallow his pride and move on, turning to Dimitru. "Do you happen to know if Bohden is still in town? I want him to go to the capital and watch over my father until I can set out myself."

Dimitru nodded. "He can travel with my father and me to the capital if he wishes. I'll give Bohden your message. My father is still waiting to depart, so I'll have to take my leave."

With a short bow, Dimitru let Kanat show him out of the hall.

A teacup found its way into Cyril's hands. He stared into its depths, wondering what he should do. Could he travel into the heart of Vodomeria himself? He'd purposely stuck to caravans traveling outside Vodomeria after he'd left home. Ford Town was barely in Vodomeria, and he'd had the protection of Petru Novadi. Symon had been a small boy when he'd left all those years ago. What kind of young man had his brother grown into?

"We should talk about how to best help your family," Daumantas said. He took the teacup and set it aside.

Cyril gripped Daumantas' arm to steady himself as he stood. "I'm not sure I can handle walking up all those stairs." Though he felt nearly normal, he found himself easily winded and was still tired from the trip down to the main hall.

"We'll be taking the lift up to my private room." Daumantas smiled at Cyril's puzzled look.

"Lift?" Cyril asked, walking slowly as he used Daumantas to keep his balance. They walked past the stairs to a doorway with a matching gate he'd seen near his own room.

"No sense in taking you all the way back up to the Infirmary since you're all but recovered now." Daumantas pulled a cord, and with a whirring sound, a booth lowered itself into the empty space behind the gate.

A bell chimed, and the gate opened. The elegant interlocking metalwork flexed and compressed to make way. Daumantas had to guide Cyril into the lift because he kept looking around, awed by the sleek wood and metal contraption.

"Mind the gate, please," Daumantas said, maneuvering an astounded Cyril onto the lift.

With another chime, the gate slid closed behind them. Daumantas pushed a lever around a dial marked with numbers, and the lift took them up several floors faster than Cyril was expecting. He clung to Daumantas, both to hold himself steady and to disguise his distrust of the machine. After one more chime, the door opened once more.

"I've heard of mechanical lifts being used in mines. Is this something similar?" Cyril asked as they stepped into a hall much like the one for the Infirmary.

Unlike the previous floor Cyril had been on, this one had a long rug running its length and assorted plants in pots lining the windowed wall. Daumantas led him to a door at the far end of the hall and produced a key from his robes. He unlocked his private chamber and opened the door with a bit of a flourish.

On the other side was a room with walls nearly covered floor to ceiling with shelves. Along with books, there were strange items and artifacts on display. Two doorways interrupted the shelves on two walls with a long window on the third. Cyril looked around the room and felt like he was seeing more of Daumantas than he ever had before. Seeing this room with Daumantas' personal effects made it painfully apparent how little they really knew of one another's personal lives.

"I should have known you weren't a tailor," he murmured.

"What do you think I am?" Daumantas asked as he gestured to a pair of plush chairs. Cyril sat in one as he took the other.

Cyril mused aloud while he scratched his chin. "Hmm…a spy? Or perhaps a smuggler of some sort. Someone who trades things with people in the know, dealing in secrets."

Daumantas chuckled at Cyril's assessment. "I suppose you aren't far off. Among other duties for the Sorcerer's Guild, I transport artifacts and records between Tors."

"So, you're a sorcerer? Along with your colleagues?" Cyril asked, though the answer seemed obvious.

"I am, and they are. Though I wasn't trained in old Finndrigairian techniques originally." Leaning back, Daumantas fixed his eyes on a point on the ceiling. "I never meant to lie. I do trade fabric goods, and I do love to sew. I begged my mother to teach me." He closed his eyes as he spoke and looked as though he remembered something both wonderful and painful at the same time. "Svetlana and I being twins made us special beyond our station. I excelled in magic from a young age, so my path was a bit predetermined."

Try as he might, the plush chair proved much too comfortable, and Cyril found himself nodding off despite the gravity of the moment. The news and activity had taken what little strength he had, and he slipped into sleep.

When he woke, he found he'd been placed into bed once more. From the look of the room, it had to be Daumantas' private bed chamber. He took a moment to savor lying in Daumantas' own bed. It smelled nice, rich with his lover's scent, and was much softer than anything Cyril had slept in anywhere else.

Reluctant as he was to leave the bed, Cyril made himself sit up and slide out. He found the untidy room very amusing, considering the neat and fastidiously kept way Daumantas presented himself. A heap of clothing dominated one corner, and several more articles were draped on a chair. Elsewhere, a stack of books teetered on top of a low chest of drawers. A large, finely carved wardrobe stood by the door. The floor had a finely woven rug situated under the somewhat plain but sturdy bed.

Curious, Cyril picked the topmost book off the stack sitting nearest the bed. He'd never seen anything like it. He couldn't be sure, but it looked to be written in Old Finndrigairian. The text was paired with elaborate diagrams. They seemed to be illustrations of elaborate clockwork mechanisms. He turned the tome this way and that, attempting to make sense of the pictures.

"That's a book on Finndrigairian vehicles," a voice said.

Cyril jumped and slapped the book closed. Daumantas gestured for him to follow him out of the room.

Placing the book back on its stack, Cyril hurried after his lover. "You can read Old Finndrigairian? I thought that was a closely guarded secret only priests and high-ranking Grendairan sorcerers knew."

"You can learn Old Finndrigairian in Grendair if you can pass the rigorous exam they give at the University. I had a friend who helped me with my studies. Learning magic in Grendair was a very different experience from learning magic in the Khanate."

Daumantas smiled softly as he led him back to the plush chairs, which now shared the room with a table laden with a fresh pot of tea and an assortment of small sandwiches. Before he could sit, Cyril grabbed hold of one of Daumantas' long, decorated overcoat sleeves.

"I've been wanting to tell you something." Cyril's heart fluttered as Daumantas turned to face him.

"Oh?" The ogre looked down at him, his face both curious and a little concerned.

Cyril felt overwhelmed with emotion. "I should have told you that I have strong feelings for you a long time ago." He made himself look Daumantas in the eyes. "If I'd died..." He swallowed hard, ignoring the stray tears falling down his face. "If I'd died, I would have left without telling you I love you." They embraced each other, and Cyril buried his face in Daumantas' chest to hide his weeping.

"I love you, too. Though, I'd have hated to lose you regardless." The words were a rumble deep in Daumantas' chest. They stood for a long moment, simply holding one another.

"I'm sorry." Cyril pulled away, wiping his face. "I'm just feeling overwhelmed right now."

Daumantas took Cyril's shoulders and gave him a firm kiss on the lips. "You've been poisoned, and you just found out your father has been, too. Your brother is also missing, and no one knows who's behind it or where he is. To say these past five or six days have been difficult would be an under-statement."

The plush chair and relative comfort he found himself in began to grate on Cyril as he ate. "I need to leave and find out what's happened to my family as fast as possible," he said without turning to face Daumantas. "I know you don't want me to leave just yet, but I'll have a few days before I'm in any real danger."

Daumantas heaved an exaggerated sigh. "Since I know I can't convince you to stay, I won't try," he begrudgingly admitted. Then he asked with a touch of defeat in his voice, "Do you have any enemies that I should know about?"

Cyril thought about it for a few moments. "Hadeon, maybe? I did cut his hand off." Daumantas raised an eyebrow as Cyril explained, "Boyar Hadeon Zhupensken was the first to ever challenge me to a duel." The memory made his stomach twist uncomfortably as he recalled the ugly, hungry look on the boyar's face, and he grimaced. "He was the only man who suffered such a grave wound while dueling me. As soon as my father announced I'd only be wed to a man who could defeat me in a duel, that disgusting pig stepped forward straightaway."

"Why did you father agree to such an arrangement? I've always wanted to know." Daumantas asked.

He was teetering on the edge of his seat now. His demeanor had shifted from defeated acquiescence to anticipation as Cyril talked. The big ogre leaned forward, excited for Cyril's response.

Cyril couldn't help but laugh a little. "I think he believed I'd be beaten pretty quickly. Or that I'd give up after a few duels and agree to marry someone."

"You never lost a single duel?"

"Not one."

"*Really?*" Daumantas seemed unconvinced.

"Yes, really!" Cyril said, and they both laughed. "I trained to be a knight since I was a child. My father spent most of my young life away, fighting an insurgency at the Wall. I lived with an old boyar named Orest and his wife, Lilya." The fonder memories made Cyril relax, and his stomach calmed. "My father had no idea I'd been allowed such an education, or that I'd been allowed to live as a boy while he was away."

Daumantas took a sandwich and brought it to his mouth without taking his eyes off Cyril. He'd become totally engrossed by the tale of Cyril's youth. "Was the training hard for you? I mean, since you were…ah…" Instead of finishing his statement, Daumantas took a big bite of one of the small sandwiches instead.

"Since I was born a girl?" Cyril laughed again. "I played with the other boys all the time. There weren't any other young girls my age living in Orest's old castle. So Orest simply started including me…well, after a lot of begging on my part." Cyril's tone became dreamy as he remembered a time long gone. "I hated being separated from my friends, so we split my time. Orest taught me knightly duties in the morning, and Lilya taught me my letters and what womanly things she could fit into our afternoons together."

Cyril paused to help himself to a sandwich. These memories were all a little bittersweet now. Talking about it made him feel isolated. His youth had been full of warmth but coming into adulthood with a body that didn't suit him had been hard.

"What about you?" Cyril asked Daumantas, looking to change the subject. "What was your childhood like?"

"Pampered and boring, I'm afraid." Scoffing into his teacup, Daumantas continued, "I thought my father would appreciate all the knowledge I'd accumulated as a young man, but he only cares about how I can use it in service of the Tsardom of Farizhniya and not about greater service to all peoples." His gaze became lost in his cup. "I really wanted to make a name for myself, and I *have* among sorcerers…but not anywhere else."

Daumantas looked up when Cyril reached out and put a hand on his knee. Their eyes met, and Cyril gave him a warm smile.

"I'd love for you to tell me more about the magic you've been studying some time," Cyril said.

The smile Daumantas returned didn't reach his sad eyes. Cyril understood all too well how it felt to be rejected by one's father.

"I think I'd like that." Daumantas' eyes grew wide, and he sprung from his chair unexpectedly.

It caused Cyril to start. "Are you alright?"

"I have to take your measurements if I'm going to have everything ready for us to depart in a timely manner!" He held out a hand to help Cyril up, and he took it.

Curiosity bubbled inside him as he stood. "What needs finishing, exactly?" Cyril asked, confused.

Daumantas grinned, glee returning to his face and sparkling in his eyes. "Enchanted clothing for our journey!"

Seven

DAUMANTAS SHOWED Cyril into a workshop that, at first glance, seemed to be an ordinary tailor's workspace. There were bolts of fabric along one wall, a rack with spindles of thread, and a workbench with books and tailor's tools strewn across it. Upon closer inspection, though, he found many of the tools were engraved with strange patterns, and the books laying open here and there were filled with esoteric diagrams. Pinned to the walls were sheaves with Daumantas' own notes: spells and symbols for a variety of purposes.

"My primary field of expertise is the enchantment of objects," the large ogre explained as he pulled out a measuring tape. "I want to make enchanted disguises for our journey." He beckoned Cyril over to a stool and had him stand on it in front of an impressively large three-paneled mirror.

"This clothing you'll be making will be enchanted? How, exactly?" Cyril asked.

He'd only witnessed magic being worked on a small handful of occasions—and mostly by monks at Vuretsiv. Since they exclusively practiced healing magicks, he was unsure how enchantments or other types of magic worked. Would Daumantas be using focus objects, like those employed by the Vuretzian monks?

"Most of my tools and materials are already imbued with the properties I need them to have," his lover explained. "All I need to do is assign them a specific purpose." He measured Cyril with practiced efficiency and used a wax tablet to record his findings. Once he finished taking Cyril's measurements he walked away, examining the numbers. Satisfied, he hung the tablet from his belt, and with a clap and sing-song voice, Daumantas called out, "Come to me, come to me! Time to work!"

Cyril watched in awe as the various tools—scissors, needles, thread, and fabric—all lifted themselves up from where they rested and flew over to meet Daumantas in the middle of the room. Cyril's astonishment writ large across his face made Daumantas smile.

"You may want to step outside," he cautioned. "Things are going to get quite busy in here."

"Oh, uh, of course!" Cyril replied after several stunned moments.

Floating objects made way as he walked back to the door and out of the room. He lingered in the doorway for a few moments as Daumantas picked from the fabric lazily suspended in midair around him. With a coy smile, Daumantas gestured at the door, and it closed itself. Bemused and more than a little awestruck, Cyril browsed the books to pass the time as Daumantas worked. He could occasionally hear what sounded like muffled singing from the other side of the door.

The work consumed the rest of the day, and Cyril only saw Daumantas briefly for dinner and bed. They awoke the same time the next morning, and Daumantas told him that his work on their disguises would take the whole day to complete.

Much to Cyril's relief, Kanat came up to Daumantas' chamber to check in on him. "This will be your last day in Craighan Tor, and I'd like to assuage your fears of these structures, if possible." The slim ogre bowed politely to Cyril.

Glad for the company, Cyril happily agreed to be shown around the Tor. Using the lift, they made their way all the way down to the cellar and kitchen.

"Now, before we proceed, I'd like for you to know that we have automatons working in place of living beings in these spaces," Kanat informed Cyril as he showed him around.

He gestured to the entrance to the kitchen, and inside, Cyril observed several humanoid assemblages working. They were baking bread, chopping vegetables, roasting meat, and bundling meals to be sent to the residents living and working within the Tor.

"This is absolutely incredible!" Cyril stepped into the kitchen, but Kanat pulled him back.

"They aren't self-aware, so it is best to stay out of their way," the ogre advised.

The clockwork workers continued their tasks, unaware of the visitors as they returned to the lift.

"Is this the Nameless Tor just north of Ford Town?" Cyril asked as they rode up to the next floor.

"That is what the locals call it, yes," Kanat replied, stepping into the corridor leading to the main hall where Cyril had met with Dimitru the day before. "We let the story of monsters continue to circulate to keep the locals away. It doesn't stop everyone, though."

The main floor contained mostly unused meeting rooms with the great hall at its heart. Cyril noticed small groups of people—other sorcerers, he presumed—watching him and Kanat tour the building. Several of them looked at Cyril with suspicion from across the room.

"Do only sorcerers inhabit the Tor?"

The tall, slim ogre nodded. "We have some contracted porters who occasionally bring supplies from Olten, but the only full-time residents are sorcerers." Kanat pointed to a large map mounted on one of the walls. "There are only a half-dozen intact Tors within the borders of what was once Finndrigair still standing. At the peak of the Empire, there may have been hundreds." Kanat smiled slightly as they made their way back to the lift. "Daumantas maintains an apartment here, but he actually lives in Olten. Many of his colleagues think he's aloof."

"Is that so?" Cyril asked, unsure of Kanat's intent.

They rode the lift quietly for several moments, then Kanat said, "Don't misunderstand me, but he trusts outsiders much more than the average sorcerer."

His words felt heavy on Cyril's ears. The Tor still made Cyril uneasy, but he also felt guilty for fearing a place Daumantas and Kanat called their home. The lift stopped, and they disembarked onto a floor with many strange instruments pointing up through a skylight in the ceiling.

"Most of the other floors are private apartments," the ogre said, "and you've seen the floor that houses the infirmary, so we'll be going up to the Observatory and the roof."

They walked along the windowed colonnade encircling the top floor to a small set of spiral stairs. Kanat led Cyril up to a gallery, then up another flight of steps and through a door to the outer parapet. A warm wind buffeted them both as they gazed out across the landscape. The Tor stood on a bluff above the Zult River, and the top of the tower was several stories above the crowns of the surrounding trees. Cyril could see Ford Town from where he stood, fuzzy and miniature in the distance. The residents believed the Tor to be sealed with no way in and crawling with monsters besides.

Cyril understood the advantage to encouraging such a story. Magic was respected by most, heavily restricted by many a church decree within the Voivodates, and often feared in the territories that were once part of the Finndrigairian Empire. While magic saved lives and was used in maintaining the Great Monster Wall, it had also wreaked havoc on the land and created the insect-like monsters the inhabitants of the Voivodates now feared. Being a warrior, Cyril understood any tool could be a weapon in the hands of a malicious person. Magic was a powerful force that, when wielded with malice, had destroyed an entire empire practically overnight. It understandably struck fear into people's hearts.

"Why do some old Finndrigairian structures produce monsters, while others don't?" Cyril asked as he squinted out across the landscape, gazing towards the hazy cluster of buildings of Ford Town in the distance.

Kanat rubbed his chin, pondering an answer to Cyril's question. "That's something we're eager to answer ourselves. There are these...let's call them 'black boxes'...in some structures. They somehow produce the Inferni." he explained, "They can be destroyed, but we've only achieved this by either collapsing the surrounding structure upon them or with some other equally physically destructive force."

It was a little reassuring to know the sorcerers here were as concerned about the Inferni as anyone else in the Voivodates. "Thank you for showing me around today," Cyril said. "I know a lot of people regard anyone from the Voivodates as barbarians and consider us...uncultured." He thought of the diminutive sorceress in the chair and her assessment of him.

Kanat stood still, gazing over the river and into Vodomeria. His heavily embroidered silk robes flapped in the wind around him. "You are very humble, for a prince." Kanat bowed respectfully.

Cyril found it unusual to be referred to in such a way, and the title made him a little uncomfortable. "I haven't been among other royals in a very long time."

Tiring of the hot sun and summer wind, the pair retired back inside the observatory.

"But you are a prince, are you not?" Kanat fanned himself as he tried to cool off back in the unusually cool and comfortable interior of the building.

"I was...I was always at odds with my father, so I never felt very princely." Cyril fidgeted with the cuffs of his sleeves attempting to dodge the question.

They made their way back to the lift, and Kanat took them to the floor with Daumantas' apartment. They paused before parting ways.

Kanat gripped his shoulder. "I hope that the Voivodates will be more accepting of our craft one day." The look in the slim ogre's eyes was intense. "I'd like to be able to further our research so that we may not need the Monster Wall. Our predecessors never meant for it to be permanent."

"I could speak to the boyars on your behalf, perhaps," Cyril said as he shook Kanat's hand.

Kanat nodded solemnly, then boarded the lift and left him alone in the hallway. Cyril's stomach lurched from the little lie he told. Bringing the end to the monsters would be a dream come true. How he'd sway the boyars or the next Voivode of Vodomeria, Cyril had no clue.

Cyril spent the rest of his afternoon idly flipping through Daumantas' expansive collection of books. Nothing held Cyril's attention very long, as anticipation of their pending departure ate away at his mood. Could they make it into Vodomeria's interior unmolested? What if Tymor succumbed to the poison and the realm fell into chaos before they arrived?

The door to Daumantas' workspace opened, and Cyril jumped, the book he was holding tumbled from his hands.

The big ogre sagged with fatigue, but he gave Cyril a warm smile. "Everything should be ready for tomorrow." He closed the door behind him and locked it. "The final spell needs to be activated in a specific way, and I don't want any ambient sounds triggering it too early."

Cyril nodded, even though he was confused by what Daumantas had said.

Cyril used the rest of the evening to organize what would come with him on the journey. Dimitru had brought Cyril's personal effects to the Tor with him during his visit. His sword and matching dagger got a polish and sharpening before being hung close by. The fact that all his possessions fit in one rucksack made him smile sadly. Though it had been some years since he'd stopped traveling, he still lived like a man on the road. Outside of a few books he treasured and didn't want harmed, most everything else stayed packed in the traveling sack.

Prepared and anxious, Cyril sought comfort in Daumantas' embrace. The two made love until they could no longer move that night. Cyril felt like this may be one of the last times they'd be able to enjoy one another so completely for a while.

The next morning saw the pair reluctantly out of bed. Cyril steeled his resolve for the journey ahead. Before either could dress beyond their small clothes, Daumantas lead him back into his work room. They stopped at the door. "I need you to think of what you want yourself to look like as a disguise," he told Cyril just above a whisper. "You can be vague or very detailed, but pick traits far from your own."

Cyril contemplated his words, taking a few moments to ruminate on an ideal disguise.

His lover must have sensed when he finally settled on something because he said, "If you know what you'd like, make sure to speak it clearly, and nothing more for several moments. Do you understand?"

Daumantas stared intently as Cyril nodded; only then did the ogre unlock and open the door.

Two brand new outfits stood on mannequins in the middle of the room. The larger mannequin was clearly Daumantas'. It was a dark brown cloak paired with a humble tunic and overcoat in a Vodomerian style, a simple affair in comparison to what Daumantas typically wore. The intricate embroidery decorating the garments made the ensemble feel more opulent than the materials that made it.

Daumantas placed his hands on the breast of the mannequin. "Human." Cyril gave Daumantas a curious look but didn't speak a word. He couldn't be sure, but the embroidery seemed to shift and move for a few moments. With a mysterious smile, Daumantas donned the clothing right off the mannequin, and Cyril had to suppress a surprised gasp. Daumantas appeared mostly the same, but he was a full head shorter and missing his horns. His ears were also no longer the long, pointed ears of an ogre. Daumantas smiled broadly at Cyril's expression and pointed at Cyril's own mannequin.

Taking a breath, Cyril placed his hand on the breast of his traveling outfit. "Old man." The cloth felt warm and cold at the same time, and Cyril could have sworn he felt the embroidery shift under his palm. He wondered how he'd look to himself as he dressed. His ensemble had a midnight blue cloak and overcoat, very similar to Daumantas in cut and styling.

"Come see!" Daumantas clapped his hands excitedly. "I had my doubts when you spoke the words, but I think this disguise will work brilliantly."

Cyril openly gaped at the vision of himself reflected from across the room in the large three-paneled mirror. He was fully twenty or thirty years older, wrinkled and gray-haired. If he held his hands right to his face, they appeared normal, but if he looked at them a short distance away, they appeared wrinkled, and age spotted.

"How does this spell work?" Even his voice sounded aged beyond his actual years.

"The enchantment is projected by the clothing itself, and the embroidery is the spell," Daumantas explained. The glee in his voice was palpable. "Some people will still be able to see through the spell naturally or by practice, though the innate skill to see through enchantments is quite rare."

Cyril's eyes roved up and down the now human-looking Daumantas, fascinated.

He smiled at Daumantas. "I hope to look like this one day. With time, of course!"

Daumantas appeared confused at first, then smiled and nodded. "I hope to see you happily aged in the future as well, if you'll have me for that long."

The two lovers gazed upon one another, taking in their disguised appearances. Cyril hoped Daumantas would be at his side for as long as he could stand to be. The man had agreed to go on this dangerous journey with him, and Cyril knew tougher men who'd shrink from such a fraught and deeply personal task. Perhaps if they made it through this, the two of them would still be together when they were both old and gray.

Eight

DARK and twisted dreams haunted Tymor Valentin. He appeared
to be home in Triadoara. The palace felt both normal and foreign to
him, the building appeared distorted and oddly lit. The halls were
full of people reveling, but they hung immobile and suspended
around him, their figures like ghosts in the halls. He frantically
searched for someone, but they were nowhere to be found.

A young man he recognized brushed passed him. He reached
out, clutching his arm.

"Let me go."

———

Tymor woke up from the dream, gasping and still reaching for the
phantom. He felt a hand grip his in the darkened room.

"It's just me, darling," someone said.

It took Tymor a few moments to recognize Milena's voice.

"Where's the boy?" he croaked.

"Symon went with Octavius."

Symon? Tymor realized she meant their younger and her only
child.

Milena gripped his hand firmly between her own. "I know you've been struggling these last few days."

Tymor's head swam with half-formed questions. Milena pushed a cup to his lips, and he greedily drank the water that was offered.

"We have to get out of here." Milena's voice sounded strained. "Hadeon has taken control of the capital. I don't think he's going to let you walk back into the palace once you're well again."

Tymor listened to his wife's blunt assessment. "Hadeon is a fool, but I never believed he'd resort to murder for my throne."

He laid back and became lost in his thoughts. Hadeon had been calling for his removal as Voivode for some years now. A few ambitious boyars entertained the idea, but Hadeon had gone largely ignored over the years. Tymor had hoped Hadeon's arrival in the capital after so many years away heralded a thaw in their relationship. Hadeon was almost too gleeful to be present, and while Tymor had felt something amiss about it, he hadn't believed Hadeon would enact a plot against him.

The poisoning had been much more insidious. Many more than himself had been made ill in the palace, and some of those less fortunate than himself had died. Many more would have lost their lives if not for the priests of Saint Nauen attending the feast that day. Tymor had become delirious and confused while trying to help others get medical attention.

Visions of his elder child haunted him, and he feared it an ill omen. With a great effort, he sat up. No time to waste, he had to think.

"Where are we, exactly?" he asked.

"The Monastery of Saint Nauen, just outside of Triadoara." Milena glanced about, looking for eavesdroppers. "The abbot had you brought here when you fell ill."

They were outside Triadoara's walls. It improved their chances to escape.

"Have you noticed any men lingering about the place?" Tymor asked, the fog slowly lifting from his mind. "Anyone not of the clergy?"

Milena thought for a few moments. "The abbot hasn't allowed

anyone else into the monastery since we arrived, outside of other sick people in need. One of Hadeon's men—Ruslan, I think—has come by once or twice demanding to see you. I've seen a few suspicious characters by the road, but I can't be sure of their intent, to be honest."

Milena's shrewd vigilance would be their saving grace. They would have to leave by cover of darkness and not take the road.

"Someone much smarter than Hadeon has put this plot together, I think." Tymor tried to keep himself upright, but his body slowly sagged back into the bed.

"Please rest." Milena gently encouraged him to lay back down. "We should be safe here for a few more days at least."

Try as he might, Tymor could not stay awake and drifted back into slumber.

———

The next time he awoke, he felt much more in control of his body. He eagerly departed the bed, bathed, dressed, and ate a modest meal on his own. As well as he felt, caring for himself still took a great deal of effort. He debated on whether he should tell Milena about Cyril. Octavius had confirmed his presence in Ford Town. He'd told Tymor that Cyril had chosen to take the letter but declined to visit his father.

Octavius described Cyril as a lean and strong man who resembled Tymor in a lot of ways, albeit twenty years younger. It would explain why Tymor sometimes heard rumors of himself having a bastard son wandering the territories adjacent to Vodomeria. Cyril's presence in Ford Town gave the old rumors new life, spurring Tymor to send Octavius.

Tymor tried to picture his daughter in his mind. He could only imagine the young man he'd refused to recognize all those years ago. The brash young man who fought all those men right in the main hall of the palace, holding back waves of suitors stretching over several years with just a sword and his wits. The same young man who'd cut off Hadeon Zhupensken's hand, and the one who'd hit Tymor when he'd tried to force him to marry without his consent.

Tymor found himself wondering how Cyril fared now. Had his assassins targeted Cyril as well, or was he safe due to his estrangement? He'd told Octavius to take Symon and flee to Ford Town. Tymor prayed his elder child was well and able to aid his half-brother.

If Cyril was unwilling or unable to care for his younger brother, Octavius would continue to head east into the deep forests of the City-States. Symon might have to live as an exile in a strange land, but at least he'd be alive. Tymor tried not to dwell on those dark thoughts too much.

His elder child had chosen years-long self-imposed exile. Cyril had already proven to have a deeper determination and grit than Tymor could have ever imagined. He hoped it meant he'd overcome any potential attempts on his own life. Cyril's choice to return to Vodomeria baffled Tymor and he now feared for both his children's lives.

Milena protested, but Tymor went to walk the abbey grounds. He hoped the walk would chase away his grimmer thoughts. It was a slow trip to the main church at the center of the compound, and the Voivode had to stop several times to catch his breath. The bright white walls towered over the cluster of buildings, making Tymor feel secure. The blood pumping in his veins and the warm sun felt good as they warmed his sluggish body. He pushed through the fatigue to reach the church.

He passed through the church doors, and it took his eyes a few moments to adjust to the dim interior as he crossed the threshold. A series of high arches and columns marched down the middle of the structure with the ceiling bowed between them. A dome at the heart of the church filtered sunlight into the interior. Tymor gazed at the prolific gilded images painted on every surface. They depicted the War of Madness, the Great Exodus, and various miracles being enacted by the seven major saints.

The church was quiet and mostly empty, save for a few souls praying in the apses. High, narrow windows gave the vaulted ceilings a far-off glow, making the gold accents on the frescoes glimmer and shine where the light touched them. Large chandeliers and hanging lamps provided illumination for the parts of the interior not reached by sunlight.

Tymor walked to the main altar, where a tall, beautiful wooden iconostasis stood separating the main interior from the tabernacle at the far end. The time-darkened panels were decorated much like the church—the wood carved with climbing vines and geometric shapes. Larger-than-life portraits of Saint Nauen and Saint Vodomor stood on either side of the main tabernacle doors. Clusters of minor saints decorated the panels at either end. Tymor contemplated praying, but he hadn't felt the urge in ages and wasn't sure he knew how to anymore.

Never a devout man, Tymor wondered if anyone would really hear any prayers he may offer. But even with his skepticism, he could see the merit of the practice. He found comfort in believing the saints could still hear and aid those in need in this world. Though she was more myth than anything, Tymor felt he had Nauen to thank for delivering him from otherwise certain doom. She'd inspired followers to practice potent and effective medicine long after her death, and the saint's followers had saved his life.

Shouting and the distinctive creaking and clanking of heavily armored men turned him back to the church's main entrance. Flanked by soldiers wearing Hadeon's colors, Ruslan appeared in the doorway. Tall and rugged, Ruslan had thick blond hair and sharp blue eyes set in an angular, clean shaved face. He wore the expression of a hunter cornering its prey. Once a friend of Cyril's, something had transpired between them on the road to Vuretsiv and it had turned Ruslan hard and bitter towards his former companions—and Tymor by proxy.

"So, you did survive," Ruslan said, disappointment dripping from his words.

The soldiers kept angry monks from entering the church as Ruslan slowly—menacingly—approached Tymor. The light from the lamps danced on his dark blond hair. While Ruslan was handsome, it was a dangerous beauty akin to that of a sleek predator.

Though unarmed and weak, Tymor resolutely stood his ground. If the man decided to strike him down in a church, there would be little he could do to stop him.

A few common folks who'd been praying quietly fled the armed men through the deacon doors set into the iconostasis to hide in the tabernacle beyond. One recognized Tymor as the Voivode and paused a moment to mumble a "highness!" before darting away. Ruslan stood not ten paces away now. He contemplated Tymor, who swayed before the icon of saint Nauen.

"Killing your Voivode in a church would be dooming yourself," Tymor said.

He did his best to appear calm and confident. The look in Ruslan's eyes told him the other man contemplated the idea. Tymor had fought heretics trying to bring down the wall for ten long years, so he knew the murderous look well, even after all this time.

Ruslan smiled slightly. It did nothing to soften his hard face. "I don't need to kill you, but your death would make things much easier for me." His smile turned into a snarl. "You're just as stubborn as that girl."

Tymor felt white hot rage surge inside him. "If you've hurt either of my children…!" The sudden overwhelming emotion made his heart hammer against his ribs, and he nearly collapsed. He took a hard seat on the floor, struggling to catch his breath.

Ruslan laughed harshly at Tymor's predicament. "Maybe you'll die all on your own after all."

Ruslan started to step closer, but something held him back. His head swimming, Tymor willed himself to move and saw a priest walking slowly through the royal doors out of the tabernacle. Their hands twisted curiously, and all their attention focused on the armed men.

"Those with Intentions Impure must leave this place 'til next morn'!" they cried.

The simple spell chanted by the priest made Tymor's ears tingle. He watched in awe as Ruslan, against his will, began to jerkily turn and walk towards the door. The soldiers with him followed suit, moving like puppets controlled by invisible strings.

"It's like my boots are walking themselves!" one of the men shouted as the soldiers awkwardly filed out of the church, fighting their own bodies as they went.

The priest sagged with relief and turned to Tymor. They were stocky and thickly built with close cut hair and a benevolent air about them. A life of the cloth had given them a soft, rounded body. The priest offered Tymor a hand up. His knees weak, he was grateful for the assistance as he climbed back to his feet. The common folks emerged from hiding while several priests filed in. They looked over their shoulders as the shouts and protests of the armed men filtered in from outside.

"Abbot Gavril!" One of the priests, a dark-skinned older man with a long gray beard, rushed to the abbot's side. "Is everyone unharmed?"

Gavril nodded and pushed their octagonal glasses back up their nose.

The bearded priest pointed at the door. "Those men. Did you…?"

"I took care of it." Gavril wiped sweat from their brow. "The spell will only last until dawn, but they won't be able to come back near the abbey until then."

Tymor stood unsteadily, holding onto the abbot for support as they spoke to the other priests.

"Please take the Voivode back to his chambers so he can rest for now," Gavril said. "Then we can decide how to handle the situation."

The bearded priest did as he was told. With wrinkled but strong hands he helped Tymor return to his room, where he became lost in his thoughts again while lying in bed. Once Tymor felt his strength return, however, he took to slowly pacing about.

"What now, darling?" Milena's words broke through Tymor's swirling thoughts.

"We'll have to sneak out of here. Tonight, if possible." Tymor went to cross the room once more, and his legs nearly gave way.

Milena helped him back into a chair. "Are you sure?" she asked, though Tymor's stubbornness meant they would as long as he had the strength.

"I'm certain. I'll be limping, but I can't risk another attempt on my life." Tymor scratched his chin. "We'll get some peasants clothes and leave as soon as we can. I also want to speak to the Abbot."

Milena's expression was doubtful, but she kept them to herself, saying instead, "I'll fetch the abbot, then." She stood and left the room.

A brief while later, Milena returned with Abbot Gavril in tow. Tymor noticed their youthful appearance compared to some of the other priests here. They peered at Tymor with concern through their octagonal spectacles.

"My lord," they said, wringing their hands, "I don't believe you are quite well enough to travel." Milena had clearly talked to them on the way.

Tymor scoffed with false bravado. "I am a seasoned tactician and your Voivode, young man."

"I'm not a man." The Abbot's tone was flat.

"My apologies, young…?"

"Person."

"Person?" Tymor was confused but pushed through it. "Ah. Well, it's imperative that the Princess Consort and I get somewhere safe."

The Abbot pursed their lips. "Then I should come with you," they said after a few moments of contemplation. "If flight is the only way you see to preserve your life, then I shall escort you and make sure the poison hasn't done any more damage to your body."

Tymor thought about arguing. A…person of the clergy wouldn't be a fleet-footed companion. But priests of Saint Nauen were very capable healers. They weren't the miracle workers like the priests of Saint Vuretz, but they exercised incredible knowledge in practical healing techniques. Gavril also had some magical talent, as well, and Tymor was painfully aware of his inability to contribute to their defense in his current state.

The Voivode nodded, agreeing to allow the Abbot to depart

with them. "Alright. I suppose it's all for naught if I die on the road."

Gavril smiled. "I'll make arrangements for our departure."

After they left, Tymor turned his attention to Milena, feeling unsure of himself. "Did anyone come with you from the palace?"

"Only Antoniu. I don't think he'd ever leave you."

Antoniu was the head of the Royal Guard and one of Tymor's oldest friends. The Voivode hated the feeling of utter defeat, but he had no good choices before him. He'd have to get somewhere safe before attempting to contest the coup.

Tymor planned to seek out Orest, the old soldier and minor boyar he'd entrusted Cyril to when he was off at war. Orest may not move to help restore him to his throne, and despite what Tymor had done to him, he felt certain Orest wouldn't betray him.

He remembered the day he banished Orest, and it now wracked him with guilt and regret. The man had stood there and stoically accepted his punishment. He'd allowed himself to be taken to Triadoara and tried for treason after taking Cyril to Vuretsiv. He defended his actions by telling a court of his peers taking the princess to The Healing City had been a matter of life or death. Tymor was furious at the time. The man had had the gall to come back to the capital and dress him—the Voivode—down in a public forum. He'd told him if Tymor had been a more attentive father, then none of this would have happened.

The boyars who heard the case agreed Orest had betrayed the Voivode's trust but that he'd acted in what he believed was the best interest of the child. Tymor had wanted him executed at the time, but the other landholders felt that punishment was too harsh, and he'd been forced to relent. The court of boyars decided instead to strip Orest of his holdings and sent him and his wife Lilya to live in exile to the south.

The irony of his current situation didn't escape Tymor. He'd be following Orest into exile if things went poorly and the boyars gave Hadeon his throne. The Voivode spent as much of the rest of the day as awake as he could, attempting to get his own affairs in order before nightfall. The poison's lingering effects robbed him of his strength, and Milena had to help him back into bed. Tymor cursed his aging body as he fell back to sleep.

A sudden light woke Tymor from his slumber. The Abbot Gavril, Milena, Antoniu, and a small handful of priests stood in the room.

"Your highness, it's time to go."

Tymor was fuzzy from sleep, and it took him a moment to realize they were acting on his own orders.

Abbot Gavril took a step forward. "I've told everyone in the abbey to pack anything useful and head to any safe haven they think they can reach. I fear they may be in danger if they stay."

Tymor nodded, his face serious, then rose to dress and depart.

The quickly emptying abbey would be a good distraction to ward against prying eyes. Out in the corridor, priests and patients alike packed and hurried by. The priests only took things that would be most useful on their journeys, and much would be abandoned. With so many people fleeing, it was a huge undertaking. The air was charged with fear despite how calm they all appeared, and there were signs of fraying nerves everywhere: a crying woman here, a priest barking orders there. One priest had an old woman on his back as he made his way out.

Tymor's party had already prepared for their journey, so the small group made their way for the main gate with the steady stream of people and into the darkness. Many of the priests had strange lanterns to light their way on the dark road. The small lamps had glowing crystals in place of flames at their hearts. Gavril pulled one off their pack and activated it with a click. The cool, bright light was enough to keep them from stumbling on the otherwise dark road.

Blinking and looking around, Tymor gasped. There were dozens of him—or copies of him, anyway—all along the column of people leaving the abbey. He turned to Gavril; his mouth opened with unspoken questions.

Gavril smiled. "I know a little magic." Their tone was mirthful. "This enchantment will also fade in a few days, but hopefully it'll last long enough to throw any potential pursuers off our trail."

The abbey's doors were left open, the interior quickly darkening as its inhabitants poured steadily out into the night.

"Your people will be in danger," Tymor said, gesturing around at the priests risking their lives to protect him.

"Any who would harm them deserve the punishments they'll get," Gavril said simply.

It was considered blasphemy to harm the monks and priests who dedicated their lives to the saints, especially those who dedicated their lives to the healing saints. Gavril, the now-former Abbot, clearly counted on the sacrosanctity of their lives to protect the enchanted members of the diaspora now on the road.

Tymor hoped for their sakes the ruse would work and that these people would stay safe against the forces that might desire to do them harm.

Nine

A HOT BREEZE cut through the thick foliage on the road north of Ford Town. The summer heat was stifling, even with the shade provided by the trees lining the dirt track. Cyril and Daumantas walked along, a quiet hung between them. Cyril's thoughts rushed through his head, too quick to focus on or give voice to, and Daumantas respected his companion's silence.

That is, until he asked a curious question. "What would happen if your father dies? Do the boyars really choose the next Voivode?"

Cyril jumped when Daumants broke the silence, but quickly recovered. "They do. My father was elected when he was a young man. Though, sometimes someone will declare themselves Voivode, and occasionally elections are bought." Cyril's brow wrinkled as he frowned, and he glanced over at Daumantas. "You aren't thinking they'd try to elect *me*, are you?"

Daumantas gave him a small, secretive smile. "Well, they *could*, couldn't they?"

Cyril opened his mouth to say 'no', but he had a point. He'd never considered that a possible outcome.

"I'm not a boyar, though," he said a bit weakly after some thought.

"But you *are* a prince."

"Former princess, yes."

"Former?" Daumantas stopped walking, clearly confused. "Did the title disappear?"

"What are you getting at?" Cyril snapped.

"I'm simply making a statement that you didn't stop being royalty when you left."

The heat and the conversation were starting to wear on Cyril's nerves. It would be a half-day's journey on foot to cross the river and re-enter Vodomeria. Cyril would rather talk about the merits of interlocked stitches than his lineage or Vodomerian politics. But this was Daumantas, whom he loved, and he felt a little bad about getting upset.

"What's your point?" he asked, shoulders slumping.

Daumantas grew quiet and they walked in silence once more. Cyril thought he'd given up his pursuit of the subject, until he asked, "I hate to admit that I don't know much about Vodomeria." He gazed into the trees, avoiding Cyril's eyes. "I've traveled through many parts of it, but I've never learned much about its history or people."

Cyril scoffed and kicked at a rock in his path. "I've always hated how people think the kingdoms and Voivodates bordering the Monster Wall are backwaters filled with uncultured yokels."

Daumantas stared at his feet and said nothing for a few moments. "I've never fully understood why people think that, honestly." He glanced furtively at Cyril. "The Grendairan kingdom has some of the most extensive libraries in the Northern Territories. You'd have to travel southeast to the Shining Sultanate or into the Khanate to the east of the steppes to find better."

"Grendair is where a lot of Finndrigairan elites settled after the Great Exodus." Cyril kicked up dust in a childish display of frustration. "Vodomeria, Hredera, Monor, and Boritz are where the majority of the common folk and Animalis ended up."

He had never had the pleasure of traveling to Grendair himself, but many of the dark-skinned Grendairans Cyril had met were all very gracious and highly educated, though they did talk down to him on occasion.

Every place Cyril had visited around the world had felt more exciting and majestic, and yet homesickness had won out in the end. He'd returned to Ford Town to be close to what he knew. Vodomeria may be viewed as a backwater by its neighbors, but it was Cyril's home. He'd missed the brightly painted church interiors, the smell of freshly baked apple cake on a cold winter day, and the sound of his mother tongue on the lips of friendly people.

Cyril felt a stab of concern for the fate of his people, but he didn't believe he could prevent a war of succession if one broke out. He sincerely hoped things wouldn't become that contentious.

"I think you should be prepared to rally boyars around you if things become dire." Daumantas became quite serious.

Cyril turned to protest once more, but the grave expression on his lover's face made him fall silent.

"Petru and Dimitru Novadi know who you are," Daumantas said. "They clearly feel some allegiance to you. We're going to need allies as we travel."

"You never struck me as the political type before." Curiosity slowly overcame Cyril's discomfort around the subject. "What's gotten into you?"

Daumantas scowled. "Court life is ostentatious where I'm from, and fraught with danger." He stared into the distance as he spoke. "It's part of why my trips home are few and far between." His face had become a hard, unreadable mask. "Everyone even remotely related to the current Tsar believes they should be his heir, and even children aren't safe from their games. It's why Svetlana and I spent so much of our childhoods away from home."

The connection suddenly became clear to Cyril, and he gaped at his companion. "Your *father* is the *ruling Tsar* of Farizhniya?"

Daumantas grimaced. "My sister is his heir by five minutes." He closed his eyes. "A lot of people think I'm jealous, but the pressure was a lot on us as children." He gazed upon Cyril with sad eyes. "Some people thought we might be cursed because we were twins.

We sneaked away to Vuretsiv when Svetlana realized she couldn't keep being a woman in secret."

Cyril's chest tightened. Svetlana and Daumantas never talked about it at length, but he'd always known Svetlana had left for Vuretsiv against her parents' wishes. Cyril's time of healing at the monastery had come to an end when Svetlana arrived, and they'd met by chance because he stayed at the monastery between jobs at the time.

"Svetlana said your letters always gave her such comfort." Cyril smiled up at Daumantas, trying to lighten the mood. "She was overjoyed when you were finally reunited."

Daumantas' gloom began to pass. "I dislike how much our lives have kept us separate. I'm just glad it's made Svetlana and I closer in the end." He wrapped an arm around Cyril's shoulders. "I also met you, thanks to her."

Cyril felt his cheeks flush. "You and Svetlana both mean the world to me. I really don't know what I'd do without either of you."

He was overcome with emotion, and Daumantas kept his arm wrapped around him as they walked, handing him a handkerchief to dab the tears from his eyes.

The day passed without incident, though it was hot and dusty. The only other people they saw on the road were headed into the City-States. Some were clearly pilgrims, and some were making the long journey to Vuretsiv for healing. The pair went out of their way not to pass directly through Ford Town. Though they had disguises, Daumantas worried that their familiarity with the people in town may allow them to see through their enchantments. They walked the north road that bypassed Ford Town and walked a time after dark, stopping at a roadhouse on the main road that would take them west.

The barkeep sold them a simple meal and a bed to share upstairs. "Where are you headed, old man?"

Cyril had forgotten his disguise and choked a bit when he realized the barkeep was talking to him. "My daughter is naming her firstborn. I want to be there to see the child when they get their name," he lied.

The barkeep appeared unconvinced. "And you are...?" He turned his attention to Daumantas.

"Ah! I'm his physician. He has a condition, and I want to make sure he arrives safely."

"Right..." The barkeep scratched at his head. "Look, I'm not here to judge how you treat a lonely heart, just keep it chaste while you stay in one of my beds. Agreed?"

Daumantas and Cyril both turned scarlet but acquiesced to the barkeep's request. They quietly finished their meal and went upstairs. There were no private rooms here. The space above the bar was one big open room. Other patrons were already asleep across a dozen or so beds that shared the loft.

"Is it that obvious we're lovers?" Daumantas whispered as they got ready for bed.

Cyril laid himself in bed, and Daumantas wrapped himself around him. "I didn't think it was that obvious, but I suppose the barkeep has seen all sorts of couples pass through here."

Gentle snoring was the only other sound in the loft as the two tried to sleep. Cyril felt uncertain of their enchanted disguises and slept uneasily that night.

————

Morning came, and the pair roused themselves early to continue their journey into the heart of Vodomeria. It wasn't a very large country, so one could walk east to west across the whole of the voivodate in eight days. They could walk all the way to Triadoara in roughly five.

Cyril supposed they should keep their eye out for any traveling bards for information. Bards, whether they loved or loathed one another, often heard all the talk in the towns they visited and shared it between one another. Cyril figured the fastest way to find Symon would be to first locate Octavius or another bard who might have information.

A good day's travel took them to a small town with a large ursus bard strumming tunes in the main square for coin. Most of the townsfolk had escaped inside or to other shaded oases to hide from the heat of the afternoon sun. She hid under the awning of a large merchant's tent, trying fruitlessly to escape the pervasive summer heat. Cyril and Daumantas were both sweating through their tunics and in need of respite themselves, so they decided to speak with her later.

They walked into the local tavern to cool themselves. A few scattered groups were quietly sipping cold ale. The barkeep fanned himself behind the bar as he talked to some local patrons. Two heavily armed men sat in the far corner, removed from the other patrons and they watched Cyril and Daumantas intently.

Cyril sat so he could keep an eye on the men in the corner without being obvious. He and Daumantas ordered two weak ales and drank quietly. The barkeep was far more interested in his own conversation than with the two of them, and he turned quickly back to the locals he'd been chatting with.

Cyril noticed the two men in the corner having a heated discussion. One made the mistake of pointing at him. Trying not to be too obvious, Cyril stood and slowly made his way out the door, and Daumantas followed suit. Before long, the two men from the tavern appeared behind them, just far enough back that anyone else would believe it a coincidence.

Daumantas' face grew serious as they walked, and Cyril leaned in and dropped his voice to a whisper, "We'll head into that church and see if they follow."

Two pairs of men walked north along the road—one pair pursued and the other pursuing. It was a low-speed affair, and both groups became more suspicious of one another as they moved along the road. Cyril and Daumantas made their way into a small church of Saint Julia the Fair. He hoped that the two men from the tavern wouldn't follow an old man into a church, but he was disappointed when their shadows crossed the threshold.

"Now what?" Daumantas said in a tense whisper.

"We're going to pray. Just pretend if you have to."

Cyril calmly walked to the iconostasis and clasped his hands together. He began to recite the only prayer he knew quietly to himself. Daumantas thew Cyril an incredulous look, but he bowed his head in silent contemplation anyway.

"We want a word with you, old man," one of their stalkers demanded gruffly.

"Can't an old man pray in peace anymore?" Cyril grumbled as he turned to face his pursuers.

One of the men had a very serious face and a thick mustache. The other had a thin chin beard and looked less sure of himself.

"A traitor escaped us some days ago in these parts." The thickly mustached man took a step forward, clearly the one in charge. "There's a felis bard wanted for the murder of the Voivode and the kidnapping of the crown prince. We think he may be hiding in the area."

Cyril tried to act as casual as he could. "Oh, do I look guilty of aiding a murder?"

"What? No, we—" Mustache sputtered.

"You're clearly not locals," Chin Beard said, picking up where Mustache sputtered out. "And we just wanted to know if you'd seen any suspicious characters on your travels."

He looked as though his companion's overly aggressive nature frayed his nerves. Cyril decided to use it to his advantage.

Cyril laughed. "I've been too busy chasing skirts to notice any ugly men on the road."

Mustache and Chin Beard exchanged a look. Mustache was clearly furious with Cyril's lack of interest in their search.

"Now, see here, old man!" Mustache went to grab his tunic, and Cyril took a step back.

Chin Beard grabbed his companion and pulled him away. "I told you this was a fool's errand!"

The two argued for a few moments before Mustache agreed to leave.

"I'm very sorry for my grandfather's behavior!" Daumantas called as the two left. A soft "ahem" turned them both back to the iconostasis.

Standing in front of the royal doors was an elderly priestess. She wore a deep look of disdain. "If you two are finished praying, I'd like you to take your lecherous selves elsewhere."

Cyril and Daumantas sheepishly turned and took their leave. Once out of the church, the pair laughed as they continued back into town.

"I wasn't sure what you were planning." Daumantas chuckled between his words.

"Guess I'm a lecherous old man and you're...my grandson now?" Cyril laughed even harder.

"I'll admit I didn't put a great deal of thought into my own persona." Daumantas wiped a tear from his eye.

Their mood became more somber once they entered town for the second time. There was clearly something to learn here.

As they walked by, Cyril tossed a few silver coins into the ursus bard's tin cup. "I don't suppose you know any felis bards?" he asked. "I saw one in Ford Town a little over a fortnight ago, and I was wondering if he'd been through here."

The large ursus gave him an odd look. "I haven't seen any in person, but I've heard some things. If you buy me a beer, I'll tell you what I know. Name's Brea, by the way."

The large ursus woman straightened her bright skirt while she stood and led them back into the tavern. Cyril got three more mugs of weak ale to quench their thirst and sat with his companions.

"Thank the Saints!" Brea said as she brought the cool ale up to her lips and took several large gulps. She lowered her voice to a surprisingly soft whisper. "What in the name of the Saints has Octavius done? You're the second pair to ask about him in two days."

Cyril and Daumantas exchanged glances. "I don't believe he's done anything wrong," Cyril answered, "He may have been entrusted with something very important to me."

Brea leaned close. "Tell me why you're wearing those fancy magic disguises, and I'll tell you a little more."

Cyril sputtered as Brea finished off her beer. Smacking her lips, she slammed the mug down on the table.

"Not the best ale in town, but certainly the coldest!" She gave them a large and toothy smile. She leaned in again to whisper, "Finish your own beers and meet me at the merchant camp outside of town, and we'll talk about this in private. Just follow the road leading north past the church of Saint Julia the Fair. The merchant camp is by the creek just past the church."

She left them sitting and contemplating their next move. "Do you think it may be a trap?" Daumantas asked as he sipped his beer.

"I think she knows something but doesn't exactly trust us." Cyril took a swing out of his own mug. He wasn't discounting they were possibly being scammed, but he didn't believe Brea harbored any malicious intent.

They followed the bard's directions to the camp, and Brea waved them over to a circle of wagons situated in a stand of trees as they approached. "Did those men from the tavern give you a hard time?" she asked once they were in earshot.

"A little, but we were able to deal with them without resorting to blows," Cyril answered with a shrug.

Brea looked relieved. "They've been hounding everyone passing through town. I overheard them talking about how much money they'd been offered to capture poor Octavius."

She glanced around furtively before motioning for them to follow her deeper into camp. Here and there were people napping in shaded areas, waiting for the heat of the day to pass. Brea took them to a tent towards the back of the camp, deep in the trees. Lines of what Cyril assumed were Brea's personal laundry hung between the trees in the area around the tent.

"The poisonings in Ford Town really hurt my prospects there," Brea said as they followed behind her. "Rumor has it that it was all to kill Voivode Tymor's bastard son…or his daughter, depending on who you ask."

Cyril's stomach lurched, but he said nothing. Daumantas looked wary and held his silence as well.

The heavy silence made Brea visibly uncomfortable, "I guess we can discuss more in a moment." She said simply and held the flap of the tent open for them. Cyril cautiously stepped inside. The interior was dim, and it took his eyes a few moments to adjust. Something in the back of the tent moved, and he gripped the hilt of his dagger.

"Voivode Tymor?" a familiar voice called softly.

"Octavius?" Cyril moved closer to get a better look.

In the back of the tent sat Octavius, though he'd been seriously beaten. One of the felis bard's eyes was swollen completely shut, and one of his ears bore a notch that wasn't there before. His ears flattened against his head, and he gave a feral hiss as Cyril approached.

"It's me! It's Cyril!" He looked back at Daumantas, desperate to remove the disguise.

"Take off the tunic, and he'll be able to see you." Daumantas instructed, removing his own. Cyril followed suit and turned back to Octavius.

Confused but calm, Octavius stood to move closer. "My apologies," he said with a small bow. "As you can tell, I've had a rough couple of days."

A thousand questions pushed to the front of Cyril's mind, but one leapt out of his mouth. "Where is my brother?"

Octavius grunted and sank into a pillow on the floor. "I'm not sure. Some of Hadeon's soldiers caught us for a time and did this to me. Symon helped me escape, but we were separated, and I haven't seen him since." Octavius shook his battered head. "Tymor was spouting nonsense when I saw him last. He thought your brother was you."

Cyril's stomach did a somersault. "Do you know if he's alive? Tymor, I mean." He sat down on the floor of the tent across from Octavius.

Brea spoke up. "Rumor has it that a hundred Tymors left the monastery of Saint Nauen a few days back. I thought you were one of those decoys at first."

"This could still be an asset to us, if we use your disguise wisely." Daumantas looked deep in thought as he spoke. "It can sow a lot of doubt and chaos among our unseen enemies."

Cyril nodded, but the news made him tense. He turned back to Octavius. "Do I really look that much like my father?"

Octavius nodded. "I could see the resemblance quite clearly the first time I laid eyes on you. No one who knows him would doubt you were Tymor's child. The disguise makes the resemblance uncanny."

They spoke with Octavius for a little while longer before departing. Brea agreed to keep him safe and tend to his wounds until she could get him to safety. Cyril agreed to clear his name, if it was within his power.

Since they now knew Symon was somewhere in the area, Cyril and Daumantas decided to set up camp a little way upstream from the merchants. Hot and irritable, they both stripped naked and climbed into the stream to cool off. Daumantas quietly hung a line and rinsed their traveling clothes while Cyril sat on a rock, half submerged in the water.

"I hate this," Cyril mumbled as he leaned back, letting the stream run through his long hair.

He closed his eyes and felt the cool water flowing around his body. It gently gurgled and babbled as it ran over stones and through its course between the mossy banks. Even though the rest of his body felt relaxed, his chest still felt tight. Cyril still didn't have any real answers, though his brother may be somewhere in these woods.

Since the water only reached above his knees, Daumantas was forced to rinse himself using a ladle. He sighed contentedly as he poured cool water over his sweaty body. "An unfamiliar young man in the area shouldn't be hard to find," he said. "I only hope we can find him first."

Cyril thought about the child who'd been caught stealing bread in the market. "A thief." He sat up suddenly. "We should ask around and see if anyone's had anything stolen from them."

Daumantas turned to face him. "Oh?" He paused to look at Cyril, his bare body glistening in the dappled sunlight filtering through the trees.

"Symon might be stealing from local farmsteads to keep from going into town" Cyril explained. He stood and walked over to Daumantas. "Even if they haven't seen Symon, it may be a sign he's nearby."

Daumantas smiled and nodded. "Ah! That's an excellent point."

He leaned down, and Cyril stood taller to meet him for a kiss.

Ten

THOUGH HE WAS loath to tell his lover, Daumantas had traveled to Vodomeria as a representative of his ruling house many years ago…

———

Daumantas Borzhegov, second child of Hovanes Borzhegov and Tsarevich of Farizhniya, wandered around Triadoara. Traveling bards had brought the tale of the Dueling Princess of Vodomeria to the Farizhniyan court, and Daumantas had become enthralled by the story. His father saw an opportunity to toughen his son, and he'd pressed Daumantas into a strict training regimen to prepare for this journey and to challenge the princess. His actual arrival in Vodomeria's capital seemed…less grand than he'd imagined.

The way people stared at him as he walked through the streets made it clear that not many ogres visited the capital, though it could've also been his very fine—and obviously foreign—style of dress attracted so much attention. An unattended aristocrat must have been an equally unusual sight. Daumantas had been forced by his father to take the journey alone.

Triadoara was a pleasant enough place, with clean, neatly cobbled streets; cheerily painted brick-and-plaster buildings; several grand churches; and a size-able "palace." More a fortress than a palatial dwelling, it sat on a bluff overlooking the main town nestled on the north bank of the Tria River.

Daumantas spied his destination rising above the rest of the town, but the twisting streets he took didn't lead to his goal. He gave up on finding the palace on his own and stepped inside a bakery for directions. The woman behind the counter nearly dropped an armful of loaves when she spotted him approaching the counter.

"Hello!" He smiled and waved in what he hoped was a friendly way. "You are knowing way to palace?" His thickly accented words drew the attention of the entire room. Daumantas wished he'd been afforded more time to practice his Vodomerian before his journey because he *knew* he'd messed something up there.

"I...the palace?" She set her bread down, wiping her hands on her apron.

A few other patrons were gawking at Daumantas, who noticed their eyes on him as he glanced around.

"Ah! I buy bread!" Daumantas thought it a bit rude of him to not give the shop his patronage. He pulled a handful of coins from his pocket and slapped them on the counter, beaming at the baker. "Loaf now, then directions...yes?"

The customers around the shop began to gather around to watch the exchange.

"This is...this is too much," the baker mumbled as she counted his money on the counter. She handed Daumantas back a handful of coins and went to pick him a loaf. She hefted a particularly large oblong loaf of bread and handed it to him, though she was still befuddled by Daumantas. "I don't really, um... I can't leave the shop to take you..." The baker tried to explain while walking around to the other side of the counter. "I have an idea. You still got the coins I gave back to you?"

Daumantas couldn't quite follow what she said exactly, and he tried to hand the baker the coins.

"No, no!" She waved her arms, loaf and all. "Not to me. Here…"

The other patrons shook their heads as the baker looked pleadingly around at them. They were not eager to take a foreigner to the palace in place of the baker. Shaking her head, she opened the door to the shop. Several curious children stood sheepishly where they'd been peeking through the window.

"Would one of you like to take him to the palace for me?" the baker asked while the children talked amongst themselves.

A lanky boy towards the back of the small crowd waved his hand in the air. "I will!"

The baker gestured to Daumantas, miming the exchange as she talked. "Give him money, and he'll take you to the palace, okay?"

Daumantas laughed and handed the boy a few silver coins. The baker heaved a relieved sigh and closed the door behind Daumantas as he left with his purchase. These children had been following Daumantas most of his way through the city. He felt silly for not thinking to ask them to take him in the first place.

Daumantas and the flock of children followed the lanky boy through the winding streets of Triadoara. He could tell when they were nearing the palace because the buildings became larger and more grand—grander than those near the outer wall of the large town, anyway.

They rounded a corner, and the main gate came into view. He broke apart the bread and spent some time distributing it among the urchins before turning to talk to the confused guards standing watch at the gate.

"I can have audience with Tsar, for duel?" Daumantas asked, hoping he'd gotten his point across.

He waited patiently as the two men sorted out what he wanted.

"You want to speak to the Voivode about dueling?" one of them asked.

Daumantas nodded enthusiastically, and the two guards talked briefly between themselves before coming to a decision.

"Alright, follow me." One of the guards led him into the palace while the other continued to stand guard at the gate, shaking his head.

Daumantas didn't believe the lukewarm reception boded well for him, but he followed the guard in the hopes of getting an audience with the Voivode.

They walked across a small yard and through the main palace doors. The guard led him around a corner and to a small room.

"Wait here, please."

Daumantas nodded and stood patiently as the guard stepped out of the antechamber. The walls were a clean, white-washed plaster, and the ceiling and floors were made of dark wood. The furnishings were a bit worn but well cared for. Daumantas took a seat on a padded bench.

Did the princess get betrothed or wed before I arrived? he wondered idly as he sat. He'd heard rumors of an impending marriage during his journey, but his limited Vodomerian kept him from understanding all he'd been told.

Voices on the other side of the doorway caught his attention. Daumantas could hear the guard walking down the hall and talking with another man. They stopped, and the other man left. He could hear the guard huff and tap his foot as they were both now being made to wait. Finally, yet another person approached.

"Someone is here to duel the princess?" This voice sounded incredulous.

Daumantas frowned as he listened through the door.

"Yes, my lord," the guard said. "A wealthy man from outside the Voivodates, from the look of him."

The guard reentered the room, followed by a very well-dressed man Daumantas assumed was the Voivode. He had long hair, copper streaked with silver, and a well-trimmed copper and silver beard to match. The Voivode wore simple but very finely woven clothing in the local style: a dark green great coat over a fine linen tunic and wide trousers that spilled over the tops of a pair of soft leather boots.

"What is your name, young man?" He eyed Daumantas up and down from where he stood.

"I am Daumantas Borzhegov, second son of Hovanes Borzhegov, tsarevich of Farizhniya." Daumantas gave a low and formal bow.

"I am Voivode Tymor Valentin, ruler of Vodomeria," the man introduced himself. "It is very nice to meet you, Daumantas." Tymor gave a slight bow back to Daumantas in greeting. "I hear you came all this way to duel the princess, is that correct?"

Daumantas nodded.

Tymor pursed his lips. "Come with me, young man."

They walked through the doorway into a fair-sized meeting chamber. Members of the nobility sat talking to one another in small clutches. Some peered at them curiously as Tymor and Daumantas walked across the room.

"I'm afraid the princess is gone," Tymor said. "Several years gone in fact." He patted Daumantas on the shoulder. "There is no one for you to duel. I'm sorry. It must have been a long journey for you on foot."

Daumantas sighed. He'd come all this way for nothing. What was he going to tell his father? "She is bested?" Daumantas asked gently.

Tymor scoffed, and his face hardened briefly. "Gone! Just…gone. The stubborn child…" His face wore a pained expression. "The princess went to Vuretsiv to live as a New Man, or so I've been told." He talked quietly as if he didn't want to be overheard.

Tymor led them to an alcove with benches built into the white-washed brick walls. He motioned for Daumantas to sit across from him and quietly asked a servant to bring them tea. The tea came swiftly, and Tymor leaned over, piercing Daumantas with a hard gaze.

"Why did you come all this way to duel? Trying to prove something?" Tymor's face became a hard mask. He clearly didn't think too highly of the men who'd trekked all this way to duel his child. "Si…Cyril was the best swordsman at court. Probably still is, I suspect. No one finer with a blade. I—" Tymor's words caught in his throat momentarily. "I wish I'd never pitted him against young men like you, even if he asked to be." The Voivode stared into his teacup, lost in his own memories.

Daumantas also stared into his dark cup of tea. "I have… nothing to prove. I came to make friend." It sounded silly to say out loud, but he'd wanted to see if the princess was like his own sister. He looked up at Tymor. "Princess sounded like own sibling. Strong and good fighter. Would have liked to meet. Nothing more."

Tymor's demeanor softened, and he nodded, contemplating Daumantas' response. "You may rest the night here in the palace, if you wish."

He stood to leave, and Daumantas grabbed his sleeve. "Please, what is…New Man?"

Tymor's eyebrows knitted together at Daumantas' question. "It's… Well, it's when someone born a woman has the heart and soul of a man, or a man has the heart and soul of a woman. If they choose, they can become a New Man or New Woman, and some go to Vuretsiv to do that."

"Vuretsiv is…not place of dark magic?" Daumantas' father had insisted he couldn't go there to study, as they still practiced forbidden Finndrigairian magic.

Tymor laughed, not unkindly. "You've never heard it called 'The Healing City,' have you?" When Daumantas shook his head, the Voivode explained, "There are those who find their techniques… controversial, but that's because there's such a bias against ancient Finndriairian techniques. The Grendairans are the only ones that know more about the ancient magicks than those in the Grand Monastery of Saint Vuretz."

Daumantas stood and followed the Voivode, much to Tymor's annoyance.

"Was there something else?" Tymor stood, clearly indicating he wished to conclude this meeting.

"I want…learn more about Healing City." Daumantas fumbled with his limited Vodomerian vocabulary.

"I see." Tymor waved an attendant over to them. "Please take this young man to the Monastery of Saint Nauen." He turned back to Daumantas. "The priests there can assist you much more than I can. Farewell, and I hope you find what you're looking for!"

After Voivode Tymor hurried off, Daumantas allowed himself to be led away by the attendant. Thankfully, he didn't have to walk all the way to the monastery. The attendant took him to the stables, and they rode in a simple horse drawn buggy to their destination.

The monastery had similarly thick, white, plastered walls like the palace, with a steep-set, red-tiled roof. The main buildings and church were ringed by a thick outer wall, which was a building unto itself, with chambers to shelter people in times of crisis. The complex had several tall watchtowers overlooking the countryside. The attendant quietly slid away once Daumantas was safely deposited within the care of the monks of Saint Nauen.

Daumantas spent several days poring over documents with the monastery's chief librarian, Gavril. The long trip to Vodomeria was finally bearing fruit, and he was concocting a plan in his mind to help his sister. When Daumantas concluded his studies, the librarian kindly helped him gather supplies for his journey home.

"I made you a list of authors and historians for you to look for," Gavril said, handing Daumantas a piece of paper.

"Thank you." Daumantas took the list from his new friend, feeling some relief after his misadventures wandering Triadoara. "Are you…New Man?" Daumantas ventured cautiously.

Gavril laughed. "I'm a New Person. Not a man or a woman, really. Though I do lean a bit man-ish." They laughed. "It's a bit rude to just ask like that, though. It can be hard to be a New Person, after all."

They shared a friendly embrace, and Daumantas departed the Monastery.

The two-and-a-half-week journey back to Farizhniv rushed by. Daumantas was eager to speak with his sister, his mind on fire with ideas. This taste of freedom from court life had made him hungry for more, and he planned a trip to Grendair in his mind as he walked home. He felt a deep desire to embrace his true passion and become a great sorcerer. He also now bore vital information to help his sister live more comfortably as a New Woman.

Eleven

DAUMANTAS GAZED over at the man he shared his tent with. Cyril's long, rose red hair spilled around his shoulders, his chest slowly rising and falling with the deep, even rhythm of sleep. His neatly trimmed goatee was beginning to get a little long and untamed, and stubble sprouted in patchy spots across his normally clean shaved cheeks. Daumantas wondered if fate had brought them together. His failed attempt to duel him as the princess of Vodomeria had led them to meet later at Vuretsiv, and in time they had fallen in love.

He gently placed a hand on Cyril's stubbly cheek. Daumantas had never met a man quite like him; Cyril had no equal in all the realms he'd traveled.

"Are you watching me sleep?" Cyril mumbled. His eyelids fluttered but remained closed.

Daumantas smiled. "Maybe a little."

Cyril took Daumantas' hand and kissed his palm. He held the other man's large hand against his face. "You're odd," Cyril said sleepily, opening his eyes.

Daumantas couldn't help but chuckle. "I'm odd? Why? Because

I love you?" He dared to speak the words. It wasn't easy to admit it aloud.

Daumantas felt triumphant when Cyril reddened a little. It was cute, as was the sleep still clinging to him.

"We should probably get up," he deflected, reluctantly pushing his body off the ground.

Daumantas leaned towards him, and their lips met for a soft kiss. "I know you're anxious to find your brother."

The tension in Cyril's demeanor was palpable. It had been ever-present since he'd received word his family had been attacked and forced from their home. Though they were estranged, Cyril clearly didn't wish harm on his family, Which Daumantas understood. He hadn't been home in years because of how his own father had treated him. Yet he still longed for news of his family. Daumantas was always glad to have Svetlana tell him about life in Farizhniya and of their mother and father.

The lovers reluctantly extracted themselves from their humble bedding and exited the tent.

"I think we should go undisguised today," Daumantas said as he shook out some mundane clothing from his bag.

"Oh?" Cyril rummaged around for some clean clothing in his own rucksack. "Going undisguised as its own disguise? I think I like that idea, especially after yesterday." He put on his baggy trousers and pulled a simple tunic over his head.

Daumantas dressed himself in a simple wrap robe. It made him appear to be a man of humble means from the Tsardom, but it was elegantly tailored. His taste for finer clothing was something he couldn't shake from his former life as a tsarevich. His father had insisted on the most rigorous education for his children, but this also came paired with highly pampered and indulgent living.

They ate a simple breakfast, broke camp, and headed back into town. It felt a bit odd to be retracing their steps from the other day. Daumantas saw the priestess from the church glowering at them as she swept the church steps. He smiled and gave her a friendly wave. Her cautious expression softened, and she gave a small wave back.

While not unheard of, ogres weren't very common in the Voivodates. Daumantas had so many connections through his work, both as a tailor and a sorcerer, that he sometimes forgot he was a bit of an oddity within Vodomeria.

Daumantas and Cyril heard a commotion as they approached the village square. The two men from yesterday were trapped in a heated argument with about a dozen locals. Several frustrated town wardens tried to make sense of the situation. The crowd made Daumantas nervous.

"This doesn't concern us," he murmured and tried to sneak to the tavern.

He and Cyril had almost made it to the other side of the town square when a familiar sounding voice rang out. "That man there is a Keeper of the Peace from Ford Town! He can help settle this!"

Cyril grimaced before turning to face the crowd now moving towards them. As soon as he did, the cacophony of voices rose once more. Daumantas scowled. Who here had recognized Cyril? Whoever they were, they'd managed to stay hidden in the throng.

An onslaught of complaints roiled over Daumantas and Cyril, and it was hard to tell who shouted what.

"These two have been stealing my eggs!"

"We've done no such thing!"

"They've been scaring off my customers and they haven't paid me for the food they've eaten!"

"We're looking for a criminal! You should be supporting us!"

"You haven't done anything useful since you arrived here!"

Daumantas' stomach churned. He disliked conflict and didn't want to be involved in this town's squabble with the two hired men who were searching for Octavius.

Cyril put on his hardest face. "Enough! If it can be proved they committed a crime—stealing eggs, for example—then they should be handed over to the wardens."

The crowd grew quiet to listen to Cyril speak. Daumantas had never witnessed him at work, and being a Keeper of the Peace was a dual role; he acted as a mediator and, sometimes, a judge to settle disputes between feuding parties.

The farmer with the missing eggs spoke up. "I caught them on my property just this morning near my chicken coop! My eggs started disappearing the day they arrived in town."

Mustache and Chin Beard were equally infuriated at the accusation. "While it is true we were at his farm this morning—" Mustache began.

The farmer pointed wildly at him. "There, you see? He admits it!"

Cyril's eyes flashed, and he made a gesture for the farmer to hold his tongue. The farmer sullenly obeyed.

"As I was saying," Mustache continued, "we heard about the thefts and were simply investigating for ourselves."

Chin Beard nodded in agreement. The farmer went to speak again, and Cyril shot him a withering look that silenced him instantly.

Satisfied the farmer wouldn't interrupt, Cyril turned back to Mustache. "Why not talk to the farmer first? If you weren't stealing, that is."

Mustache sputtered. "W-we don't need to go around announcing ourselves!" He quickly lost his composure. "We have a quarry we're trying to catch!"

Jeers from the crowd prompted Mustache to argue with the disgruntled villagers once more. Daumantas groaned. This town disagreement wasted precious time they didn't have.

"Enough! *Enough!*" Cyril and the wardens forced the crowd to become silent once more. "I think you've caused enough trouble. Pay the man for his eggs and leave town."

Mustache gaped, while Chin Beard dug in his coin purse. "You can't do that!" Mustache cried. "There's—"

Cyril scowled. "You've nothing to show for your efforts. It's time for you to move on. Ford Town is only a day and a half away. The wardens will escort you in that direction."

He crossed his arms over his chest as Mustache tried to find a reason they should be allowed to stay. Chin Beard reluctantly handed over a handful of copper pieces to appease the farmer and walked away.

Mustache's shoulders sagged as he realized he had no choice but to leave for Ford Town. Daumantas felt himself relax while the two were escorted out of his sight.

"Thank the Four Great Dragons," he muttered, glad to be rid of the troublesome pair. The farmer with the missing eggs trotted over to Cyril.

He happily shook Cyril's hand. "Thank you so very much!"

The farmer's delighted grin made Cyril smile sheepishly. Daumantas had to admit it was kind of ingenious. Cyril had effectively forced the pair out of town long enough to locate his brother.

The farmer balked as Daumantas moved closer.

"Don't worry, I'm…ah…" Daumantas stumbled, searching for a polite way to describe his relationship to Cyril.

Cyril glanced at Daumantas. "He's my lover." Cyril's bluntness made both Daumantas and the farmer's face redden.

"I…I see." The statement caught the farmer off guard but recovered quickly. "Can I talk to you about something?" He peered around nervously.

Cyril nodded. "I'd be happy to. What's your name?"

"I'm Gheorge." He looked at them expectantly. "And you two are?" After the lovers introduced themselves, Gheorge gestured for them to follow him. "My farm isn't far from here. Care to walk with me?"

The three of them walked along the road to Gheorge's farm, accompanied only by the sounds of buzzing insects and the occasional passersby.

"Those men say they were looking for a criminal, but I'm certain they were up to no good," Gheorge said as they put some distance between themselves and the small village.

"Aside from stealing eggs?" Daumantas asked casually.

"I saw them chasing a boy." Gheorge peered around as if he feared they were being followed.

"Did he have hair and eyes like mine?" Cyril asked, his voice strained.

The farmer examined him for a few moments as they walked to the edge of town. A breeze cut through the warm mid-morning air and made the grass and trees dance along the dirt track. Daumantas spied a humble farmhouse coming into view as they followed their guide.

Gheorge nodded slowly. "He does look a little bit like you. His hair was more golden than red." He nervously chewed his lip. "I'll admit that I'm not sure who stole my eggs. It may have been the boy, but I've caught those men on my property more than once."

They said nothing else as he led them to his humble home, which was bordered by a fence of woven sticks and had a wild garden alive with chickens and bouncing grasshoppers.

Two small children tore through the yard and greeted Gheorge and his guests enthusiastically. "Tata! Tata! That man has horns!" A little boy pointed excitedly at Daumantas. The little girl smiled and waved shyly from behind her father's legs.

Gheorge picked up his small daughter and led them into the house, his son darting between the men as they walked inside.

A woman sat in the central room, her hands busy spinning wool into yarn. "Gheorge! Did you turn those men over to the wardens?" Her eyes darted from her spinning to her husband and back.

"I think I've got everything sorted out." He set his wriggling daughter back on her feet. "I even got some compensation for the missing eggs, thanks to these two gentlemen." He gestured at his guests. Cyril and Daumantas both gave small bows.

"I'm Marta. Welcome to our home." She gave them a friendly smile and finished the spinning in her hand. "Have you seen—" Marta paused, staring at the two strangers in her house pointedly.

"I haven't. I'd imagine the heat is keeping him away."

"Those out-of-towners chasing him around haven't helped matters." Marta huffed as she sliced some bread to offer to Cyril and Daumantas. "So, what brings a New Man and an ogre to our humble farm?" She smiled and handed them both slices spread generously with butter.

Cyril sputtered. "How did you...?"

"How did I know? I've been to Vuretsiv and met many New People there. The monks helped me with a diseased leg." She pulled up her skirt a little, revealing a prosthesis, before handing her children some bread as well.

Daumantas chewed thoughtfully on the home-made loaf. The butter was rich and slightly sweet and complimented the slight tang of the sourdough well. Then he swallowed and found his words since Cyril had forgotten his. "We're hoping to find my companion's family."

"The boy is your family?" Marta asked, her face both worried and full of suspicion.

Cyril nodded, swallowing a mouthful of bread to speak. "He's my half-brother. Something terrible has happened to our father, and he fled home for his own safety."

Marta looked at Gheorge for reassurance. Gheorge contemplated Cyril's words. "So, is it true that something has happened in Triadoara? Did a bard really kidnap the prince?"

Rumors were clearly traveling. Daumantas wondered how the news would impact their plan to head into the interior of Vodomeria. Cyril stared at the floor, overwhelmed with emotion.

"We can't say for sure, as we know very little ourselves," Daumantas spoke up. "Our goal right now is to see my lover and his family to safety, providing no one has perished." Daumantas gave a formal bow. "I will attempt to compensate you for your aid, as long as I am able."

Satisfied with Daumantas' explanation, Gheorge agreed to help them find the young man who'd been hiding in the woods around his farm. They walked past his fields as the sun climbed to its zenith in the sky. The heat had the men sweating profusely as they walked.

"How do you plan on compensating this man, exactly?" Cyril hissed as they trotted behind Gheorge.

"No need to worry. I have plenty of coin." Daumantas glanced down at Cyril, a small smile on his face. "It'll be good for us to have the townsfolk in our good graces should...Hadeon? It is Hadeon, correct?" At Cyril's nod, he continued, "If Hadeon sends more men, they'll be even less inclined to be helpful towards them."

Cyril grunted but didn't argue. He clearly wasn't fond of

Daumantas currying favor in this manner. As they picked their way through the underbrush, he couldn't help but wonder- who had pointed out Cyril from the crowd? No one had come forward to greet him after the incident. Daumantas couldn't escape the feeling the person had involved them on purpose. But to what end, exactly?

They reached the banks of a shallow river. Gheorge stopped and whistled loudly in a distinctive pattern. A young man—his hair a bright, coppery gold—peeked cautiously over some fallen logs near the riverbank. Gheorge waved, pointing at Cyril and Daumantas. The young man moved slowly at first, clearly unsure of his own safety.

"Those two men who've been chasing you are gone! It's safe!" Gheorge shouted to encourage him.

The young man picked his way over the fallen trees and up the bank, then stopped for a moment before sprinting towards them.

Daumantas didn't know how long it had been since Cyril had seen his brother. Cyril rarely traveled from Ford Town and never ventured further into the interior of Vodomeria. The young man approaching them was tall and slim. His hair was cut just above his shoulders, and the clothes he wore were grimy from days spent hidden in the woods. He came to a stop in front of them and brushed his hair out of his face as he tried to catch his breath.

"Symon?" Cyril's voice shook.

"Are you Cyril?" The young man took several cautious steps towards them. "Octavius was taking me to meet you."

The two regarded one another with no small amount of wonder. The sight reminded Daumantas of himself seeing Svetlana for the first time after many years apart, the longing and joy that swirled inside him every time they were reunited. Similar feelings must be swirling within the two men before him.

Cyril's voice caught in his throat as he said, "By the saints… you're practically a man!"

Symon grinned. "Father told me so many stories about you. I was starting to think he'd made them all up!"

The two brothers laughed and hugged. Cyril tried to hide his tears from the other men.

"He did a shit job describing you, though!" Symon exclaimed into Cyril's shoulder.

Cyril laughed, wiping the tears from his face, and Symon began to weep. "I remember that laugh…" The young man became overtaken by sobs, his whole body shaking.

Cyril held him close while Gheorge and Daumantas stood quietly by.

They walked quietly back to Gheorge's house. Daumantas laid a hand on Cyril's back as he talked softly with his brother. Symon began to wilt as the excitement passed. The tears had cut channels in the dirt on his face. Marta had lunch prepared for all of them when they arrived back at the farmhouse. The children darted around, eating and playing as the adults sat talking amongst themselves. Everyone tried to ignore the heat, eating cool fruit and cured meat with bread between swigs of cool well water.

"So how exactly are we going to save Father?" Symon asked around a mouthful of meat and bread.

Cyril choked on his own food and had to wash it down in a hurry. "There is no 'we' in this situation!"

Daumantas couldn't help but chuckle. "Your brother has a point, though." he smirked when Cyril's eyes flashed. "What is the plan, exactly?"

Cyril's eyes ran back to the floor. "You aren't coming."

The words stung Daumantas, and he wagged a finger accusingly at Cyril. "Oh? And why not?"

Cyril's eyes didn't leave the floor. "I want you to take Symon out of Vodomeria."

"Pity. Neither of us is leaving."

"Daumantas! Please!" Cyril stood and finally raised his eyes to meet Daumantas' own.

Daumantas firmly held his ground. "If we split up, we risk being picked off." He hoped he could make Cyril see reason. "If you go on alone, you may not make it to your father."

Their eyes remained locked for several tense moments. Cyril

wasn't prepared for this much resistance from Daumantas. The ogre held his stance until Cyril broke eye contact.

"Alright, fine," he relented, "but I'm trusting you to help me keep Symon safe, understand?"

Daumantas smiled, gripping Cyril's hand. "I understand."

"Father's been teaching me to use a sword, and I have my dagger!" Symon piped up, eager to prove he could be useful.

Cyril patted him on the shoulder. "I'll test your technique at camp tonight. We should get you a bath and some clean clothes, too." He turned to Daumantas. "Is it possible to…ah…"

"Don't worry, I'll make sure your brother has proper travel clothes." Daumantas stood and bowed low to their hosts. "Before we depart, I'd like to bestow a traditional ogre blessing upon our hosts."

"Oh, you don't owe us anything!" Gheorge sheepishly insisted. "We're just happy to finally be able to help Symon here. Poor thing's been living in the woods for days. He was afraid to stay here on the farm with us because of those men."

"It won't take but a moment!" Daumantas promised.

Gheorge and Marta watched him pull multiple red cords from his bag. He hummed to himself as he tied them in intricate knots, hanging each one on a tack in the four corners of the small house. They thanked their hosts for the meal and headed back to their camp with Symon in tow.

Cyril walked close to Daumantas' elbow while Symon ran ahead. "What did you do, exactly?" Cyril asked quietly as Symon strayed out of earshot.

"I simply set up a protection spell. No one with ill intentions will be able to set foot on their farm."

Daumantas wanted to make sure Gheorge and Marta had some form of protection. He hated the thought of a terrible fate befalling them after they departed town. The spell wouldn't last forever, but it would hold for plenty long enough to see them safely through the current turmoil.

Twelve

CYRIL FELT GREATLY RELIEVED NOW that Symon was safely in their care. He kept a close eye on the young man while he darted around, exploring the small village sights along the road on their way back to camp.

"Which way?" Symon shouted back to them as the three approached the area where Cyril and Daumantas made their camp.

"We're up in a clearing past the merchant camp!" Cyril pointed into glades by the stream.

Some of the merchants who'd been camping off the road had left, including Brea and the small band of performers she'd been with. Cyril prayed they'd make it out of town and across the Zult River safely. They walked into their humble camp, and Symon immediately stripped and threw himself into the creek nearby. He laughed and splashed around in the cool water, rinsing the layers of dirt and grime off his body.

Cyril tossed him a bar of soap, and Symon began to lather it liberally across himself. Daumantas made a face as he hefted Symon's dirty clothes. He took off his outermost robe and began to wash them with a great deal of vigor.

"How do you two know each other?" Symon asked Daumantas as he rinsed the suds away.

"Daumantas and I are…" Cyril hesitated. How would he explain this to someone Symon's age? While not a child, Symon was far from being a worldly adult.

"Is he your manservant?" Symon asked, trying to get an answer.

"Manservant!" Daumantas grumbled and slapped Symon's tunic against a rock, muttering curses in the language of the Tsardom under his breath.

"No, no! Absolutely not!" Cyril gestured wildly against the idea.

"We're fucking!" Daumantas barked.

Daumantas rinsed Symon's clothes viciously. Cyril reddened as Symon gaped at them. A little embarrassed "oh" escaped the young man in response.

Symon climbed out of the water, and Cyril handed him a cloth to dry his body and a tunic to wear while his clothes dried. Symon's burst of energy waned now that he was clean. He sat on a log by the fire pit as Cyril struck up a flame and blew it into life.

Symon stared into the fire, his elbows on his knees and his chin on his hands. "Father said you left home to become a New Man. What does that mean?"

Cyril tried to think of the words to explain. "I've always been a man," he said, sitting nearby. "I just needed some help to be the man I always knew I was." He placed a hand gently on Symon's back. "The monks at Vuretsiv helped me. They…changed my body and made me feel better. They made me feel complete."

They sat quietly, listening to the crackling of the fire. Daumantas hung Symon's clothing to dry and gathered firewood out of earshot to give them some privacy.

"Tymor told you all that?" Cyril asked his younger brother. "*He* told you I left to become a New Man and that my name is Cyril?"

Symon perked up and nodded. "He told me that he should have respected you and that he didn't want me to remember you as something you weren't."

Cyril's chest tightened with emotion. Tymor must have had a change of heart after he'd left. Perhaps their reunion wouldn't be as awkward as Cyril first feared...providing Tymor survived the attempt on his life.

Daumantas returned and dumped his armload of firewood on the meager pile left from the previous evening. "We should start planning our next steps," he said as he sat with his companions.

"I think we should keep heading towards the monastery of Saint Nauen for now." Cyril said, trying to picture the villages and town between their current position and the monastery.

"Boyar Novadi may have closed the road," Symon chimed in. "While sneaking around in the woods, I saw a column of soldiers headed down the highway that leads west out of his fief."

Cyril's eyebrows knitted together. "I wanted to leave in disguise, but I may need to go without it to get by. If there are any guards I know, I might be able to get us through."

Daumantas threw some wood on the fire as they sat, the sun getting low in the sky and the last light of day cutting through the trees. Symon yawned and rubbed his eyes. Cyril wondered how long it had been since his brother had had a good night's rest.

"Let's worry about the rest after we leave here," Cyril declared as he got up.

He needed a moment to himself. As darkness descended, he walked back to the road. The warm, peaceful evening was at odds with the storm in his heart.

Cyril was starting to feel like he'd embarked on a fool's errand. He didn't know where his father was or if he was even alive. He walked to the church and sat on the low wall surrounding the humble building.

"Have something on your mind, young man?" The priestess' voice gave Cyril a start. She chuckled as she finished closing the distance between them, settling on the wall beside him.

"I feel a bit lost at the moment," Cyril said, a bit cautiously. He didn't want to burden this stranger with his problems.

The priestess chuckled. "You seem like someone who's done their fair share of both causing and solving problems." She smiled knowingly. "Those were mighty clever disguises, but I can see right through that kind of stuff. Studying magic is a perk of my job." She nudged Cyril in the ribs with a bony elbow, and he laughed. "My name's Pamina."

"Cyril."

Pamina smiled, and the wrinkles on her face flexed and deepened. "Go ahead, tell me what's bothering you."

Cyril let out a slow breath. "I want to help my family, and I don't know how." He also wasn't sure he could, but he didn't want to tell Pamina that.

She tapped a finger on her chin thoughtfully. "I think you have to get where you're going first." She looked at him, her face serious, her dark eyes clear in her wrinkled face. "You fear what will happen when you reach your family, and it's softening your resolve." Cyril opened his mouth to argue, but Pamina held up her hand to silence him. "If you want to mend this relationship, you have to at least try. No son hesitates to help his family unless he feels he's been wronged."

Cyril stared down at his hands in his lap. "How did you know all that?" He asked.

Pamina chuckled. "A wayward child off to help his stricken father? I'm old, but I'm no fool." She stood, dusting off her vestments. "The Princess of Vodomeria was once called 'The Steel Rose' because of her rose red hair and fearsome swordsmanship." Pamina's eyes roved over Cyril knowingly. "You have rose red hair and are on a quest to help your stricken father. The Voivode was attacked some days ago. It isn't hard to put together." She turned her gaze on the darkening road. "Help the Voivode if you feel you must, but don't feel obligated to say you love him as your father if you don't." The elderly priestess stood slowly and began to walk back to the church. "No need to break each other's hearts twice."

Cyril thought about Pamina's words while he walked back to camp. Purple twilight had come, casting deep shadows across the road. Twinkling fireflies and the lingering summer heat followed him back to camp. He could smell food being cooked as he neared. Symon had succumbed to weariness and was curled up on a blanket, sleeping soundly. Daumantas quietly tended to a meal, fish baked by the fire with greens foraged from the clearings along the road.

Daumantas handed Cyril a plate as he took a seat by the fire. "How was your walk?" he asked, delicately pulling the skin back on his fish to reveal its tender white flesh.

Cyril nibbled at his own meal. "I don't want to see my father," he said, staring at his plate, "but I know I have to if we keep going."

"We could take Symon back to Craighan Tor and let the scenario play itself out." Daumantas suggested.

Cyril shook his head. "I think Symon would just try to come back on his own." He set his plate aside, feeling his appetite wane. "I wish I could talk to Orest about this. He knew my father fairly well." Cyril felt a deep longing for Orest and Lilya. They'd worked so hard to raise him and he felt lost without them.

"Maybe we should go to him."

"Go where?" Cyril was confused.

"Go to talk to Orest." Daumantas poked at the fire. "We can take Symon there—and your father, too, if we can find him."

Cyril's heart swelled with renewed conviction. "That's a great idea!" he almost shouted, curbing his enthusiasm as Symon rolled over. "Orest lives just over the border in Monor. It wouldn't be hard to get to him from here."

Cyril picked his plate back up, tucking in with renewed enthusiasm. Daumantas smiled at him from the other side of the fire.

———

When Cyril awoke the next morning, he felt refreshed and filled with renewed hope. He told Symon of their plan while they broke camp.

"What if we don't find father?" the young man asked as he helped bundle bed rolls.

"Orest is the least likely to turn Tymor over to Hadeon, and he gave Ionia Voinescu Orest's small fief." Cyril neatly tied his bedroll to his pack. "I think it makes sense that Tymor might head that direction. Ionia's fief borders Monor, and she's also in charge of monitoring Orest. Otherwise, we have to assume the worst."

Symon looked concerned and a little frightened. Daumantas donned his disguise while Cyril left his own in his traveling pack. Symon was given a braided cord to wear around his neck, which Daumantas explained wouldn't change his appearance but would make him less noticeable.

The three walked briskly towards town. Symon was less inclined to wander today, opting instead to chat casually with Daumantas about his enchantments. As they approached the church, Cyril veered off toward it.

The elderly priestess Pamina stood outside, gently sweeping the steps of the church. She gave a friendly wave as he approached. "Need any more advice this morning?" she asked with a smile on her face.

Cyril offered her a palmful of coins. "For your services. And for putting up with our antics a few days ago."

She set the broom aside and took Cyril's hand in both of her own. "May the Saints watch over you and help you on your journey." She deftly scooped the coins out of his palm and dumped them into one of her apron pockets.

Cyril chuckled and jogged back to his waiting companions.

"Is this where you got off to last night?" Daumantas asked as they meandered away from the church.

Cyril smiled. "We had a good talk."

They stopped briefly in town to top off some of their provisions before they continued to the westward road out of the Novadi fief. Outside of some locals, they saw no one traveling along the normally busy highway. It didn't take long to have their fears confirmed; a caravan rolled by, and the people informed them the road was indeed closed.

Undeterred by the news, they pressed on. Before the sun was very high in the sky, they'd reached the blockade. While normally busy this time of year, the guardhouse, inn, and trading post were swollen beyond capacity with a large detachment of liveried guards wearing Novadi's colors and disgruntled travelers and traders hoping to still make their way through. People were camping all along the road, and some traders were making the best of it. Small makeshift stalls dotted the roadside as merchants sought to ply their wares to stranded travelers as well as each other.

"I'm going to try and find out who's in charge if you two want to go to the inn," Cyril said.

But before he could say anything else, a large man strode towards him and grabbed him forcefully by his tunic. He shook Cyril's entire body while he spoke. "You bastard! How could you send him on your fool's errand?"

Cyril was caught off guard, so it took a moment to realize it was Dan, the blacksmith from Ford Town.

"Bohden is an old family friend!" Cyril tried to explain himself as he was jostled to and fro." He's also a grown man who can care for himself!"

Calmly, Daumantas seized one of Dan's thick forearms. "Release my companion, please." His words, while calm, were cold and sharp.

Dan's hot gaze turned on Daumantas, Cyril's tunic still clenched in his fists. Daumantas twisted the other man's forearm, and with a grunt of pain, Dan released his hold and pulled back.

"By the Saints, Dan! What are you *doing*?" Iuliana came running through the crowd towards them. She skidded to a stop, sending clouds of dust into the hot summer air.

Cyril groaned. "Iuliana! What are you both doing here?"

Iuliana's fist darted out, and she hit Dan on his meaty shoulder. "Someone has to keep an eye on this fool!" She put her hands on her hips, her expansive chest still heaving from the effort of her sprint. Then she stabbed a finger at Cyril. "*You* aren't excused! I thought you died!" A sob caught in her throat.

Cyril folded Iuliana into his arms, holding her as she began to weep. "I'm sorry I didn't try to get word to you," he said, stroking her chestnut hair to comfort her.

Iuliana sniffled and pulled away from Cyril, wiping her eyes. "Who are these strange men you're traveling with?"

Cyril thought it best to get out of the sun, "I'll explain everything once we sit down."

They headed to the inn with Dan and Iuliana in tow. It was busy but not bustling at this time of day, so the group was able to find a table in a corner where they could talk.

"This is Daumantas and my brother, Symon." Cyril gestured at each as they settled in around the table.

Dan and Iuliana shared a skeptical glance. "Why does Daumantas look like that?" Iuliana asked, confused.

Dan scowled. "Magic." He grunted, crossing his arms. "I should've known you'd be a sorcerer. I haven't seen magic like this since my time at the Wall." He squinted at Daumantas, trying to see though his enchantment.

"Cyril has an enchantment, too, but he thought it best if he remained undisguised to negotiate a way across the border," Daumantas explained, frowning and squirming uncomfortably under Dan's scrutiny.

Iuliana sat up in her chair. "They say someone saw the Voivode in a town not far from here. Was that *you*?"

Cyril nodded. "I chose to be disguised as an old man." He shrugged. "Though now I think I should have chosen something else."

Dan chuckled. "Those two men working for boyar Hadeon Zhupensken were caught trying to sneak past the blockade the other evening. Said they saw the Voivode at a church. They must've doubled back to report back to Zhupensken after you made them leave for Ford Town."

"That was *you* in the crowd!" Daumantas' nostrils flared angrily. "The one who spotted Cyril and pointed him out!"

"We had places to be, and we weren't allowed to leave town until the egg thieving was resolved." Dan scoffed and waved a dismissive hand. Then he gave Daumantas a small, sad smile. "We're all in the same boat now. No one can leave while Hadeon controls the capital. According to some of the other travelers here

I've spoken to, his men are harassing caravans and stealing goods."

A barmaid came over and took their order, either not noticing or pretending not the notice the tension at the table.

As she walked away, Cyril glanced between Iuliana and Dan, "I think you two should come with us—if we can even get out of the fief."

Daumantas shot him a questioning glance.

Making steady eye contact with Dan as he spoke, Cyril said, "I want you to know I wouldn't send Bohden into a situation I'm not willing to put myself in."

Anger flared on Dan's face for a moment, then dissipated. After a moment, he gave a nod, his expression sinking into worry.

They had a round of cool ale and let their nerves settle for a bit before moving on. The others agreed to let Cyril approach the guards himself. He had a decent reputation with Boyar Novadi's guardsman, but he wondered if it would be enough to buy them passage into the heart of the country. Cyril walked towards the checkpoint, heads turning at his approach. Some of the guards must have recognized him, he caught them pointing at him and whispered among themselves.

One guard broke from the group. "Cyril!" the guard called out to him as she jogged towards him.

It took Cyril a moment to recognize her in full armor. Nena was one of only a handful of female guards in Petru Novadi's employ. A swarthy woman with black hair and sharp blue eyes, she'd almost beaten Cyril in last year's fencing contest at the Feast of Saint Vodomor.

"I heard you collapsed at the wrestling competition!" she said. "After the mass poisoning, boyar Petru had us come up to the border."

She and Cyril briefly clasped hands in greeting.

"Is anyone allowed to pass through?" Cyril asked, trying not to sound too desperate.

Nena made a face. "Old man Mihena isn't letting anyone use the road unless they live in the neighboring fief. He's got people patrolling the fields, too. Farmers have been complaining that some people have been trekking through their crops to try and get to the capital."

Cyril frowned. Mihena was a grizzled older man who believed in strict order and often enforced the rules to a fault. Talking to him would be a challenge, but trying to sneak across the border would be worse for their party.

"I know you've probably heard this a thousand times by now," Cyril said, "but I need to speak to him. It's urgent."

Nena pursed her lips, then turned and gestured for Cyril to follow.

Cyril mentally steeled himself for the fight ahead as they entered the guardhouse. Mihena was talking quietly with several other guards as they approached him.

Nena saluted smartly. "Sir! I have Cyril Valentin from Ford Town. He wishes to speak with you."

Mihena affixed Cyril with a wary eye. Cyril gave a formal, if less enthusiastic, salute. "All of you leave. Now."

Mihena's order stunned his subordinates, but they did as they were told.

Nena gave Cyril a lingering look as she headed out last, closing the door to the cramped cabin behind her.

The grizzled old guard crossed his arms, managing to appear both casual and threatening at the same time. "Is this where you finally admit to being Tymor Valentin's child and not a simple peasant from the Valentin fief?"

Cyril sat himself in an abandoned chair, deciding not to play games. "As much as it pains me, yes. I am the child of Voivode Tymor Valentin. I need to cross the border."

Mihena chuckled. "Do you remember when you dueled Dimitru?" He slowly paced the room. "I was just a hired hand back then. My job was to keep Dimitru from getting robbed on the way to the capital. I couldn't believe my eyes." He shadow-fenced an invisible opponent. "You disarmed him so easily! He took it well, all things considered."

Cyril's throat went dry. "What do you want?" He felt intense discomfort listening to Mihena talk about his past.

Mihena stopped and faced Cyril. "You could be doing anything, yet you seem content to be a Keeper of the Peace, hiding in Ford Town. Why is that?"

Cyril frowned. "What does that have to do with anything?"

Mihena smiled. "A man like you should be more ambitious is all." He strode over to Cyril and clapped him on the back. "I can't have any of those poor good folks I've waylaid seeing you, so you and your party will have to go the long way 'round tonight."

Cyril was stunned, but grateful he didn't need to plead his case. "Thank you! I don't know what to say." Cyril stood, and they shook hands.

"Don't thank me just yet. You have a hell of a task ahead of you!" Mihena chuckled, patting Cyril on the shoulder. "I need you to rescue some poor souls taken captive by Hadeon Zhupensken's soldiers. They've rounded up a group of priests not far from here."

Cyril's stomach dropped. *Of course*, there would be a catch.

Thirteen

BOHDEN FOUND that most people don't take kindly to being asked if they've seen a strange old man. He'd been steadily making his way southwest for several days, and he wasn't sure he'd accomplish the task he'd been given. He'd accosted a couple returning home after a wedding, a man walking into town, and some poor older man in the woods taking a piss—some children thought it would be funny to send Bohden after him. So far, his search hadn't panned out. People finding was clearly not in his skill set.

Bohden sat stewing in his thoughts and chewing dejectedly on a stale piece of bread while bathed in the late morning sun. Dimitru had sent him southwest in the hopes he might learn something noteworthy about the Voivode. Petru Novadi believed, if Tymor still lived, he would seek out Ionia Voinescu.

Yesterday afternoon saw a breakthrough: a man frantically telling a wild tale about a thousand men with the same face leaving the monastery of Saint Nauen the previous evening. The men matched Tymor's description, and many had headed south. The news renewing his resolve, Bohden threw on his pack and headed south once more. Cyril was counting on him, after all.

Bohden finished his meager breakfast while he walked down a

dirt track. The roads crisscrossing the area were mostly farmer's tracks linking fields and scattered villages. A vast swamp marked the southern border Vodomeria shared with Monor. The inhabitants near the southern border capitalized on the abundant water to farm. The current stretch Bohden walked was flanked by fields left fallow too long. Young trees slowly overtook the long un-ploughed earth on either side.

Movement ahead made him pause. A person was gathering plants at the side of the road ahead of him. He grinned when he recognized the vestments of a priest of Saint Nauen.

"Good day to you!" Bohden smiled and waved. "I was wondering if you could help with—"

Before he could finish, the strange priest balked at his presence, grabbed their basket, and ran into a stand of young trees.

Cursing under his breath, Bohden gave chase. He wasn't going to lose his only good lead in so many days. The priest crashed through the thicket, following an animal path ahead of them. Bohden plowed forward, following the same narrow path at a frantic pace.

The young stand of trees met an older patch of wood, and the priest broke through and darted away, struggling to keep up such a rigorous pace. They pushed ahead with great effort. Bohden grumbled and started sprinting but was cut short. To his surprise, a man with a two-handed sword stepped out from behind a large tree. Bohden barely managed to stop without running into the blade trained on him.

"Who are you, and what do you want?" the guard demanded. Aged as he was, he held his blade steady. He stood in a defensive stance, blocking the way forward.

Bohden raised his hands. "I'm just looking for someone," he said rather innocently.

The man seemed familiar, but he couldn't quite place why. "Why are you chasing a priest through the woods?" His blue eyes bored into Bohden uncomfortably.

"I just wanted them to answer my question!" He gritted his teeth. "Who are *you*?" He threw the man's question back at him.

"Bohden?" Hidden in the wood, a familiar voice said his name.

The swordsman became irritated. "Sire, it isn't safe!" But the guard lowered his sword as another man approached.

Bohden grinned when he recognized Tymor walking cautiously towards them. His smile immediately dropped, though, when he remembered he was supposed to be in exile.

"Voivode Tymor!" Bohden offered what he hoped was his most respectful bow. "Si—uh…" He'd started to use Cyril's childhood name, then thought better of it. "Cyril sent me."

"Cyril? Is he well?" Tymor walked up and tugged on Bohden's arm.

"Sire!" the old swordsman hissed. "What if he's an assassin?"

Tymor waved away man's concerns. "Antoniu, please. Bohden, do you intend to harm us?"

Bohden shook his head aggressively. "Absolutely not! Cyril sent me here to see you somewhere safe!"

Antoniu grunted and put his sword away. Tymor patted Bohden's arm and led him to their meager camp.

"Let's try to keep the noise to a minimum, at least?" Antoniu grumbled as he followed behind the Voivode and Bohden. "I'd like to at least *pretend* we're in hiding."

"Oh! You asked about Cyril!" Bohden lowered his voice when Antoniu shot him a sharp look. He leaned closer to Tymor as they sat down in the deeper shade under a large tree. "He's well enough. Someone poisoned him at the Feast of Saint Vodomor, though." Bohden's stomach knotted as the memory of Cyril's limp body being protected from the crush of the crowd flashed through his mind.

Tymor nodded, his face solemn. "Are you and Ruslan still friends? Have you heard from him recently?"

Bohden shook his head. "We haven't been friends in a very long time."

"Why is that?" Tymor asked, his brows knitting together. "He left with you for Vuretsiv, yet he returned a full month ahead of you and Orest. What happened all those years ago?"

Bohden frowned. "I don't really feel like I should say." He stared down at his lap, not wanting to meet Tymor's gaze.

The Voivode huffed at Bohden's deflection. "I suspect Ruslan tried to kill both Cyril and me. I'd like to know what's poisoned the man against me."

Bohden scratched at his beard, ruminating on how to answer. "Ruslan has always wanted to be powerful, so that much isn't new. I think he saw his friendship with Cyril as a way to become a boyar."

Bohden and Ruslan were both foundlings Orest had taken in and raised as his own. Bohden had lost his parents to disease, and Ruslan had been abandoned at the gates of Orest's ancient fortress. Bohden had nothing but gratitude for his surrogate family, but Ruslan had always wanted more than their love and affection.

"He proved how cruel he could be when we went out to the brothels once. Ruslan was always rough with prostitutes, and I didn't approve. I never thought—" Bohden stopped himself. He balled his hands into fists and stared hard at the ground.

"You never thought what?" Tymor urged.

Bohden slumped. "He tried to violate Cyril. They'd been arguing on the trip, right before we got to Vuretsiv."

Bohden squeezed his eyes shut. He didn't want to remember that horrible night—Cyril's strangled cries for help piercing the night air; the sight of him fighting while pinned underneath Ruslan, whose undone trousers gave away his malicious intent; the torn clothes they later burned after they reached a safe place to stay the next evening.

"By the saints…" Tymor placed an arm around Bohden's shoulder. "I let that man stay and sent you into exile!"

"I don't care about that!" Bohden's voice was hoarse with emotion. "I'm just glad Cyril is safe and happy!"

He stood, suddenly eager to be away from Tymor. The man had no idea how much Cyril had struggled, how much he'd tried to convince Tymor that him being a boy wasn't just a clever ruse to keep himself safe. Bohden tirelessly supported his friend during what Cyril described as the worst years of his life, but the man before him now had made it immeasurably more difficult.

He sat down hard by the small campfire, watching the priest he'd chased through the woods brewing tea and talking softly with another woman.

The priest came up to Bohden and offered him a cup, "I'm sorry I ran from you earlier. My name is Gavril." They held out their hand for Bohden to shake.

The big man took it and shook it gently. "I'm Bohden Stanescu, a friend of Cyril Valentin."

"Who is Cyril, exactly?" the priest Gavril asked, leaning towards Bohden intently. "Is he an…illegitimate child of the Voivode?"

The woman at the fire scoffed. "He's the first child of Tymor Valentin. He was Princess Si…" She trailed off when Bohden's eyes flashed. He hadn't recognized her at first, but Milena clearly hadn't changed. She cleared her throat before continuing. "Ah, Cyril's been using his chosen name since before he ran away to Vuretsiv. But he is, or rather was, The Dueling Princess of Vodomeria."

Gavril gasped. "I had no idea!"

The Voivode approached the fire, and Gavril handed him a wooden cup of tea.

"I should have been a better father." Tymor huddled by Milena, sipping gently on the hot beverage. The forest protected them from the summer heat to an extent, but it was stifling in the late afternoon. Tymor grunted and set his tea aside, waiting for the liquid to cool before drinking it in earnest.

"Yes, you should have." Bohden grumbled. He turned his attention back to Gavril. "How did you get mixed up in this mess?"

Gavril shrugged their shoulders. "Well, I had the Voivode brought to my monastery and then I kind of got myself mixed up in it, actually."

Bohden leaned in and talked softly to Gavril. "So…are you a friend of Saint Vuretz?"

Gavril chuckled. "New Person. And you look like you've never even kissed a girl."

Bohden smirked. "Not once in my entire life."

They shared knowing smiles, and Bohden chuckled before turning his attention back to Tymor.

"Where is it you're headed?" he asked the Voivode. "Last I remember, Ionia Voinescu is only friendly to you for surrendering Orest's fief to her."

Tymor grunted into his tea. "I have to cross Ionia's fief to get to Orest."

Bohden loudly scoffed. "Orest? Why Orest?"

"He's hoping Orest will actually help him, the Saints only know why." Antoniu walked over to where they sat by the fire. "We should break camp. This fool already managed to locate us. I'm loath to find out if anyone followed you."

Gavril scowled at Antoniu. "The Voivode needed to rest. His heart is still recovering from the poison."

Tymor waved dismissively. "I'll be fine. The rest and the tea are helping, and we really should go."

The party gathered their meager gear and worked their way out of the forest and back to the road. They walked together solemnly, with few words exchanged between them.

As Bohden trudged along, his mind wandered elsewhere. Going to Orest's homestead across the border in Monor would be safer than staying here, and sticking with the ragtag party would be the best way to ensure their safe arrival, too. But he had to wonder if there was much danger here. The physical border separating Monor from Vodomeria was a large and sparsely inhabited swamp. The possibility of assassins coming all this way just to kill an ousted Voivode was almost laughable.

And then the sounds of horses and men caught his attention.

Milena threw a shawl over Tymor's head, and they all stood in front of him while a column of soldiers marched past. Luckily for them, the soldiers wore Voinescu's colors and family crest. The column moved steadily past them for a bit, with a few soldiers glancing at the motley crew of travelers waiting by the side of the road.

Ionia Voinescu, the boyar herself, brought up the rear of the group. Bohden and the party he now found himself a part of tried to slip past unnoticed. No one knew if Ionia was still a friend or a potential foe, and no one in the party was keen on finding out the answer now.

Ionia's eyes raked over them, and she rode on for a moment. But then she whipped her horse around in a whirl of dust. "Hold! Hold, I said!" she cried out to her men as she doubled back to cut Bohden's party off.

She chuckled as she slid down from her horse. She cut an intimidating figure, fully armored in impressive mirror plate and chain mail, and Bohden regretted his earlier thoughts that they were in no danger.

"Milena Valentin and Antoniu." Ionia said, cocking her head to the side.

The color drained from Milena's face. "Ionia, please! We only wish to pass through."

Ionia crossed her arms, and the chain mail she wore crunched and rattled together. "The two of you step aside and let Tymor show his cowardly face."

Antoniu growled in protest, but Tymor placed a hand on his old friend's shoulder. The other man stood aside, and Tymor stepped forward, uncovering his head.

"Hello, Ionia," he said.

The armored boyar smiled. "You old fool! I thought you'd been killed for sure!"

Tymor smiled weakly. "I managed to survive—but just barely. Would it be too much to ask to accompany you back to the capital?"

Ionia's laugh was cold. "I'm afraid not. I don't want anyone to think I want to restore you to the throne. It's not personal, just politics."

Tymor sagged visibly at her rejection.

Ionia climbed back onto her horse and addressed her former Voivode, "Orest isn't far behind us. I agreed to hold talks and end his exile. You'll still be a boyar if you make it back to Triadoara for the election of the new Voivode. Maybe Orest will be more accommodating. Farewell."

The tone of her voice indicated that she expected Orest to give them a similarly cold reception. She gave a sharp whistle and galloped to rejoin her retinue, soon gone in a cloud of hot dust.

"Damn that woman," Tymor muttered under his breath.

Bohden was relieved they wouldn't be harassed any further. Dejected, the party began to walk once more down the dusty track.

A whistle grabbed the party's attention, and Bohden turned to see a porter trotting up behind them bearing a pack.

He offered it to Bohden. "The lady offers these supplies as an apology for the inconvenience." He bowed a goodbye and the porter trotted back to his own traveling party headed for the capital. Bohden took the pack, curious about its contents.

"Well, that wasn't a total loss," Bohden said, rummaging through the bag.

Inside was cheese, bread, several small quantities of dried and salted meat, a few bundles of root vegetables, a block of salt, and a small tin of what Bohden believed to be tea.

"This is a good amount of food for us."

He handed the pack off to Gavril, who peeked inside and nodded in agreement.

They continued their journey south with a little less energy in their collective steps. Antoniu, Milena, and Tymor talked amongst themselves while Bohden and Gavril walked a few steps behind.

"So, you know the Dueling Princess? What are they like?" Gavril glanced over their glasses at Bohden, trying to hide their eagerness.

Bohden chuckled. "He's a stubborn fool like his father, but he's a good man."

"What did you say his name was? Cyril?" Gavril practically danced as they walked along. "The Voivode uses Cyril, but Milena uses another name to refer to him. Cyril is his chosen name, I assume?"

"Cyril has been his name almost as long as I've known him. He chose it when we were still children."

Bohden felt a wistful longing for those simple days. They'd run and play and weren't bothered by the outside world. He wished being an adult wasn't so complicated sometimes.

Their shadows lengthened, and the heat of the day eased as the sun slowly set in the west. Though the forest on either side was punctured by small farmsteads, the nearest town wouldn't be reachable with the remaining daylight. The small group began to search for a place where they could set up camp for the night.

One farmer agreed to let them camp in a fallow field if they were willing to share the space with another party. Tired and dusty, they all quietly agreed and were led to where they'd be spending the night, Gavril quietly planning a meal for them as they walked.

The other party's camp came into view as they crested a grassy knoll. The other group had a single horse, which was more valuable than anything the Voivode's ragtag entourage possessed. They appeared familiar to Bohden but couldn't explain it, so he ignored it. Or he tried to, at least. He helped set up camp and calmly followed Gavril's instructions while preparing their evening meal, but the voices from the other camp sounded eerily familiar to him, and his attention kept wandering.

An older lady from the other camp trotted over to greet them, and Bohden jumped from where he chopped vegetables. "Lilya!" He ran and embraced the woman who'd practically raised him.

"Oh! I thought I heard you! Is Cyril with you?" Lilya asked, her voice muffled against Bohden's chest.

"Ah, well..." Bohden didn't know how to reply.

They broke their embrace, and Lilya looked at the fire. It was plain on her face that she didn't consider it to be surrounded by friends.

"Cyril wanted me to look after his father," Bohden mumbled awkwardly.

Lilya nodded as Tymor and Milena stood. "Milena," Lilya said, trying to sound pleasant and failing.

"Lilya," Milena returned curtly.

Tymor attempted a warmer greeting. "Lilya! I wish we were meeting again under better circumstances."

"As do I, Tymor." Orest's raspy yet orotund voice cut through the air as he strode towards them. "I'd half hoped you'd been done in by some feckless usurper."

Tymor didn't shrink from the hard words of his one-time friend, instead he strode to where Orest stood on the edge of the firelight. "I can fully admit now that exiling you was an overly harsh punishment."

The two older men stood sizing each other up. Bohden held his breath as Tymor extended a hand to Orest.

"My only goal here is to live and protect my family," Tymor said. "I promise not to impede your return to the country."

Orest regarded Tymor for a few moments, then took his hand and shook it firmly. Bohden let the breath out of his aching lungs.

"My apologies, but can I get some help prepping supper?" Gavril said, breaking the tense silence with their modest request.

Milena and Lilya both happily moved to Gavril's side to aid them in preparing the evening meal, while Bohden settled in with Tymor and Orest. Bohden hoped this meant the biggest of his worries were now behind him, and he could focus on getting Tymor to safety.

Fourteen

THE NEWS of their imminent crossing and the task given to him
by Mihena burst from Cyril as soon as he returned to his companions. Serious-faced, Daumantas took Symon to restock their
supplies and reorganize what they had. Dan and Iuliana retired to
their camp with some other travelers from Ford Town, and Cyril
broke away for some time alone. He found a paddock tucked into
the woods for guard training that suited his needs.

Pacing back and forth, he wove his sword from side to side,
windmilling the blade slowly at first to work his shoulders. He
picked up speed as he loosened up, and the blade quickly became a
blur of steel. Sweat poured down his face, he loosened his belts and
pulled his tunic off, tossing it over a worn-out sparring dummy. He
picked a dummy in better shape to shadow spar with.

The blows came fast and furious; parries, thrusts, and slashes
rained down on his mock adversary. His nervous energy expended,
Cyril halted his assault on the straw and wood enemy, his chest
heaving from the effort.

"How did you get so good?" Nena's voice made Cyril jump.

He shrugged. "I was the personal guard and general to the
reigning Sultana of the Shining Sultanate for a time."

Nena crossed her arms. "That's not why."

"I fought 108 suitors. They all lost." Cyril wiped his blade and placed it back in its scabbard.

Nena offered him some water, and Cyril hefted his own water bladder. They refreshed themselves in silence.

Eventually, though, he said, "I don't like to talk about it because the memory is painful." Cyril felt vulnerable talking about his past with Nena. As hard and sculpted as his body was, he still felt the urge to cover himself out of a sense of deeply ingrained modesty.

Nena chuckled. "You were much too respectful to be anyone but the Dueling Princess. I'd secretly hoped you were, but not so I could best you."

Cyril laughed. "Why on earth would you want to duel me and lose?"

Nena smiled. "Because you get it. You know what it's like to face ugly leering men all day."

Cyril grimaced when the words hit him, and the memory of all those hungry faces from his past swam before him.

Nena hefted her own blade, silently asking if he wanted to spar. Cyril nodded and drew his weapon once more. They lazily batted at one another.

"Half the people in Ford Town are convinced you're Tymor's bastard child," Nena said, parrying Cyril's swings with a practiced hand. "The other half thinks you're just some sword for hire who bears a passing resemblance to the Voivode." Even at their slow pace, Nena had to focus to deflect Cyril's deft strikes.

"The legend of the Dueling Princess is so strong that even *I* can't live up to it!" Cyril laughed and dodged one of Nena's swings.

"It's ridiculous, given how highly skilled you are."

Nena was sweating profusely along with Cyril now. They ended their sparring session and retreated to the shade provided by a large tree.

Cyril splashed himself with some water from his waterskin as he spoke. "In the end, I'm just a person. No real person could ever live up to a legend like that."

They sat and chatted for a while in the shade, and time finally began to pass at a pace Cyril was happy with. He'd been anxiously awaiting nightfall since he'd spoken with Mihena.

The sun hung much lower in the sky when Cyril caught back up with Daumantas and Symon. They beamed at Cyril; their clothes rumpled from their afternoon activities.

"What did you two do while I was away?" Cyril asked, dabbing the sweat from his skin with his tunic.

"Daumantas taught me some unarmed combat from the Khanate!" Symon excitedly jabbed at Cyril with his fists.

Cyril smiled and batted the younger man's fists away. "I did some sparring myself. The wait for nightfall is killing me!"

Daumantas smiled and gestured towards the small inn. "Why don't we get some supper and relax for a bit?"

Cyril agreed, and they returned to the inn.

Only the most well-heeled travelers gave the inn any business, and it was only nominally busier than it had been earlier that afternoon. The trio settled in, and a barmaid quickly took their order.

"Stuck here, too?" she asked, though her attention was on the bar, and she left before they could respond.

Both Cyril and Daumantas shrugged at each other, then the three of them dug in once the barmaid brought their dinner. The fare here was simple but of a decent enough quality. Cyril couldn't decide if he preferred a memorable meal or a forgettable one at this moment.

"I want to free the priests of Saint Nauen as quickly as possible," Cyril said to his companions around mouthfuls. "I don't want this detour to slow us down too much."

Daumantas nodded along as he ate, but Symon fidgeted and toyed with his meal.

"Will you fight Hadeon?" Symon asked Cyril, his eyes sparkling.

"I hope not," Cyril managed with his mouth full.

He hadn't thought much beyond getting his family to safety, and he didn't want to contemplate the maneuvering and scheming over the Vodomerian throne that was inevitably coming.

Symon frowned. "Why not?"

"Well." Cyril swallowed the lump in his throat and took a swig of ale. "I'd like the boyars to settle this themselves, if possible."

Symon's frown deepened, unsatisfied with his answer.

"Hadeon Zhupensken is a brute and a horrible man, and fighting is what he's good at." Cyril fixed his younger brother with a stern gaze. "It's what he knows. It'll be better to let the other boyars settle it."

"I just thought that…" Symon stared at this plate and fiddled with his meal. "I thought that we'd save the day."

Cyril gripped Symon's shoulder. "Sometimes saving the day doesn't mean defeating an enemy."

Fear clouded Symon's face. "Do you think Mother and Father are alright?"

Cyril pursed his lips. "Father is tougher and smarter than most people think, so I'm going to say that he's probably fine. Milena, too."

Thankfully, this soothed his younger brother, who said no more about it while they ate.

Later that evening, Cyril, Symon and Daumantas met up with Dan, Iuliana, and Nena at the agreed-upon spot behind the inn. The moon wasn't quite full, and the light aided their careful walk through the dark forest. Nena led the way, showing a missive Mihena had drawn up to any other guards who attempted to halt their progress. Cyril was impressed with how many were stationed in the woods. light from the fires at guard posts flickered in the dark, stretching a good way in either direction from the crossroads.

The trek wasn't far to the road on the other side of the woods, but the late hour and the frequent guard stops made it feel much longer. Everyone in their party kept deathly silent. Cyril suspected that they all feared they may squander their good fortune by being too boisterous. They stepped away from the trees and onto the dusty track on the other side of the blockade.

"We'll head into the woods on the other side," Nena said, adding, "A group of Zhupensken's soldiers have been pretty active on this side of our blockade."

They found a hollow in the woods to camp in and made themselves as comfortable as they could in the dark. None of them slept well that night, and they were all awake by first light.

When Cyril donned his disguise in front of his companions, Symon's eyes grew wide, and Iuliana gasped at his visual transformation, while Dan simply scowled. Nena was unaffected.

"Is the magic necessary?" Iuliana asked quietly as they picked their way through the woods.

Nena had them avoiding the road in order to keep them hidden from the marauding band holding the priests captive. Dark clouds had rolled in, and the air was thick with the smell of rain.

"It is if it keeps Zhupensken's soldiers off my father's trail," Cyril said.

He feared looking like the Voivode might attract too much attention, but he was certain they'd fair far better against Hadeon's men than his own aged father or any of the disguised priests.

Rain started to fall and grew heavier as the day wore on. Nena led the party through the wood until it gave way to farmer's fields. The side of the well-traveled track became quite muddy as they trudged along. The wet sound of hooves in the mud and jingling armor alerted them to the approach of soldiers. They dove into a wheat field as a band of armed men passed by, and Cyril did his best to stay well out of sight. They wore Hadeon's colors and bore his family crest, but thankfully the driving rain removed any interest they may have had in a group of soggy travelers standing in a field.

Keeping slow and staying far behind, they followed the group of Zhupensken's soldiers until they arrived at a fair-sized village. Nena had them hang back as the soldiers entered the village inn.

"This is where the group of priests are being held captive," she said, brushing the rain from her eyes and pointing at the building. "Most of the other villagers are hiding in their houses."

Nena led them south of town to a farm where they could shelter for the night. A soldier was standing guard outside, wearing Boyar Voinescu's crest.

The guard's eyes fell on Cyril, and he groaned. "By the Saints, not another one!"

"He's not one of the disguised priests, I promise!" Nena laughed. "I'll explain once we're out of the rain."

The guard led them towards a hay barn, where a small cluster of soldiers waited inside, talking quietly among themselves.

Nena gestured at Cyril, and he removed his enchanted tunic. "This is Cyril Valentin," she said. "He's going to help us free those priests."

One of the soldiers, a big ursus man, stepped forward. "How is this going to help, exactly?" He sounded exasperated.

"I should be able to make them think I am the real Tymor Valentin," Cyril explained as he pulled his soggy tunic back on. "I can try to negotiate, or we can run them out of town. It could go either way."

A tabby striped felis soldier scratched at her chin. "It could work, even if they aren't totally convinced of your identity." She surveyed the motley group that had entered the barn, her concern plain on her face. "We don't have much more on them in terms of numbers, though."

"Hadeon's numbers are smaller than when they started," the soldier who'd led them in said. "They were twenty strong about a week ago, but there are maybe eight or ten Zhupensken mercenaries now. Their leader is a harsh man, and some of the soldiers have fled his command." He made a frustrated grumble. "Lady Voinescu recalled all her other soldiers to go to the capital a few days ago. The other boyars seem to have the rest of Zhupensken's forces trapped at Triadoara, but its left us with no support to handle this band in a timely fashion."

"Mihena has been stingy with help, too." Nena nudged a pile of straw with her boot. "He doesn't want to commit a force to handle it himself." She looked at Cyril. "That's why he tasked you with dealing with them."

Cyril shook his head. "Mihena is too conservative." He turned his attention to the Voinescu soldiers. "If our enemy is already demoralized, it should work to our advantage. We'll head out at first light and try to catch the soldiers at the inn."

The rain began to taper off, and they moved to an unused part of barn the soldiers set up camp in. In exchange for a modest sum, the farmer kindly supplied them fresh bread and vegetables to eat. Cyril and his companions worked to dry themselves around a campfire, and they discussed their strategy for the following day with the Voinescu soldiers.

Iuliana and Dan agreed to stay at the farm with Symon. Symon took some convincing, but he eventually agreed to stay behind for his own safety. They shared a simple meal with the soldiers and bedded down for the night, still damp from walking in the rain.

———

Morning came, and Cyril, Nena, Daumantas and the Voinescu soldiers headed back to the small village. "They're holding the priests captive in the inn," the leader of the Voinescu soldiers explained. "The Zhupensken mercenaries have been occupying the building and extorting the villagers for food and drink."

As they approached, a heated dispute could be heard happening outside the town inn. A half dozen men—armed a bit haphazardly but still clearly dangerous— demanded unreasonable quantities of food, gold, and other supplies from the small village. Cyril and his small party observed cautiously from a distance, trying to go unseen.

"We simply don't have—" one man protested.

A gruff-sounding older man cut the villager off. "What *do* you have then? You all were happy enough to give food and drink to those damn traitor priests! Stop holding out on us!"

The gruff man was brandishing a straight-bladed, double-edged sword popular further west. He slashed at the villagers and laughed when they flinched away.

Cyril clenched his teeth and tried to keep himself where he was. Six men, even poorly armed, could be dangerous. The gruff one had a breastplate and bracers on his forearms, but no other protection. No pole arms to worry about. Would it be too flashy to take six men at once? Cyril wondered to himself. Daumantas stood behind him with a serious expression and a sword already drawn.

"I want my money, my food, and my booze!" The gruff man lunged aggressively at the small group of villagers desperately trying to appease him.

They huddled together, staying defiant but clearly intimidated. Cyril couldn't stand to watch any further and marched forward. The gruff man and his companions quickly noticed his approach. Now clearly in view, Cyril spotted Chin Beard and Mustache from several days before. They balked at the sight of his disguised self.

"That's the Voivode!" Mustache shouted, pointing while keeping his companions between himself and Cyril. "He used magic to make himself look young in a village east of here!"

Cyril recognized the brutish man as a servant of Hadeon from his time at court many years ago. "Ladislaus Zhupensken." He strode within a few feet of the gruff man's party.

Ladislaus was stunned by his appearance but recovered quickly. "So, you *were* hiding here." An ugly smirk spread across his face. "I haven't seen you since the feast of Saint Vodomor. You recovered from your stomachache I see."

Cyril put a hand on the hilt of his sword. "Leave these people be."

Ladislaus snorted. "You don't have any power anymore." Ladislaus pointed his sword at Cyril. "Who's that with you? Antoniu in a magical disguise? And those cowards who work for Lady Voinescu?" He laughed. "Come on, boys! This lot are worth more than anything in this miserable town!"

Ladislaus sprung at Cyril with the confidence of a veteran. Cyril quickly unsheathed his sword and batted Ladislaus' blade away. Beside him, Daumantas whipped his own blade through the air beside him, easily pushing Ladislaus' men back on his own. Cyril and Ladislaus circled one another, and the older man renewed his attack.

Ladislaus Zhupensken fought like a desperate man. He was clearly suspicious of Cyril and was trying to end the fight quickly. His sloppy, fevered swings left gaps just big enough for Cyril to take advantage of. Cyril kicked Ladislaus below the ribs to throw him off balance and followed with a savage slash at the other man. Unable to bring his sword up to parry in time, Ladislaus shouted, his eyes growing wide as Cyril's slightly curved saber bit deep into his neck.

"Princess…Si…." Ladislaus gurgled; sudden recognition of Cyril's identity made his eyes bulge. His blade dropped out of his hands.

"My name is Cyril," he said calmly, beheading Ladislaus with a savage heave that drove his blade the rest of the way through Ladislaus' neck.

He stepped over Ladislaus' lifeless body to find the other five men defeated or running from Daumantas. One man lay a crumpled corpse, and another man, wounded but not dead, had collapsed near Daumantas' feet. Chin Beard and Mustache had taken Ladislaus' horse and were fleeing without putting up a fight. One final man still fought halfheartedly against Daumantas. Seeing Cyril standing over Ladislaus' body, the last soldier threw down his pitted sword and fled towards the woods on foot.

"You've been hiding a sword?" Cyril asked incredulously.

It felt strange, seeing Daumantas with a bladed weapon in his hand. The blade didn't differ much from Cyril's own, though it was a bit longer and had a deeper curve. A bright red tassel hung from the gilded pommel.

Daumantas glanced at him but said nothing. He turned to the wounded man, who clutched his arm and sat in the mud. "If you agree to leave these people be, we'll give you aid."

The man sobbed and howled in fear when Daumantas effortlessly hauled him from the muck. "I promise! I promise I won't hurt these people!" he cried.

Daumantas steered him towards the inn. The small crowd of villagers who'd been negotiating on behalf of their settlement approached Cyril and Daumantas carefully.

"Are you really Voivode Tymor Valentin?" the one who'd been speaking to Ladislaus asked.

Cyril shook his head. "I'm not, though I used to live at court."

The villagers consulted amongst themselves, occasionally glancing over at him. Eventually, the man who'd been speaking for the village broke from the group and held his hand out to Cyril. "I'm Radu. While I appreciate your assistance, I'll admit I fear for the safety of my small village." Radu wrung his hands. He wasn't *quite* saying they were unwelcome, but his discomfort was plain on his features.

"I understand," Cyril said. "We'll take care of this mess and be on our way."

The Voinescu soldiers had gone into the inn to free the priests inside, but there were still the bodies to take care of in the street. When Cyril turned, he saw Daumantas holding onto the side of the building, looking unwell, and Nena stopped to check on him before trotting over to Cyril.

"Is he alright?" he asked.

Nena shook her head, then pointed at the corpses in the mud. "I'll help you with these two."

They dragged the bodies to a clearing near a stand of trees and heaped dead wood on top of them. Several villagers came over to wordlessly help them build the improvised pyre. The wood was still damp from the previous day's rain, but Cyril eventually got the wood alight. Once the fire burned strong enough, some of the villagers stepped in to keep it burning, and Cyril took his leave of it.

As he and Nena walked quietly to the inn, he took a few moments to clean his sword.

"You did the right thing." She patted him on the shoulder, attempting to assuage his grim disposition.

"I don't like killing people." Cyril's voice was flat.

In all his years as a sword for hire, he hadn't taken many lives, but he'd grown to know the look of a man ready to kill. It made his stomach turn uncomfortably.

"I know," Nena shook her head. "They didn't give you much of a choice. That man—Ladislaus, was it? He would have killed you if you'd given him the chance."

She patted Cyril on the shoulder one last time before leaving him to his own devices. Daumantas sat outside the inn, slumped over on top of a barrel. Cyril walked over to him and put a hand on his back.

"I didn't mean to kill that man," Daumantas murmured.

Cyril stood beside him in silence.

"I don't enjoy violence," he continued. "My father thinks I'm weak." He seemed to shrink as he talked, the weight of his conscience crushing him.

Cyril felt indignant at Daumantas' words at first but remained calm. His lover's aversion to physical conflict sometimes irritated him, but Cyril suspected Daumantas had witnessed much more violence and conflict than Cyril imagined—even with his seemingly pampered background.

"Those men were after our lives," Cyril said, trying to console him. "You made the right choice to defend the town."

"It's been a long time since I've killed anyone. I'd hoped to never have to do so again."

That shocked Cyril, but he chose not to comment on it. "We should go." Cyril tugged gently on Daumantas' arm, urging him off the barrel. "I promised we'd leave as soon as I took care of things."

Daumantas slowly stood, then nodded. "You're right. I shouldn't sit here feeling sorry for myself anyway."

A pang of guilt hit Cyril, but he just wasn't sure how to handle the situation. He quietly made his way inside the inn, where the Voinescu soldiers searched for the priests. Upstairs were two more Zhupensken mercenaries who'd surrendered to the Voinescu soldiers. The ursus soldier waved Cyril over to a door.

"The priests won't let me in," the ursus man huffed. "They want proof we are who we say we are."

"Please, we mean you no harm," Cyril called through the door. "I was sent here by Mihail Novadi to assist you."

An elderly priestess cracked the door open to peek out. She took stock of Cyril's disguised self, then threw the door wide and beckoned him inside. The room was packed with almost a dozen priests and priestesses. They collectively backed away, frightened for a moment when Cyril stepped into the room. A dark-skinned, bearded priest towards the back of the room stood up.

"Remove your enchantment," the man demanded, though not harshly.

Cyril obeyed, pulling the enchanted tunic over his head. Gasps punctuated the room gasped as his long, rose-colored mane spilled out across his shoulders and down his back.

The bearded priest stepped forward. "Who are you?" he asked, scrutinizing Cyril uncomfortably closely.

"I was born…" Cyril trailed off and started again. "I am Cyril Valentin. First child of Tymor Valentin and Princess Consort Erzbet." His late mother's name sent a pang through his heart.

"How do we know he's not an imposter?" one of the other priests asked.

The bearded priest shook his head. "This man must be who he says he is. Erzbet is all but forgotten since she passed so young." The priest pointed to the scars on Cyril's chest. "Furthermore, this is the work of skilled Vuretizian monks. I'd heard rumors the Dueling Princess had gone to Vuretsiv, but I didn't believe it." He stepped back to give Cyril space. "My name is Darius. I cared for your father when he was ill in our monastery."

"Th-thank you," Cyril said, for it felt like the most appropriate response. "Why are you here?"

Darius took a deep breath, looking much more relaxed in Cyril's presence. "A man named Ruslan threatened to cut Tymor down in our own church."

Cyril could taste the hatred rising in his throat at the mention of Ruslan, but the priest was continuing his story.

"Our abbot, Gavril, took the Voivode and fled south at Tymor's insistence. He claims he has at least one ally there, though who I'm not sure. Hadeon tried to take all the priests of Saint Nauen into custody until the boyars encircled him at the capital."

Cyril thanked Darius for his time and informed him they were free to go. He left the crowded room to meet his party downstairs.

The Voinescu soldiers agreed to take the Nauenian priests to the Novadi fief with Nena. Villagers began to venture out of their houses and gave the priests and soldiers food for their journey. Daumantas took a humble bundle of foodstuffs from a villager and thanked them for their kindness, then he and Cyril walked to the road and started towards the farm where Iuliana, Dan, and Symon waited.

"Wait! Please, wait for me!" Cyril turned to see Darius sprinting towards them. He skidded to a wobbly stop, doubling over from the effort. "I'd like to join you, if you'll have me."

Cyril looked at Daumantas. "Do you object?"

The big ogre scratched his chin. "I think it would be wise to have a fully trained healer among us."

Cyril nodded, and they continued on the road south and away from the village.

Fifteen

THEY MANAGED to make the crossroads and onto a route towards Cyril's intended destination before nightfall. A light rain began to fall again, and they sheltered in an abandoned barn at the edge of a field for the evening. Rain pattered though holes in the ruined roof, but plenty of the interior was still dry enough to camp in for the night.

Cyril slept in fits and starts. Visions of his duels with suitors haunted his dreams. He dreamed he lost a fight to a faceless man, and he'd been forced to marry him. He had another strange dream where Daumantas came to Triadoara, and they ran away together. There were many more dreams he didn't remember, but they all left him uneasy.

First light touched his eyelids, and he was instantly roused from his restless sleep. Resigning himself to wakefulness, Cyril quietly extracted himself from the bedroll he and Daumantas shared and sat in the doorway of the dilapidated barn. Steely pre-dawn light intruded upon the darkness of the night sky to the east, highlighting the high, wispy clouds lingering from the evening's rain. Several rabbits hopped among the tall grass as he listened to the chirping of crickets that had yet to retire.

Iuliana startled Cyril with her sudden appearance. She offered him a smile as she sat beside him. "Rough night?" She put a hand on his knee and leaned onto his shoulder.

Cyril sighed. "Just some strange dreams." He glanced over at her and returned her smile.

Giving him a small kiss on the cheek, she murmured in his ear, "I'm glad you're alive."

"Why are you here?" Cyril asked.

Iuliana frowned. "Honestly?" She took a deep breath, squeezing his knee. "I couldn't stand the thought of living in a place where your memory would haunt me, so I followed Dan on his ridiculous journey to protect Bohden from himself."

Cyril laughed softly. "I didn't take you as the sentimental type." Iuliana slapped his knee.

She sat up and looked at Cyril earnestly. "We were lovers, weren't we?"

His mouth fell open. "I didn't realize…"

Iuliana groaned and rolled her eyes. "Did you think I was servicing you for free? Oh, by the Saints!" She stood and walked briskly away, then turned to face Cyril with her hands on her hips. *"Really?!"*

He jogged to her, pleading with his hands "Iuliana!"

She wrapped her arms around him, pressing her body against his. Cyril's mind burst with thoughts of them tangled together in pleasure.

"It's alright. We never put words to it," she said, smiling softly at him.

He wrapped his arms around her in kind. "I really did enjoy the time we had together." Cyril kissed her softly on the cheek.

"But you need love, and I can't offer you that." Iuliana sighed, breaking their embrace. "Truth be told, I didn't want you to fall in love with me."

Cyril smirked. "You knew I was in love with Daumantas the whole time, didn't you?"

She smirked over her shoulder as she headed for a stand of trees nearby. "I can't hear you! I'm going to take a piss!"

Cyril laughed and shook his head.

Dawn came, and the others began to awaken. Dan passed Cyril and Iuliana, grunting a greeting as he stumbled outside to relieve himself, followed by Daumantas. He came and wrapped his arms around Cyril.

"Did you sleep well?" Cyril asked.

Daumantas gave him a squeeze. "Not too well, but then, neither did you."

Cyril let out a long breath. "I'm sorry if I made you feel like you were…lesser yesterday."

He half expected Daumantas to push him away, but the big man held him tighter. "I…I shouldn't be upset about you defending yourself or the town. And I shouldn't be mad at myself, either." Daumantas relaxed, unconscious tension leaving his body.

"You don't have to like it. The violence, I mean." Cyril gazed over at Daumantas. "I'd rather resolve a situation with words than my sword any day."

Daumantas chuckled. "I know what kind of sword you'd *really* prefer," he whispered against Cyril's ear.

"By the Saints! Such a filthy mind!" he hissed back, and they both laughed softly.

Darius and Symon finally arose from their slumber, and the party shared a simple breakfast before departing once more, following the road headed south. The warm morning air was quiet, save for the call of the occasional bird and buzzing insects.

After a time, Symon fell into step beside Cyril. "Do you think I could learn to fight like you?" he asked.

Cyril put his hand on Symon's shoulder. "A sword is a tool and a burden," he said, locking eyes with his younger brother. "If you learn to wield one, you must never draw it in anger. Do you understand?"

Symon's face was solemn as he nodded. Cyril turned his attention back to the road ahead, where Dan had stopped and signaled for them all to do the same.

"Is that smoke?" Iuliana asked, staring at the thick could of dust rising off the road ahead of them.

"That's a large column of men on the road." Dan turned to his companions, his face serious. "What should we do?"

The road on either side was flanked by farmer's fields, and some were occupied by people tending to the plots. It left them no real cover.

Cyril's chest tightened with worry, but he was determined to press forward. "It's probably a boyar headed for the capital. If we remain calm, they probably won't pay us much mind."

They started walking again, keeping to one side as they went.

The column of soldiers met them quickly. It was a mix of people on foot and horseback. Many were Vodomerian, but there were dark skinned Grendairan mercenaries and a few wearing Monoran style armor as well. Cyril tried to keep his head down, but he noticed several among their number pointing towards him and talking amongst themselves. More than half the company of soldiers had passed when their number began to slow, and men flanked them on either side.

Iuliana pulled a hefty cast iron pan from the side of her pack, and Dan defensively wielded a large smithing hammer.

"Everyone, remain calm..." Cyril entreated his companions.

Daumantas stood close to Symon. His hand loosened on the hilt of his own concealed sword, but he kept his hand close to the handle of his blade. Darius stood close to Cyril, unsure of himself.

A woman wearing mirror plate armor rode towards them on a snorting horse and dismounted. She drew her blade and pointed it at Cyril. "You aren't Tymor Valentin, so who the hell are you?"

Cyril studied the older woman's face while contemplating his answer. She waved her sword, attempting to intimidate an answer out of him.

"Madame, please!" Darius cried, drawing a dangerous glare from the woman. Frightened by her hard gaze, he took several steps back. "This man is disguised for good reason!"

Cyril held his hands up, conscious of the blade level with his chest. He squinted; certain he recognized the woman. "Boyar... Voinescu?"

She'd attended many of his duels at court. Ionia sheathed her blade, curiosity plain on her face. She gripped a fistful of Cyril's tunic and rubbed the fabric between her gloved hands.

"Magic!" she grunted, and she ripped through the garment's elaborate border.

The strange physical shock that resulted from Ionia breaking Daumantas' enchantment startled both Cyril and Ionia. She quickly released him with a curse. The crowd of soldiers began to murmur as Cyril's true visage became visible.

"Is that Tymor's first born?" he heard someone in the crowd ask.

Ionia reached for Cyril's face, her gloved hands gently trembling against his cheeks. "By the Saints!" She gently held his face now, turning him this way and that to study his features. "What Orest said was true, then. You did go to Vuretsiv to receive the blessings of Saint Vuretz. What are you called now, child?"

"Cyril." His voice was thick with emotion.

Ionia smiled. "What a fine name. It suits you!" She released him, her smile growing broader. "You always had such fire. I always thought your father a fool for not nurturing your obvious strengths. You could have made a fine general!" Ionia turned to her men, getting their attention with a high-pitched whistle. "We keep heading towards the capital! Nothing more to see here!" Before remounting her steed, she turned back to Cyril. "Your father isn't far behind far, as long as Orest hasn't sent him further south. Good luck to you!"

They stood on the side of the road while the remainder of Ionia Voinescu's company filed past. Many openly stared at Cyril as they rode by. Bards and gossips had woven fanciful stories of him after he'd left Vodomeria, and he'd only ever heard a fraction of them. The fact that he was alive and well must have been a surprise to some. Many songs had woven him a tragic demise.

Dan and Iuliana beheld Cyril with no small amount of awe. "So, you are...or were... or...are formerly the Dueling Princess?" Dan stumbled to ask while shaking his head, clearly overwhelmed by the revelation.

Cyril was hit with a wave of intense self-consciousness from the scrutiny.

Iuliana kept glancing at Cyril and blushing. "I can't believe I bedded royalty!" she murmured to herself a bit too loudly.

Cyril imagined his face must be as red as the hair on his head. He stared at his own feet until he felt a hand grip his arm. He looked up to see Symon's pained face.

"That woman said Father shouldn't be far," Symon said.

Cyril patted his hand and gave him a small smile. "We'll see him very soon."

The thought filled him with conflicting emotions. What would Tymor do when he saw Cyril? Would he even recognize him? Cyril's stomach twisted and turned, though the mood around him had lightened considerably.

Daumantas slapped him on the shoulder, breaking his solemn train of thought. "Looks like we'll finally achieve our goal, and not a moment too soon!" Daumantas smiled down at him, but concern clouded his eyes. "You don't have to greet them if you don't want to."

Not quite knowing what to say, Cyril absentmindedly ran his hands over the rip in his tunic, and Daumantas heaved a dramatic sigh.

"My hard work ruined!" he groaned, wrapping an arm around Cyril.

"Do you think you can fix it?" Cyril asked. "I rather like this tunic."

The warmth of Daumantas' body against Cyril's comforted him, though the heat of the day made it almost unbearable. This close, Cyril could see through his disguise at times, his true face appearing through his enchantment like a mirage.

Daumantas stroked his chin. "It should be repairable, but it won't be quite the same."

They walked past busy farmsteads and fields heavy with crops nearly ready for the harvest. Whatever unrest there was elsewhere didn't penetrate far into the Voinescu fief, and life moved along undisturbed. They stopped briefly so Dan could help a man with his cart. He moved swiftly, knocking the metal that had begun to protrude from the wheel back into place.

The big blacksmith was an enigma to Cyril, and though they both lived in Ford Town, Cyril realized how little he knew about him. He walked beside the burly man for a bit, hoping to remedy that.

"So…you fought in the war?" Cyril asked. "I was just a child when the Heretic Wars raged at the Monster Wall myself."

Dan's face clouded. "I was just a boy myself for most of it." He flexed his hands as he spoke. "Hadeon did a lot of damage, trying to track the heretic army." He turned to Cyril, his face pleading. "That man cannot be Voivode." It was a simple statement, but it was filled with Dan's unspoken pain.

Cyril grunted. "He…threatened to have his way with me at court in front of everyone before our duel. Hadeon Zhupensken is the last man I want to be the next Voivode."

Dan grimaced. "I had no idea."

"Many men threatened to do worse to me. He was one of the first, but far from the last." Cyril felt bile rising in his throat, and he fell silent.

Dan put one of his big hands on his shoulder. "Men can be horrible beasts sometimes."

Cyril laughed. "I hated it, but it gave me fuel. I was furious that they couldn't see that I was just as much a man as any of them. I vowed to never act like them after the way they treated me."

"You're a better man than any of those fools." Dan squeezed Cyril's shoulder.

They walked side by side for a long time. The sun slowly climbed higher in the sky as they went, its rays unrelenting. As they were about to step off the road to wait out the heat of the day, another party of travelers appeared around the bend.

One of the members of the other party came sprinting towards them. Startled at first, Cyril reached for his sword, but he soon recognized Bohden's large frame hurtling towards them. With a cry, Dan ran to meet him, and the two large men collided, embracing. Then Dan grabbed Bohden's face and pulled him close for a rough kiss. Iuliana trotted over to them and got scooped up in an embrace as well, all of them hugging and laughing.

"Mother! Father!" Symon sprinted off towards his parents as he spotted them, and Darius joined behind at a slower pace when a member of the other party called to him by name.

Cyril stopped, keeping his distance. His father and stepmother embraced his brother, the three of them overjoyed to be reunited. Then Cyril's eyes lifted to the woman sitting astride a horse. It was Lilya, watching Cyril with a mix of joy and worry. On the ground beside her stood Orest holding the reins, his head cocked to the side, regarding Cyril with curiosity.

"We should go." Cyril took a few steps backward before turning away. His chest had grown uncomfortably tight at the sight of his father, and he knew Lilya and Orest would understand if he didn't speak to them at this moment.

Daumantas said nothing and followed his lead, falling in step with Cyril.

"We can cut though one of the villages we passed and make it halfway to Triadoara by nightfall," Cyril said to Daumantas as he walked resolutely away from the reunion behind him.

"What's the plan when we get there?" Daumantas asked, diplomatically avoiding the conversation Cyril didn't want to have.

Moving with purpose again lifted the dread Cyril felt, "We'll see if we can find Petru and Dimitru Novadi and make camp with them. After that, I'm not entirely sure."

"Wait! wait!" someone shouted from behind.

Recognizing the man's voice, Cyril stiffened his resolve and kept moving away, determined to keep heading north. Daumantas hesitated, looking back.

"Please, wait! For the love of the Saints!" the man called out.

Cyril drew in a sharp breath and turned around. Tymor was running towards them, his breaths labored from the effort.

Joy, fear, dread, and a fair amount of anger warred within Cyril's body as Tymor reached out for him and placed his hands on his shoulders. His mouth hung open as he examined Cyril's face. "Oh, my child, I'm sorry. I'm so sorry." He embraced his wayward child as tears streamed down his face. "My son. My amazing son.

Thank the Saints you're alive!" Tymor's body shook against Cyril as he sobbed into his shoulder.

His son…

The words warmed Cyril's soul, and he gently embraced his father, tears filling his eyes. They held each other for a long time as they both wept.

Sixteen

THE COMBINED parties now made up a sizable retinue for the deposed Voivode and his family. Cyril walked along in a daze, listening to the voices around him. His good friend's voices mingled with those of his estranged family, and he found it both comforting and a little disquieting.

Dan and Bohden laughed and talked boisterously with Iuliana, Daumantas chatted with Darius and the abbot he'd been searching for, and Milena fussed over Symon while Tymor talked quietly with Antoniu and Orest. Cyril walked in silence, as his emotion still threatened to overwhelm him. The joyous mood around him did not lift Cyril's spirits.

"Darling, are you alright?" Lilya's voice cut through Cyril's unpleasant mood.

"I'm…I'm glad everyone is alive and well," he answered neutrally.

Lilya leaned down from her mount, placing her hand on Cyril's shoulder. "I've always loved you like you were my own son."

He looked up at her, and she smiled. Her face was deeply wrinkled now, and her long hair, once dark, was now a cloudy gray.

Cyril took Lilya's hand and held it for a long while as they walked north together.

He remained apart from the group while they made camp for the night, opting to help gather firewood and care for the horse rather than mingle. Daumantas brought him his dinner where he sat at the edge of the firelight.

"I set our tent up at the edge of the wood so I can take off my disguise without upsetting anyone." Naked concern painted Daumantas' features. "You can come to bed when you're ready."

Cyril nodded to show he'd heard his lover, and Daumantas slunk off into the dark.

Tymor eventually found his way to where Cyril sulked alone. Cyril stood as Tymor opened his mouth to speak, but Cyril cut him off. "You never were a father to me."

Tymor closed his mouth slowly, then opened it again. "I am truly sorry," he pleaded, "I simply didn't know how to handle—"

Cyril huffed. "How to handle me? Orest and I both told you—"

"I thought you were just playing at being a boy! I thought it was just a phase!"

"A *phase*?" Cyril slapped his muscular chest and opened his arms wide. "Does this look like a phase?"

He turned to march away into the dark, but Tymor followed. "I'd been away at war, and I came home to find my daughter was my son! How was I supposed to feel?"

"I thought you'd be happy!" Angry tears seeped from Cyril's eyes. "I wanted you to be happy. *I wanted to be your son.*" Sadness and anger choked off any other words Cyril might have said in that moment.

They stood in awkward silence for a long time.

Finally, Tymor said, "A Nauenean priest came and spoke to me when you returned to court. They told me you might be a New Man." He stared at the ground. "I panicked. I wanted you to marry well so Vodomeria would have a blood connection to one of our neighbors. I didn't want to see you as a man because I didn't want to lose that opportunity." He took a shuddering breath. "I was a fool. I wanted you to be my daughter so badly that I ended up losing you as my son."

Cyril's anger cooled as his father wept in front of him for the second time that day. He quietly embraced Tymor and let him cry until no more tears came. Neither man said anything, not even when the let go. But as they walked away from each other, both glanced back a few times.

Finally finding his bed, Cyril laid down beside Daumantas. He felt as if years of fear, anger, and sadness had physically drained from his body. It made him feel lighter, but bone weary.

"Are you still awake?" Cyril softly asked Daumantas.

The big ogre rolled over to face him in response. "Are you going to be alright?" he asked.

Cyril let out a slow breath. "I think I will be now."

Daumantas laid a big hand on his cheek. "You don't owe them anything," he said as he planted a soft kiss on Cyril's forehead.

Cyril smiled in the dark, placing his hand over his lover's.

Daumantas rubbed his palm against Cyril's cheek. "Your face is all stubbly."

"I'll have a barber shave it as soon as I can," Cyril said with a yawn.

"Why not grow it out?" Daumantas ran his hand along Cyril's jaw, feeling the rough short hairs sprouting from his face.

"It's all patchy," Cyril grumbled. "It wouldn't look nice."

"I think it would." Daumantas lovingly patted Cyril's cheek, then rolled back over.

Cyril touched his own face and fell asleep dreaming of the possibility of growing a full beard.

———

Morning came a bit rudely as Cyril was startled awake by the sounds of a scuffle and screaming.

Bleary eyed, he stumbled out of the small tent he shared with Daumantas. Several others also arose sleepily and were observing the same scene: Daumantas, undisguised and attempting to cook breakfast, was being chased around the fire by Milena.

"Get away from our food, you awful creature!" She swatted at him with a large stick.

"I'm only trying to cook! Please!" Daumantas dodged her while also attempting to tend the pot he had over the fire.

"Milena!" Cyril marched up and wrenched the piece of wood from her hands. "Daumantas is a friend!"

"Where was your friend yesterday?" She was panting from the chase.

Daumantas grumbled and cursed under his breath, handing Cyril the wooden spoon he'd been defending himself with. "Tend the porridge, won't you?" he said, then marched off towards their tent.

Cyril dutifully went to the fire and stirred the porridge to keep it from burning while watching the others gather around.

Tymor yawned and peeked into the pot while Cyril stirred the contents. "Who was that ogre? He looked familiar somehow…"

"I can't explain it well, but he was in disguise yesterday." Cyril stared into the depths of the pot while trying to figure out how to explain his relationship with Daumantas to his father.

"Daumantas was in disguise?" Bohden asked, confused.

Cyril arched an eyebrow at him as Daumantas walked back with his enchanted tunic. With a flourish, he put it on. The enchantment took immediate effect, giving him the look of an unassuming human male.

Orest, Milena, and Tymor gasped. Antoniu grunted disapprovingly, and the two priests seemed curious but not impressed.

"*Oh!* I thought he was your manservant," Tymor said quietly.

Cyril leaned close. "He's my lover." Cyril's father's face reddened, and he stepped away from the fire and sat down.

"I don't understand. Is he supposed to look different?" Bohden asked, genuinely confused.

"Congratulations, my friend!" Daumantas removed the extra enchanted layer of clothing and clasped Bohden's shoulder. "You have a rare gift."

"I do?" Bohden was not any more enlightened than before.

Iuliana put a bowl into his hands and nudged him towards the fire. Cyril spooned in a generous portion of corn porridge.

"What was I supposed to see?" Bohden asked as he received his helping.

Cyril chuckled. "I'll explain later."

Bohden's bewildered expression stayed fixed in place as he walked away.

Cyril continued to serve the others as Iuliana distributed bowls to the rest of the party now gathered at the fire. Symon was giggling to himself when Cyril filled his bowl with Daumantas' porridge. He clearly found the whole situation very amusing.

They had a much quieter breakfast as the sun slowly came up over the trees. Daumantas distributed some berries he'd picked while everyone else still slept. Both Tymor and Cyril regarded them with a small amount of suspicion while eating them. Thoughts of the poisonous sweet cakes Cyril had nearly died from eating danced uncomfortably in the back of his mind, though the tartness of the berries was oddly reassuring to him as he slowly chewed them.

They broke camp and continued their journey northwards. The sun wasn't very high in the sky when they started encountering groups of people traveling south.

"Inferni in the capital!" one man shouted from a cart.

A murmur rippled through the party. Inferni? This deep into Vodomeria? This far from the wall?

Iuliana came up to Cyril and touched him on the arm. "Are the Inferni as terrible as they say?" she asked, frightened.

Cyril pursed his lips. "I've only seen them once or twice while in the City-States. Just Devil Ants, but they'll rip a man apart if left to their own devices."

She gasped and covered her mouth. Cyril didn't want to scare her, but there was no denying how dangerous the Inferni were. Whatever cursed magicks had created them had given them an insatiable bloodlust, and their singular, dreadful purpose seemed to be rending the flesh of sentient beings.

Bohden put an arm around Iuliana's shoulders. "Don't worry," he said, his face stern. "I did some time on the Wall, and I know how to handle those beasts."

As they continued north, activity on the road increased. The chaos in and around Triadoara frightened and displaced many people. Clusters of camps lined the road, a mix of refugees and armed people preparing to defend their homeland. Even with the crowds, though, it wasn't long before they reached the main cluster of boyar camps, just north of a small village a mile or so outside of Triadoara. The southern and eastern boyars had made camp together; Voinescu, Novadi, and several smaller fief-holders were spread out on both sides of the road.

Before Cyril's party could go much further, someone in the throngs spotted Tymor and called out, "The Voivode is here! Tymor lives!"

People began to crowd around them, and they found themselves wading through a sea of bodies.

"Make way! Make way, I said!" Ionia Voinescu came to their aid, parting the sea of people from the back of her horse. "So, you all made it?" She squinted at Daumantas. "Where did the ogre come from?"

Tymor pushed his way to the front. "I need to speak to everyone, and quickly!"

Ionia was unconvinced of Tymor's importance in the situation, but she still agreed to take them to where the other boyars were gathered within the camp.

Tymor, Antoniu, Symon, Orest, Lilya, and Milena split off and headed with Ionia Voinescu. Cyril and his original party made their way towards the Novadi camp. To Cyril's surprise, Darius and his abbot followed along with him. Cyril turned to the pair of priests.

Darius' former abbot stepped forward. "I don't think we've met properly yet. I'm Gavril."

"You're…a New Person?" Cyril shook Gavril's hand, and they smiled.

"Your father told me you were a New Man," Gavril said. "And

I'll admit I'm excited to meet you. You'll have to tell be about Vuretsiv when you have time."

Confused, Cyril raised an eyebrow. "That doesn't really explain why you've decided to accompany me and not my father."

Gavril chuckled. "Darius and I would like to offer our services as skilled healers. I don't think the former Voivode has the connections to help me coordinate my support efforts for these people."

Cyril had to admit that Gavril's observation was very astute. He agreed to help the priests and turned back to his task of finding the Novadi's.

Petru and Dimitru spotted Cyril amongst the throngs and waved him over. Cyril gave them a wave in return and turned to his companions. "Daumantas, stick close to me." Then Cyril looked at Bohden, Iuliana, and Dan. "I appreciate all your assistance over the last several days. Will you be headed back to Ford Town?"

Dan crossed his arms over his chest. "I'm not leaving until the Inferni are dealt with." Bohden nodded in agreement, his face serious.

Iuliana stepped forward. "I'm not leaving until I know you all are safe and well." She looked around with a smirk on her face. "Besides," she said, a playful gleam in her eye, "there's potential in this crowd, and a girl like me could make some good money in a place like this."

They laughed, and everyone embraced before parting ways. Cyril strode with Daumantas towards the Novadi's, his demeanor growing serious.

Dimitru walked forward to meet him, saying as the two of them embraced, "I heard you found your father."

"It felt strange to see him after all this time," Cyril admitted. It was the first time he'd really said that out loud. What he didn't add was that he was finally feeling better about the whole thing. Instead, he asked, "What is this I hear about Inferni in the capital?"

A scowl darkened Dimitru's face, as well as Petru's. "Scouts say they've seen Devil Bugs patrolling around Triadoara," Petru said. "But so far, no one has been attacked by them." Petru led them to a large tent and held the flap open for them to step inside. "The behavior seemed odd to me, so I contacted some allies to assist us with the problem."

On the other side of the table stood Kanat and the slim ogress with the strange walking chair. A smile played across Kanat's face briefly when he saw Cyril and Daumantas walk in with Petru and Dimitru.

"Cyril! I wish we were seeing each other under different circumstances." Kanat gave a small bow.

The diminutive ogress pursed her lips briefly but said nothing.

"I want to thank you both for the care you provided me," Cyril bowed low to show his respect for the ogres on the other side of the table, "I wouldn't be here without your help."

To his surprise, the slim ogress smiled slightly. "I apologize for not introducing myself the day we first met." She spoke flawlessly in the language of the Voivodates. "My name is Lyazzat. I'm the guild master of Craighan Tor."

Daumantas stepped up to the table with a confidence Cyril rarely saw from him. "Master Lyazzat, please tell us more of these Inferni."

"Most of what we know is from simple observation at a safe distance," she said, folding her hands on the table. "These Bugs simply do not move as they are usually observed to. We suspect it's an illusion, but none of the locals wish to inspect them up close."

"If we had some disciples of Dragos the Mad, we could make a determination more quickly." Petru grunted. "But people this far from the wall have no practice fighting Inferni."

Daumantas slapped his large hands on the table and startled everyone in the tent. "Bohden! Bohden saw through my enchantment!" He turned to Cyril, a mischievous glint in his eye. "We could take Bohden to the imposter Inferni and have him tell us what they really are."

Petru and Dimitru exchanged looks. "Bohden Stanescu?" Dimitru asked, confused. "He can see through illusions?"

Daumantas laughed. "I don't have time to explain the particulars, but he does have a gift for it, yes."

Petru suggested they meet back at the war council tent in the morning. Before they left to find a place to set up camp, Cyril made sure to introduce Petru to Gavril and Darius.

Kanat chased after Cyril and Daumantas as they exited the tent. "We brought your wagon here with us," he told Daumantas. "There's no need for you to sleep rough."

He led them to a circle of several wagons; one belonged to Kanat, one Cyril did not recognize at all, and the other was Daumantas' familiar, cheery wagon.

Daumantas heaved a relieved sigh when he saw his traveling abode. "The Great Dragons bless me this day!" He practically giggled at the sight of it.

Sitting at the fire in the middle of the wagons was Claudia, the felis sorceress Cyril met at Ford Town the during the Feast of Saint Vodomor. She waved enthusiastically when she saw them approach. He waved back, then groaned when he saw who was sitting beside her—his father.

Tymor stood and hurried towards them. "I want to speak to you more before…well, before whatever happens here happens."

Cyril felt the urge to send his father away quickly rise in him, but Daumantas put hand on his shoulder. "Go be with your father for a few moments," he whispered. "I'll make sure there's food and a bucket of clean water for you to scrub down with ready for you when you return."

Cyril nodded and let Daumantas and Kanat walk away while he strolled with Tymor along the edge of the sprawling camp.

"I just wanted to say that I should have been the one to take you to Vuretsiv," Tymor told him. "You should have never been made to go in secret."

Cyril cast his gaze up into the quickly darkening sky and to its many stars. "You've been talking to Orest?"

Tymor nodded. "He says you still have my sword."

The sword hung at Cyril's side, feeling like an old friend. He pulled it from the sheath and handed it to his father.

Tymor turned the blade over in his hands. "It looks so well cared for. Why keep it?"

He handed the blade back to Cyril, who re-sheathed it, "I'm not entirely sure. I'd always dreamed of wielding this blade, and it's served me well."

A chuckle escaped Tymor. "I thought you were going out for an evening with your friends!"

Cyril looked incredulously at his father. "You thought I snuck out to drink?"

The two laughed together.

"I gave you my sword because I wanted you to be able to defend yourself!" Tymor explained. "I never thought you'd be leaving Vodomeria with it!"

The statement made Cyril laugh even harder.

Once he began to regain his composure, Tymor gripped his shoulder. "I'm glad it's served you so well for all of these years."

Tears sprung into Cyril's eyes. "I always admired you." He turned to Tymor and saw that older man's face he'd seen in the mirror in his enchanted disguise. "Orest used to tell me stories about your swordsmanship."

Tymor squeezed his shoulder. "You've surpassed me in every way imaginable, and I'm proud of you."

Cyril tried to thank him, but the words got stuck in his throat. He also tried not to shed too many tears, but he did weep once they'd parted, and he made his way back to Daumantas' wagon.

Seventeen

THIS WAS SUPPOSED to be a day of rest and relaxation for Ruslan. He'd earned it, after all.

Their plan worked so far. While they were effectively trapped in the capital, they would soon open a dialogue with the boyars of Vodomeria, offering to turn over Hadeon in exchange for their freedom and the old boyars' holdings. For the moment, he hadn't a care in the world. And he wanted to keep it that way.

Ruslan had finished at the bathhouse and climbed into bed with some hired company when rapping on his door disturbed him. He tried to ignore it, but the unwanted visitor's knocking simply became more urgent.

"Sir! Sir! I have important news!" a man's muffled voice called through the heavy oak door.

With an exasperated grunt, Ruslan gently removed his two companions' mouths from his member and went to speak with the frantic man. He popped the door open just a crack, and the man on the other side started at the sight of his naked body.

The interloper had a prominent mustache and turned himself slightly away from Ruslan's nudity.

"What do you want?" Ruslan growled, causing the mustached man's eyes to dart quickly to and away from him.

"The...ah...Cyril Valentin is alive," the man said. "I pursued him, thinking he was Voivode Tymor, but he was wearing some kind of clever disguise."

Of course, Cyril lived. The Princess had proven to be as stubborn as her father.

Ruslan pinched the bridge of his nose. "I'll inform Hadeon. Make yourself useful and join the garrison patrolling the walls."

The mustached man opened his mouth to speak again, but Ruslan slammed the door on his face.

He turned back to his naked companions. "I want to take both of you at least once before I leave. Hurry up!" Ruslan climbed back into bed, pressing the man's and woman's heads back down into his crotch when they didn't move quickly enough. "Don't disappoint me now!"

They resumed working his member again with nervous urgency.

Once his carnal needs were met, Ruslan left to find Hadeon Zhupensken and tell him the news. He'd confronted Tymor at the Monastery of Saint Nauen outside Triadoara before Tymor escaped. The Voivode hadn't been faring well, but Ruslan never got close enough to finish what should have been a clean assassination. Hadeon was content with just chasing Tymor out of the capital. The now ousted Voivode's humiliation was more important to Hadeon than his death. And Ruslan still didn't know what to make of Laurent's reluctance to outright kill Tymor Valentin. Knowing that Cyril also survived would mean the country's boyars would move against them sooner and he'd have to act fast.

Ruslan hated being allied to such a crude and simplistic man as Hadeon, but they shared a distaste for the Valentin family, and he used it to his advantage. He found the old boyar bathing in Tymor's old bedchamber.

"This better be important!" Hadeon grumbled, unconsciously rubbing the stump where his left hand should have been.

Ruslan bowed low. "Cyril Valentin has also survived."

Hadeon stared at him blankly. "Cyril *who*?"

"The Princess, my lord."

Hadeon growled. "That bitch." Though they both had been spurned by the princess, Ruslan hated how Hadeon talked about her. Hadeon coveted her womanhood while Ruslan felt he'd tried to save it.

Though he'd never been close enough to be spotted, Ruslan spied upon the princess in Ford Town several weeks prior. She'd fully taken to playing at being a man—growing a beard and every-thing. It made Ruslan sick. How could she profane her body in such a way? In their youth, he'd tried to convince her not to go to Vuret-siv, not to alter her body with their magicks. He'd even tried to teach her the joys of womanhood, but she'd fought him, and he'd only succeeded in clumsily spilling his seed on her thigh. Bohden broke his nose, and Orest walked him to a guard post along the Pilgrim Road. They completed the journey without him, and Ruslan hadn't spoken to any of them since that day.

"We have the capital! We'll simply hold it until the other boyars declare me Voivode!" Hadeon's words broke through Ruslan's thoughts. He leaned back in his tub, fully confident in what he believed to be his own plan.

"You and I both know they won't do that." Ruslan kept his voice level, trying to subdue his rising temper. He approached the tub. "They all know you tried to kill Tymor, even with our deflections. It's only a matter of time before they try you for your crimes."

Hadeon chuckled. "They'll have to drag me out of the palace first!"

No longer able to contain his rage, Ruslan forced Hadeon under the water and held him there. The older man writhed and thrashed against him, but Ruslan held him under the water with a fierce determination. Only when Hadeon stopped fighting did he release him. Ruslan frowned as he looked down at himself, now soaked from Hadeon splashing about. Hadeon's body bobbed face down in the tub while Ruslan dried himself best he could. He left his old boyar's body and went to find some men to help him remove it from the palace.

The servants had largely fled the palace once Hadeon took control of it, outside of a small handful of servants too scared or too stubborn to leave. None of them would approach anyone associated with Hadeon. Ruslan made his way to the former guard's barracks to fetch a few soldiers and talk to Hadeon's commanders.

"I have unfortunate news," he told the assembled lieutenants. "Hadeon Zhupensken drowned in his own bath."

They murmured amongst themselves. "Do you suspect foul play, sir?" one of the soldiers asked.

Ruslan shook his head. "I believe he slipped and hit his head getting in the tub. Poor fool was dead when I found him."

None of the lieutenants asked any further questions and helped Ruslan take the body down to a chapel to be held until Hadeon could be buried.

It was unfortunate how Ruslan's distaste for Hadeon had gotten the better of him. He'd wanted to keep this ruse up a little bit longer. Hadeon's defeat was inevitable; most of Vodomeria's boyars shared a mutual loathing for the man many blamed for fueling the war along the Wall, and he would not be missed. But he wasn't supposed to die just yet, and now he and Laurent would need to rethink their next move.

Ruslan returned to his chambers and stripped out of his damp clothing.

"You killed the old fool and lied about it?" The voice from his bed made Ruslan jump.

He'd dismissed his hired companions after the mustached man ruined his mood, even though he'd paid to keep them all night. A familiar lithe figure now lounged in his bed. Laurent's naked form lay wrapped in the sheets, fixing Ruslan with his jewel blue eyes.

A cascade of sable hair followed Laurent as he sat up. His dark hair and bright eyes made his pale skin gleam. With a delicate hand, he beckoned Ruslan to join him. Ruslan climbed into the bed, hungry for Laurent's body. He took the outstretched hand and sucked suggestively on Laurent's fingers.

"What had you in such a mood?" the lithe man asked, cocking an eyebrow.

Ruslan reached up Laurent's thigh, but the slim man caught his hand in a vice-like grip. His question unanswered, Laurent pulled his fingers from Ruslan's mouth and extracted himself from the bed in one fluid motion.

Frustrated, Ruslan growled. "The princess is here, possibly among the boyars as we speak." The loathing he felt for the former princess of Vodomeria burned in the pit of his stomach.

Laurent filled a basin with water and frowned into its depths.

"What are you doing?" Ruslan stood, curious.

Laurent ran a pale finger around the rim of the basin three times. "I want to see this princess you keep going on about."

An image swam to the surface of the water: Cyril arguing with Tymor in a darkened field. The amused smile fell from Laurent's face as he gazed upon the scene. He pierced Ruslan with a hard gaze.

"That is a man." Laurent's usually soft and melodic voice was hard as steel.

"She *was* a beautiful woman once!" Ruslan snarled.

The slap that hit him almost dropped Ruslan to his knees.

Laurent turned on his heel and snatched a robe from the back of a chair. "I'll see this plan through, but you don't get special treatment anymore."

As he regained his composure, Ruslan managed to grab Laurent by the wrist before he could leave the room. "You don't understand! She—"

The pale man freed himself easily from Ruslan's formidable grip. A flick of Laurent's wrist sent Ruslan flying backward. He hit the floor and lay there, dazed. Laurent walked over to gaze down at him, his face like stone.

"Vuretz was an amazing woman," Laurent said. "And though these people practice with an incomplete knowledge of her work, I will not have you sully her name by proxy."

Ruslan began to laugh. "You really believe you are the Mad Sorcerer King!"

With a sneer, Laurent dug his heel into Ruslan's sternum. "What none of you seem to grasp is that I *am* the last Sorcerer King of Finndrigair. A facsimile of him, at least."

Ruslan fought to remove Laurent from his chest. Laurent's heel pressed the air from his lungs, and his vision narrowed as he struggled against the other man's weight upon him. Just as Ruslan began to lose consciousness, Laurent lifted his foot, and Ruslan took a gasping breath.

"We will see this plan to fruition," Laurent said, "but you will get no more assistance from me once this is over."

Ruslan watched from the floor as Laurent stalked out of the room.

Eighteen

WHEN CYRIL ENTERED HIS WAGON, Daumantas was sitting naked in bed with a book propped on his knee. A grin spread across Cyril's face as he laid his eyes on his lover.

"Excited for the privacy?" Cyril asked as he stripped off his clothes and scrubbed himself thoroughly. The cloth and bucket of warm water that had been left for him were a welcome sight after not being able to bathe for several days.

A little smile appeared on Daumantas' lips. "I'm happy for something familiar," he said, flipping the page.

The rough cloth felt good on Cyril's skin as it lifted several days' worth of grime. It wasn't perfect, but it made him feel refreshed. Finished, he dumped the now cloudy water out the door.

He ate the meal Daumantas made for him as quickly as he could. All Cyril wanted was to be in his lover's arms. He crawled across the bed to where the big man sat. Daumantas chuckled softly and set his book into a nook built into the wagon's wall. Sitting astride him, Cyril made himself comfortable on the big ogre's lap whose thick legs rested between his own. He sighed and sank into his lover's arms, resting his head on Daumantas' shoulder.

"Are you finally feeling better?" Daumantas wrapped his arms around Cyril and gave him a gentle squeeze.

"I was starting to think this was all a mistake," he mumbled, listening to the bigger man's gentle breaths. "I shouldn't have avoided talking to my father as long as I did, though. I also missed Symon growing up." Cyril's voice hitched in his throat, and he fell silent.

"You were afraid of what would happen if you returned. I don't know how my own father would react if I walked into the palace now."

They sat embracing one another for a while. Cyril nuzzled Daumantas' neck, and the big man moaned. He trailed gentle kisses along his lover's shoulder, and they slowly sank together into the bed. They spent the evening making love before giving into sleep.

When morning came, Cyril felt Daumantas rise with the sun as usual.

"Why must you get up so early?" Cyril grumbled and reached for his retreating form.

Daumantas chuckled and gave Cyril a gentle kiss on the cheek. "I was always expected to get up at dawn," he explained as he dressed. "I've never been able to break the habit."

Daumantas played at being a spoiled boyar's son at times, but no spoiled child is made to wake at dawn every morning. Cyril wondered about his lover's youth, and what all had led to the man being who he was now.

Unable to stand being in bed alone, Cyril roused himself and rummaged around the wagon for clean clothing. He sleepily stumbled outside, where Daumantas was sharing coffee with Claudia, Kanat, and Lyazzat around the fire pit situated between the wagons.

"Good morning, Cyril Valentin," Lyazzat greeted him. "Would you also like some coffee?"

He nodded and gladly accepted the cup Lyazzat offered to him.

Kanat cleared his throat. "As you are the only Vodomerian here, how would you approach this situation with the false Inferni?" He met Cyril's eyes with an unexpected openness.

"There will be people who won't go near them." Cyril sipped at his coffee, contemplating the best way to tackle the situation. "If the Zhupensken fief is cut off from the rest of Vodomeria, the knights of Dragos the Mad won't be reachable to assist. Their monasteries are all along the Great Monster Wall, and most lie within the Zhupensken fief. Breaking the enchantment is going to be the only way forward. Most people this far from the wall have never even seen Devil Bugs and have no idea how to fight them."

Cyril grimaced at the thought of having to face the Inferni. He'd only ever observed them from afar, and he'd never had to fight them himself. The fiends were rumored to kill any sentient beings they come across, and this fact alone scared most folks witless.

"I can dispel the enchantment using arrows." Daumantas leaned forward. "I can remove the enchantments and reveal the true nature of these false Bugs." He frowned, leaning towards the fire, "I had a great tutor who educated me on how to defeat Devil Bugs in Grendair. If they turn out to be real Bugs, I can destroy them."

Cyril nodded. "As long as the threat is something we can handle, the boyars can tighten their siege on the capital, and we can force Zhupensken out." They stood together and made their way to the meeting tent to present their plan.

The assembled boyars appeared skeptical when they heard the plan for themselves. "What do we do if these things are some kind of *other* Finndrigairian automata?" one nervous boyar asked, wringing his hands.

Lyazzat glowered at him. "There are several seasoned sorcerers among us." She leaned forward, and her walking chair stood taller. "And we can make fairly quick work of any contemporary automata the enemy might employ."

The boyars murmured amongst themselves, clearly concerned.

Irritated with the pace of the meeting, Cyril spoke up. "If we do nothing, we waste time, and Hadeon becomes more entrenched. We need to dislodge his forces fast or you'll be committing to a full-scale siege of your own capital!"

His outburst caused the voices in the tent to swell in outrage.

"And who are you, exactly?" someone deep in the crowd shouted.

"I am Cyril Valentin, the Flame of the West, former general of the Shining Sultanate! I've actually seen a pitched battle against hardened warriors, unlike most of you!" Years of bitterness from his poor treatment at court poured out of Cyril, and the room fell silent at his hard words.

Then a different voice came from the now hushed crowd. "Aren't you Tymor's oldest? The…the Dueling Princess?"

"Ugh, yes! I am—or, rather, I was—the Dueling Princess!" Cyril's face turned as red as his hair as anger burned through him.

"So, you're the general who ended the siege of Karnatakur?" A portly boyar with a thick beard stared at Cyril with wonder in his eyes. When Cyril nodded, the boyar nodded back. "I'd heard stories of a foreign general who helped secure the current Sultana's throne, but I never thought it was a Vodomerian!"

The boyars pressed close around Cyril, and the tent filled with dozens of questions asked all at once.

"Everyone, please!" Cyril shouted. "We have business to attend to!"

Try as he might, though, Cyril couldn't quell the crowd on his own. Daumantas pressed close to him, partly to keep the crowd from sweeping him away.

A loud rapping on the central table finally grabbed the assembly's attention. "Enough! You can sate your curiosity later!" Ionia leaned on the table, and she looked as though she might jump atop it if the situation dictated. "He's the only seasoned tactician among us, so let him speak!"

Cyril cleared his throat and leaned over the table, contemplating a map spread across it. "The weakest points of Triadoara's defenses are the Old North Gate and the wharfs by the river around the South Gate. While the bluffs on the north bank make for a formidable defense, the ramps and switchbacks from the wharfs up to the city proper don't have much in the way of defensive structures. However," Cyril said, pointing to the line of defensive wall that ran parallel to the river on the map, "they can shower us with projectiles fairly easily."

"This point is our best option for breaching into the city." He pointed at the Old North Gate. "This gate is bricked up and largely unguarded. It harbors an underground passage that allowed me to leave the city undetected many years ago."

Antoniu pushed his way forward to the table. "The Old North Gate used to be a Tor." He scratched the stubble on his chin as he thought aloud. "It was used as a guardhouse for a time, but the structure fell out of use when they walled in the gate."

"The cellar is actually quite expansive, and it has a corridor that extends under the current wall." Cyril pointed to a church on the map north of the Old North Gate. "It runs to what must have been outbuildings in Finndrigairian times. Now, it's this church and a burial ground."

Antoniu nodded. "Not big enough to fit a whole army, but big enough for a large party to take a gate or two for us?" His dark eyes glittered as he locked eyes with Cyril, and the old man wore a slight smile on his face.

Cyril nodded at the old guard. "We may need to fashion a ladder to get up into the old Tor turned guardhouse, but it should be easy enough. I've been told the City Guard is in control of the Pauper's Bridge east of the city. We'll have a group meet them and sneak through the Old North Gate."

The room in agreement, they began to formulate a plan to retake Triadoara. Not long into their planning, a commotion outside distracted the assembled boyars once more.

A sentry burst in from outside and bowed low. "I'm very sorry for interrupting! But Hadeon Zhupensken is dead!"

A murmur rose through the tent.

The sentry rocked back and forth on his heels. "One of his advisors has taken his place and is demanding an audience with..." The man hesitated. "Their self-proclaimed leader, a man named Ruslan, wants an audience with the...Princess."

All eyes locked on Cyril, and his stomach twisted. "I'll go talk to Ruslan, try and see what he's playing at. Orest, you take Bohden,

Daumantas, and a small handful of soldiers and go to the church where the passage comes out at. We'll need to secure it and make sure the corridor is clear if we're going to utilize it." Cyril turned his attention back to the room. "I want you all to be ready to take the city the moment the corridor is clear. Don't worry about me. Retaking Triadoara is our first priority."

Tymor waded through the crowd to stand beside Cyril. "I'm coming with you."

Cyril tried to protest, but Ionia joined with Tymor. "Going alone would be a mistake, and you know it. I'm going with you as well." She crossed her arms and fixed Cyril with a stern gaze.

Cyril clenched his jaw but relented. "You're right. It would be unwise to go meet Ruslan alone."

The remaining boyars agreed to continue preparing for their assault on the city while Cyril, Tymor, and Ionia left to meet with Ruslan. Cyril returned to Daumantas' wagon to arm himself. He checked his sword and dagger, belted them on and made sure they were secure. A piece of paper protruding from a drawer caught his eye. Cyril opened the drawer and was stunned to find the letter Tymor had sent just weeks before. He smiled at the memory and how big of a disturbance it had felt to him at the time. None too eager to meet with Ruslan, Cyril sat and finally read the letter.

Dear Cyril,

I understand that this letter is far too late. I have sat down many times to write it, and I have failed to put my thoughts into words until now. I see now that I was wrong to reject you as you are—as Orest raised you—and I humbly admit that I was wrong to try and force you to be my daughter when I should have continued to raise you as a son.

I have only heard stories of what you may or may not have done since leaving Vodomeria, and I humbly ask that perhaps you could tell me of your exploits yourself. I understand if you feel it too late to be father and son, but I'd still like the chance to celebrate my child's achievements.

Your humbled father,

Tymor Valentin

"Cyril, are you well?" Tymor called through the door of the wagon.

Cyril brushed the tears from his eyes. "I'm almost ready!" He put the letter back into the drawer, thoroughly wiped his face, and stepped outside.

Tymor and Ionia were there, both wearing grave expressions. Tymor had a plain saber strapped to his waist. Ionia had fetched a dozen of her own soldiers to accompany them.

"Do you two want horses?" Ionia asked as she mounted her steed.

Cyril laughed. "I haven't ridden a horse in years!"

She glanced at Tymor, who shook his head. "I'll be walking as well."

Ionia shrugged but didn't argue. The small party started off towards the city.

Cyril felt odd being flanked by an attachment of soldiers rather than being a guard himself. The heat of the day failed to touch him in his current mood as they walked north along the road, towards the city's main gates.

"What's the plan?" Ionia asked from atop her horse.

"We stall until they infiltrate the city," Cyril said. "We'll have to hold our own once Ruslan realizes what's happening."

Tymor glanced over at Cyril, his confusion plain on his face. "What do you think Ruslan wants with you?"

Cyril grimaced. "To humiliate me in some way, I'm sure."

Tymor gripped his arm. "Do you think he means to challenge you?"

"To a duel? Now?" Ionia pulled back on the reins and matched pace with her two walking companions.

"Win or lose," Cyril said, "I think he plans to play the situation to his advantage. He wanted to duel me for years, but he never got the chance to. We were halfway to Vuretsiv before he confessed that he'd wanted to."

All the moments Ruslan had pleaded with him—to be his lover, to not go to Vuretsiv, to allow him to duel for his hand—played out in the back of Cyril's mind as they walked. He involuntarily shuddered at the memories, and his stomach churned at the idea of facing his former friend again. Taking comfort and strength from the others walking with him, he continued onward.

They crested a hill, and Market Town on the south side of the river came into view. While most of Triadoara lay on the north bank of the Tria River, the fortification on the south bank had grown into its own town. Linking the two was the Emperor's Span, a broad and ancient bridge constructed by the Finndrigairians. The sight of Triadoara stirred an odd mix of emotions in Cyril. He both longed to walk its cobbled streets and felt a strong desire to turn around and run away as fast as he could. Cyril shook his head, took a deep breath, and continued forward.

A small group of dark-liveried soldiers stood in a knot by Market Town's main gate. Guarding the gate behind them stood two eerily still Devil Ants. As Cyril's small detachment approached, the gathering of soldiers parted to reveal Ruslan, and a beautiful man Cyril didn't recognize.

Tymor grabbed Cyril's arm so fiercely pain shot into his hand. "By the Saints! It cannot be!"

Cyril clenched his teeth against the pain of Tymor's grip. "Let me go and tell me what you see, old man!"

Tymor's grip loosened, but his hand remained on Cyril's arm. "That's Laurent, the Mad Heretic! How can that be?"

Deep concern creased Tymor's aged face as he gazed upon the men before them. Cyril knew from stories a man named Laurent had led the rebellion in the west against Hadeon and attempted to take his fief.

"Wasn't he executed?" Cyril asked, confused.

"We did so in secret. I beheaded him myself!" Tymor took a deep breath. "Dark sorcery is afoot."

Laurent leaned in and whispered in Ruslan's ear as they walked forward. Cyril tried not to flinch at Ruslan's unwavering gaze as it latched onto him, his eyes burning with obsession.

"It's been a long time, Princess Si—"

"Get that name out of your mouth!" Cyril snapped.

Ruslan smirked. "Too bad neither of you had the decency to die." Ruslan's smirk twisted into a sneer as he turned his attention to Tymor. "Hadeon had simply wished to overthrow you with force. I barely managed to talk him into a poisoning." He waved dismissively at Tymor. "You have no power here anymore. Why even come, old man?"

Tymor drew himself up. "I'm here to give my son council and to bear witness, nothing more."

He and Cyril exchanged a glance, and Cyril felt fortified by his father's words.

"What is it that you want, Ruslan?" Cyril asked, placing a hand on his sword.

The mood grew cold as Ruslan contemplated his answer. "I want Hadeon Zhupensken's fief and titles and our guaranteed safety. In exchange, we'll return the capital to the boyars and allow them to start the process of electing a new Voivode"

"There's something else." Cyril pursed his lips. "What is it?"

Ruslan's gaze dug into him uncomfortably. "I want to understand why you mutilated yourself so!"

"I'm not mutilated!"

"You were beautiful!"

"I was miserable!"

They charged one another, arguing at full volume in front of their respective parties.

Hot tears welled up in Cyril's eyes. "Trying to be a woman was killing me, Ruslan! I was dying, and I can't understand why you—"

"You were dying? *Dying*? I could have made you happy!

Besides," he said, shoving Cyril backward, "you'll let any man in that filthy slit of yours now! You've become a common whore!"

With a roar, Cyril drew his fist back to hit Ruslan as hard as he could. The other man tried to dodge, but Cyril's quick fist tapped his jaw. Ruslan returned a punch to Cyril's ribs, and the two grappled one another for a few moments before their attendants intervened.

"What in the name of the Saints are you doing?" Ionia hissed in Cyril's ear as she and Tymor pulled him bodily away from Ruslan. Cyril spotted Ruslan being similarly manhandled by the slim-figured Laurent.

"This isn't part of our plan!" Laurent's eyes were hard sapphires as he chastised the taller, bulkier blond.

This is going very poorly, Cyril thought to himself. But at least they were successfully distracting the enemy.

Fist fighting wouldn't solve their problems, but throwing a few punches at Ruslan did make Cyril feel a little better. He took several angry gulps from his waterskin before speaking. "I think we have to consider giving him the Zhupensken fief, just in case we aren't able to fully dislodge Ruslan from the city."

Ionia placed her hands on her hips. "If we give him what he wants, he'll remain a thorn in our side for who knows how long."

Ionia continued to speak, but Cyril got distracted by his father tugging on his sleeve.

"Where did those clouds come from?" Tymor asked, fear in his voice.

Cyril turned to face Triadoara. A thunderstorm was forming overhead with unusual speed. Their enemies shared panic and surprise confirmed the storm wasn't their doing. Laurent pointed at the sky while visibly arguing with Ruslan.

The wind whipped up, and Cyril felt his hair stand on end. Both parties cowered as lightning rained down on the city. With a blinding flash and mighty crack, two bolts struck the false Devil Ants, destroying the wagons they'd been all along. Great booms of thunder rolled over them, followed by a cascade of rain.

"Was this *really* that ogre's plan?" Ionia shouted through the torrent of rain now blinding them.

"We have to stop them from re-entering the city!" Cyril shouted back, grabbing both Ionia and Tymor and pulling them close.

Ionia turned to her troops and shouted orders to advance through the wall of water. Tymor gripped Cyril's arm and drew his sword as they slowly advanced on where the enemy force once stood.

Inching forward, they soon caught stragglers not moving fast enough towards the south gate of the city. The first few simply threw down their arms in surrender at the sight of them. They were bound by Voinescu's soldiers and pushed to the back of the advancing force. Moving steadily, the main body of the Zhupensken force soon noticed their offensive, and dark-liveried soldiers advanced on them through the deluge.

Tymor and Cyril stuck close together as the skirmish intensified, fighting side by side against the Zhupensken cohort. Cyril pushed into the Zhupensken forces, even though he knew the fighting would come to naught if they failed to capture Laurent or Ruslan. The rain and the chaos frustrated Cyril, who forced himself to slow his advance and gather his thoughts.

Tymor stuck with him, matching him blow for blow while they fought.

"I'm impressed." Cyril grinned at his father while he took a moment to find the best path forward.

"There!" Tymor pointed.

A group of soldiers had come to a halt, and Cyril spotted Ruslan and Laurent locked in another argument.

Ionia threw off an assailant and pushed her way over to Tymor and Cyril. "Do you see them?" she asked, panting. Her blade and her armor were smeared with blood despite the rain.

Cyril pointed at the pair they pursued through the downpour.

"Lead the way!" She shouted sharp orders, and with a mighty charge, her forces drove themselves like a wedge through Zhupensken's soldiers. The confused and leaderless Zhupensken forces parted at the charge and allowed Cyril to rush forward.

"Time for you two to decide: will you surrender or retreat?" Cyril pointed his blade towards Ruslan and Laurent. Ruslan's face contorted into a snarl, while Laurent appeared irritated but otherwise calm. Laurent grabbed Ruslan by the arm, forcing the other man to face him.

"I still wish to negotiate," Laurent demanded. His eyes were hard, and his frustration with Ruslan was palpable.

"I will not entertain this…pathetic *woman* any longer!" Ruslan wrenched his arm free from Laurent's grasp and drew his sword. "Duel me, Princess!" He beat on his chest as he shouted at Cyril.

Laurent sneered and turned away. "This is your fight, not mine." He gave a sharp whistle and roughly half of the Zhupensken forces began to march for Market Town's south gate.

"Everyone! Only fight those who side with Ruslan Zhupensken!" Cyril managed to give the order as Ruslan roared and charged him.

"A thousand gold to the man who takes Tymor Valentin's head!" Ruslan shouted as Cyril parried his first strike.

Cyril and Tymor were quickly rushed by Zhupensken troops, and Tymor Valentin fought with a tenacity of a man half his age against them.

An ugly grin split Rulsan's rain-soaked face. "Finally, the duel I've been wanting!" He charged Cyril, cutting at him viciously.

Cyril kept his form tight, deflecting the blows neatly. "You're only upset because you tried to have your way with me and failed!" Cyril goaded, hoping to keep Ruslan sloppy.

Out of the corner of his eye, Cyril saw Zhupensken troops breaking ranks and retreating. Ruslan saw as well and slowed his assault. Cyril tried to down him with a kick, but Ruslan dodged, and the blow didn't land well enough to knock him over.

To Cyril's surprise, Daumantas came charging through the crowd and headed straight for them. He stopped when he met Cyril's eyes.

Nineteen

WHILE CYRIL fruitlessly parleyed with Ruslan, Daumantas crested a hill with his small detachment and surveyed the road that followed the river below them. Some of the Vodomerians gasped and pointed at what appeared to be an Inferni automaton trundling along the road. A small camp of soldiers had barricaded the road near the bridge. The Devil Bug imposter, which appeared to be a Devil Ant, trundled to a stop but didn't approach the barricade.

A grumble escaped Bohden as he observed it over Daumantas' shoulder.

"To everyone else, that looks like a Bug," Daumantas said, pointing at the imposter. "What do you see?"

He glanced at Bohden, who squinted into the distance. "Looks like a battle wagon to me." His face was serious. "Like the kind designed to carry hand cannoneers."

Battle wagons would be tough to beat, but not as difficult as real Inferni. Daumantas had only seen cannons and Inferni while studying in Grendair. He hadn't noticed any cannons, hand cannons or otherwise, within the boyar's camp. The disguised wagons full of hand cannoneers gave their adversary a distinct advantage. But where did they come from? Grendair didn't export the technology, and the Sultanate had only just started manufacturing their own versions over the last thirty years or so. But the boyars had Daumantas, Kanat, and Lyazzat, and together, the three of them were more than capable of handling the wagons.

Funneling the small detachment in waves, they made their way towards the barricade. An officer wearing fine breastplate trotted to meet them with a smart salute. "You must be the Farizhniyan they told me about," he said. "Can you really defeat that Devil Bug?"

Daumantas smirked and waved for the captain to follow him to the barricade.

Kanat separated himself from the group of Vodomerians to trot alongside Daumantas. "So, these imposter Inferni are just wagons?"

"They're still dangerous, but a weapon of this age and not the last." Daumantas pulled an arrow from his quiver and took aim at the false Inferni in front of him. Now that he was much closer, he could tell the Devil Ant was an illusion.

"Don't break the enchantment yet!" Kanat hissed.

Daumantas sighed and lowered his bow.

Taking a fine lens and small hand-bound notebook from his bag, Kanat observed the magically disguised wagon for several minutes while furiously taking notes. "Alright, you can break the enchantment…now." He tucked the items back into his bag and became preoccupied with some other baubles.

Daumantas took aim, hummed until he felt the energy flow within him, and let an arrow fly before Kanat could change his mind. His arrow struck true, and the enchantment wobbled unnaturally before evaporating, revealing the mundane wagon. The men behind the barricade gasped and talked among themselves with shock and excitement.

Daumantas turned to the captain. "We need to take that wagon before they can get back to the main gate!"

"I can take care of it!" Before Daumantas could argue, Kanat produced a crystal on a chain and murmured an incantation to himself. "There are multiple wagons bearing the same enchantment, and I can hit them all at once!"

One of the Vodomerians cried out and sprinted towards the

guardhouse by the bridge. Realizing their cover was blown, the battle wagon lumbered towards the barricade. Blasts from hand cannons sent shots whizzing dangerously through the air.

The men near Kanat and Daumantas, including the captain, retreated from them and the sight of obvious magic. Some men tried to return fire on the wagon, shooting arrows through gaps in the barricade while giving Kanat a wide berth. The wind kicked up, clouds gathered, and Kanat's crystal crackled and glowed. Raising a hand to the sky, Kanat brought it down and pointed at the wagon.

A thick bolt of lightning struck the wagon, blowing the roof apart and setting it alight. The men inside scrambled for safety. The burning wagon eventually ignited the gunpowder inside and exploded. Rolling thunder and rapid cracks of lightning rolled through the sky, sending the remaining men on both sides of the barricade scrambling for cover.

"You fool!" Daumantas grabbed Kanat by the arm and hauled him bodily towards the guardhouse at the Pauper's Bridge.

"This was much easier than fighting them individually!" Kanat tried to justify himself while torrential rain fell and blinded them both.

Using the cobbled road to guide them in the driving rain, Daumantas managed to steer them through the fortifications to the guard house at the south side of the Pauper's Bridge. The covered bridge was thick with men attempting to escape the storm, while those who weren't as frightened formed a wall to keep Daumantas and Kanat from going any further.

The captain pushed himself to the front. "You can't bring that sorcerer over here!" He waved frantically for them to leave.

Daumantas continued to push forward, using his size to his advantage. "This sorcerer saved you a lot of time, though it's not the strategy I would have chosen."

Kanat gave a small, polite bow from where he stood at Daumantas' side. "There's a sorcerer working for the men who now hold Triadoara captive. You can't hope to fight such a person with steel alone."

The driving rain muffled the world around them for a few long, tense moments. The captain's countenance softened, but he remained wary.

"We need to mobilize the main force and take the road before the enemy does." Daumantas pointed at a scout he recognized from his own party. "I need you to go back over the ridge and tell the forces there to split in two and start moving—one part here and one part towards Market Town."

The man nodded and sprinted off into the rain.

Orest and Bohden waded through the huddled crowd towards him. "Should we still proceed to the church and take the tunnel?" Orest asked. His body shook slightly from being drenched in the rain, but the old man was fiercely determined to complete his mission, one way or another.

Daumantas thought for a moment. "I think we should. They were counting on those battle wagons to keep us at bay, and we have to take advantage of the moment in every way possible."

"We'll get moving as soon as the rain isn't blinding." Orest gave a salute and went to separate his men from the guardsmen who'd been holding the bridge.

Bohden lingered. "I'm worried about Cyril," he said simply, his brow furrowed.

The captain perked up. "Cyril Valentin?" he asked, laying a hand on Daumantas' shoulder.

Daumantas nodded. "He and Tymor are at the southern gate with Boyar Ionia Voinescu."

A murmur rippled through the guardsmen at the mention of Tymor Valentin.

The captain smiled. "I knew Cyril as a young man!" he exclaimed. "I haven't seen him since he left for Vuretsiv. And Tymor is also alive as well? That's great news!" He shouted for his men to gather round. "We need to help these men protect Boyar Valentin and his son, Cyril. If they give an order, you are to follow it without question!" The captain turned back to Daumantas. "Your man Orest is headed for the old church to the tunnel into the city, I take it?"

Daumantas nodded slowly, a bit stunned at his turn of good fortune.

"We passed through there to escape the city," the captain said. "It's become a bit treacherous, but I can help lead your men safely through."

Smiling, Daumantas slapped the captain on the shoulder. "Fantastic! What is your name, good sir?"

The captain smiled. "It's Pyotr." They shook hands before he walked over to Orest.

Daumantas turned his attention back to Bohden and Kanat. "We have to get to the south gate, and now!"

He began walking without waiting for a response. Bohden followed, hefting his long-handled war hammer. Kanat hesitated but quickly fell in step with Daumantas.

"What's the plan?" Kanat asked as they stepped back into the heavy rain.

"We don't want the enemy taking Tymor or Cyril hostage," Daumantas said. "That's our only goal at the moment."

Visibility was still poor, but the sheeting rain would hide their approach long enough for them to take the enemy by surprise.

"Try to keep up, Kanat!" Daumantas called. Bohden easily matched Daumantas' speed as he sprinted through the rain, his expression grim while he jogged past the barricade and the ruined battle wagon.

Kanat struggled with his footing, but otherwise matched their pace. "I practice my forms every day, same as you!" he shouted back at Daumantas from where he jogged at his elbow.

Daumantas took a deep breath and unsheathed his sword. Even through the rain, he could hear the chaos; the men who should have been parlaying were now fighting a messy skirmish. As they came upon the dark-liveried soldiers of the former Boyar Zhupensken, Bohden rushed forward with a roar and knocked a man clean off his feet with one swing of his hammer.

Boyar Voinescu's troops were holding their own against Zhupensken's forces so far. Daumantas cut his way through the mob, searching for Cyril. Circling around men already locked in combat, he charged a line of archers who were attempting to fire into the ranks of Voinescu's troops. Kanat unfurled a chain whip from his belt, calmly beating back the soldiers attempting to assail him.

Their lines broke as Daumantas rushed into them, cutting several down before they could run. He stopped dead when he spotted a familiar face that made his blood run cold. Some of Zhupensken's forces broke away, following a slim, raven-haired man retreating with them. Daumantas knew it to be his former friend Laurent, who smiled and waved at him while he calmly trotted towards the south gate to safety.

A blade rushing towards his face pulled Daumantas back from his bittersweet memories and into the present battle. He narrowly deflected the blade and kicked the man aside. Some of the Zhupensken forces melted away, following Laurent's retreat. Others allied with Ruslan fought fiercely against the opposing forces commanded by Boyar Voinescu. Daumantas fought brutally, using his blade, feet, and fists to part the men who stood between him and Cyril.

The enemy began to simply flee at the sight of him, and as the Zhupensken forces retreated, Daumantas saw Cyril locked in a heated fight with a stern-faced blond man. He ran towards them, but a gesture from Cyril stopped him dead.

"Keep Tymor safe!" Cyril shouted at Daumantas while dodging a lunge from his opponent. "How dare you try to kill my family!" he shouted while he parried cuts from the man Daumantas assumed to be Ruslan.

"It never had to be this way!" Ruslan shouted back. "I only wanted to save you!"

Daumantas tried to ignore the fight as he skirted around it to aid Tymor. Despite his age, he held his own; Tymor had struck down several other men, and their bodies lay strewn around him where he fought. But the former Voivode was injured and now struggling to fight off several opponents.

The man closest to Daumantas went down quickly; the soldier couldn't bring his blade up fast enough to parry, and Daumantas' blade caught him in the bicep. Before his opponent's blade could even hit the ground, Daumantas ran him through. Tymor dispatched the second man with a quick thrust to his chest. The third man broke and ran towards the gates of Triadoara to join those fleeing with Laurent.

Tymor opened his mouth to thank him, but Daumantas was already moving to tend to his wounds. A nasty cut seeped blood on one of Tymor's arms, and without asking, he ripped the sleeve right off Tymor's tunic and used it to bandage his wound.

"You need to get to safety," Daumantas told him as he tried to herd Tymor away from the skirmish.

"I can't leave Cyril!" he insisted, pushing back on Daumantas' large frame.

The rain had tapered off to a light drizzle, and most of Zhupenken's troops had either fallen or fled with Laurent. A handful of people, Tymor and Daumantas included, now bore witness to the savage duel taking place between Cyril and Ruslan. Blades whistled through the air and insults flew from their lips as years of simmering anger boiled over within both men.

"How dare you try to kill my family!" Renewed anger flared within Cyril, and he lashed out at Ruslan, forcing him to defend.

"It never had to be this way!" Ruslan shouted back. "I only wanted to save you!" They broke, circling slowly around one another.

Anger mingled with despair in Cyril's heart. "I thought we were friends! We used to do everything together!" Cyril lamented, holding out a hand pleadingly. "Why can't you accept me the way I am?"

"I loved you the way you *were*. Strong and beautiful. You were like a rose made of steel!"

"I'm not a real man to you, am I?" Cyril asked quietly.

"You are not."

The words cut the last pity and hope Cyril had for Ruslan out of his heart. The battle around them subsided along with the rain, and Cyril was painfully aware that all eyes were on them. With a smile,

Ruslan launched himself at Cyril once again. Baffled, Cyril fought hard to ward off Ruslan's primal assault. Too late, Cyril realized why—his blade had developed a bad chip. With a strange twang, the blade broke under Ruslan's fierce blows.

Ruslan's sword slipped past Cyril's broken blade and bit deep into his thigh. His triumph was short-lived as Cyril's dagger punched deep into his throat. Ruslan stumbled back, clutching at the dagger protruding from his neck. Fear and pain distorted his features, and a river of blood gushed from the ugly wound. Ruslan opened his mouth to speak, and blood poured from it instead of words. Life faded from his eyes, and he fell face-first onto the cobbles.

With a cry, Cyril collapsed along with Ruslan. The crowd rushed to aid him as darkness pressed in at the corners of his vision. Cyril fought to control his breathing while unknown hands touched him, examining his wound.

"Don't remove the blade from the wound!" Daumantas shouted as he pushed to Cyril's side. He whimpered at the sight of the blade lodged in Cyril's flesh.

Cyril laid a hand on his lover's trembling arm. Daumantas gazed upon him, his eyes filled with tears.

Still shaking, Daumantas swiftly tied a tourniquet around Cyril's leg. He howled and writhed as the ogre removed Ruslan's blade from his flesh. People within the crowd shouted for a healer.

Daumantas wept over the wound. "I can't…I'm too exhausted to heal you!" His big shoulders shook as he sobbed.

"Daumantas." Cyril squeezed his arm. "I love you."

Daumantas laid his hand on Cyril's and gave it a squeeze. "I love you, too." He managed. Cyril felt oddly calm. He wasn't sure if he would die; but if he did, he had the comfort of knowing everyone he cared about was safe. Exhaustion pressed on him, and he closed his eyes.

———

Daumantas panicked as Cyril's eyes rolled back, and he fell unconscious. The duel now finished, Laurent and his retinue cautiously approached the united Vodomerian forces.

"Let me heal him," someone said.

Laurent stood over Cyril and Daumantas with his arms raised. "In exchange for saving this man's life," Laurent said, "I would like the Zhupensken fief ceded to me and for my forces to be allowed to leave this place unmolested."

Daumantas glanced around at his companions, who regarded Laurent with deep suspicion. The setting sun broke free of the clouds, washing the scene in warm light and long shadows.

Tymor collapsed to his knees. "My son! Please!" He pleaded with Ionia. "Hadeon was the last of his line—and a bastard besides! Give the man what he wants and let us be done with this!"

With a grimace, Ionia unfolded her arms and gave a slight bow towards Laurent. "We will honor your request."

Laurent returned her bow and kneeled at Cyril's side. "This wound looks worse than it is." He locked eyes with Daumantas, his blue eyes made the ogre's stomach twist uncomfortably. "The tourniquet saved his life, but he'd most certainly lose this leg without any more intervention."

Chanting in a low voice, he placed his hand on either side of the wound. Cyril cried out as the flesh stitched itself back together, and Laurent worked the wound closed as if Cyril's flesh were clay between his hands.

"Know that I do not wish to pursue the overthrow of the Voivo-date," Laurent stood and addressed the crowd, his face calm and white as alabaster. "I hope for good relations with the rest of Vodomeria, starting with your new Voivode when they are chosen."

With Cyril healed, Laurent bowed low and walked away, joining a steady stream of people once loyal to Hadeon Zhupensken who now headed west and away from Triadoara.

Twenty

WHILE NO EXTENSIVE damage had been done to the city at large, the same could not be said for the royal palace. The larder and treasury had been ransacked, along with Tymor's personal items and those of fellow boyars who'd been visiting for the feast of Saint Vodomor just weeks before.

Tymor took it upon himself to put the palace back in order while the other boyars worked to restore peace within the city proper. Abandoned caches of looted items were found all over the city, and it was going to take some time to sort through and return everything to its rightful owners.

Most everyone fled the palace when Hadeon Zhupensken instituted himself as Vodomeria's interim ruler, and Tymor found himself sifting through wrecked furniture and other messes by himself for large parts of the day. He honestly didn't mind the work. It gave him time to consider how he was going to conduct himself going forward.

Tired from the day's hard labor, Tymor took the evening to visit Cyril. "May I come in?" he asked as he gently rapped on Cyril's chamber door.

Daumantas opened the door and welcomed him inside.

Cyril sat in bed, clearly disgruntled at being made to rest. He looked childish dressed in only a tunic. His legs dangled off the side of the bed, kicking restlessly.

"How are you feeling?" Tymor asked him with a smile.

Cyril grunted. "I have strength enough to work."

Daumantas scoffed. "You lost a lot of blood and need rest."

Cyril grumbled further but remained seated. Tymor placed his hand gently on Cyril's injured thigh. According to Daumantas, Laurent's magic had sealed the wound, but it was not fully healed.

"There will be plenty of time for work once you are well." Tymor patted Cyril's leg gently before sitting beside him.

Seeing his son awake gave him great relief after those frightening moments the previous evening. Tymor's own injuries, though minor, also sapped his energy. Milena would probably give him the same treatment once he returned to his chambers.

"Do you plan to put yourself back before the council?" Cyril asked.

The question confused Tymor. "How do you mean?"

"I mean," Cyril responded, "do you want to try and be re-elected as Voivode?"

Tymor gazed deep into his son's gray eyes, contemplating his answer. Cyril's face could have been his own, twenty years ago.

Tymor shook his head. "I haven't decided just yet," he mumbled, staring at his feet. "I want Vodomeria to be ruled by someone less self-serving than myself, I think."

Cyril nodded and turned his attention to Daumantas. "You should tell my father about Laurent." Cyril's gaze was hard on his lover. The ogre shrunk under Cyril's scrutiny.

Daumantas sighed and closed the book he'd been reading. "Laurent is a copy," he said, "There used to be a lot of copies. Apparently, this is something the Mad Sorcerer King did using ancient Finndrigairian magic before his death."

Tymor tried not to laugh. "How does a man copy himself?"

His incredulous tone made Daumantas pinch the bridge of his nose. "Please, it's very complicated." Daumantas tried to hide his irritation. "But this Laurent is different from the one you fought some years prior. I... know this one. He claims to be different from the others."

They sat in awkward silence for several long moments. A thousand questions ran through Tymor's mind; first and foremost being "How is this possible?" But he pushed his disbelief to the side.

"How *exactly* do you know him?" he pressed.

Daumamtas groaned, covering his face. "We were..." He trailed off, speaking from behind his hands.

"Tell him," Cyril commanded, jabbing a finger at his lover for emphasis.

Daumantas groaned and threw his arms wide as if pleading for forgiveness. "He was my tutor… and a friend once!" he exclaimed with a pained expression. "Though being my tutor and confidant was just a ruse on his part. In short, he used me to get access to Grendairan archives while I was studying there. I was young and... impressionable." The big ogre slumped further into his chair.

"Most of the other copies are trapped in Finndrigail Tor, at the heart of the Cursed Empire," Cyril continued where Daumantas left off, sympathy painted his features. "These copies of Laurent cannot control the Inferni, and it seems our Laurent is looking for a way to disable them."

This all felt too fantastical to be true, but Tymor had now seen two Laurents with his own eyes. He thanked Daumantas for his honesty and took his leave, the revelations weighing on his mind.

Tymor returned to his chambers and allowed Milena to fuss over him. She dutifully cleaned and re-bandaged his more severe wounds while making sure he ate a good meal. He happily allowed himself to be put to bed, sleeping soundly until the next morn.

The next day, Tymor spent most of the morning welcoming returning servants and organizing further cleaning efforts until Ionia came to him. She'd exchanged her armor for a highly refined gown.

"It's time for you to address the boyar's council," she said, beckoning Tymor to join her.

He took a deep breath before turning to follow. Tymor and Ionia walked side by side towards the council chamber. They exchanged no words as they entered together.

It was a humble room with a sunken speaking pit. Rows of chairs were built into the walls around the speaking pit for the boyars with the largest fiefs. The floor above was a gallery for minor nobles, guild heads, and other non-landed wealthy people. The nave was crowned with two seats reserved for the Matriarch and Patriarch of the Church of All Saints, who acted as impartial observers for major votes held by the council.

Ionia took her seat and gestured for Tymor to step onto the speaking floor. The Patriarch of the church stood. His aged frame remained stooped as he shuffled to the edge of the floor. "The council has lost confidence in your ability to rule but does not wish to deny you the right to keep your place as voivode," He addressed Tymor with a clear, if slightly wobbly, voice. "Do you; Tymor Valentin, wish to seek re-election?"

A thousand answers ran through his head.

"No, your grace." Tymor answered clearly. The attending council showed no surprise, though a few did lean this way and that to whisper to one another.

"Very well. Please take a seat so we may commence election proceedings." The Patriarch smiled and returned to his seat.

Tymor bowed to the Matriarch and Patriarch and took one of the seats beside Milena that were reserved for House Valentin in the lower part of the chamber. Glancing above, he spotted Cyril, Daumantas, and Orest in the upper gallery.

The Matriarch now stepped forward. She rapped her staff on the floor to silence the room. "Who here is worthy to be our next Voivode? Step forward and speak their name."

Several boyars stepped forward and spoke their own names. Petru Novadi stepped forward. Many expected Petru to speak his name, or, perhaps, that of his son, Dimitru.

"Cyril Valentin," he said instead. A murmur rippled through the assembled crowd as he took his seat. Ionia followed, declaring the same. A boyar Tymor didn't know well followed suit, also with Cyril's name.

Tymor had not planned on declaring a name, but he also stood and spoke Cyril's. He glanced up into the gallery where his son's shocked faced stared down at him before he returned to his seat.

———

Cyril stood in the gallery with his mouth hanging open. No more boyars stepped forward to declare names. Daumantas squeezed his shoulder, and Cyril snapped his mouth shut. "*Did you know about this*?" he hissed at the large ogre.

Daumantas shook his head, but a small smile played on his lips.

"Did *you*?" Cyril leaned into Orest, who grinned in response. "I talked it over briefly with Ionia," the old man said quietly.

The Matriarch rapped her staff on the floor once more. "If there are no more names to declare, we shall adjourn this meeting and commence voting tomorrow morning."

The congregation spilled out of the chamber. Most re-assembled in the palace courtyard. They mulled around, with some potential candidates working the crowd. Others stood and discussed the benefits and drawbacks of the various people proposed as the next Voivode.

Interested parties crowded around him as Cyril limped into the courtyard, aided by Daumantas. Some came over to him to simply voice their support for his candidacy. Others had questions. How did he plan to catch up on current events in the Voivodate? Could he be trusted to handle Laurent? Did he plan to use military action against the man, or would he take a diplomatic approach?

"Please! We haven't even voted yet!" Cyril pulled on Daumantas, who steered them free of the crowd. The big ogre made it clear no one was to follow as they ducked into the main building. "There's a small private chapel near the great hall," Cyril told Daumantas. "Let's go there until this crowd thins."

Cyril limped as fast as he dared while steering Daumantas through the palace. A decorated threshold marked the room they sought, and they both happily ducked inside. Seemingly untouched by Zhupensken's marauding forces, all the diminutive chapel's devotional accoutrements remained untouched.

The space was big enough for a half dozen people at best. It had two benches built into the walls with a shrine set across from the door. It had only one window set high in the wall above the shrine. Cyril pulled Daumantas into one of the plush cushioned benches to sit with him.

"Are you feeling well?" Daumantas asked as he wrapped his arms around Cyril reassuringly.

"I don't know how I feel about all of this." His hands dug into Daumantas' silken robe.

One of Daumantas' big hands slipped under his chin and tilted his face so their eyes met. "What happens if you don't want to be Voivode?" he asked calmly.

Cyril felt himself being pulled into Daumantas' calm gaze. "I can refuse," he answered. "The title of Voivode would then be awarded to whomever garners the next most votes. The remaining candidates may also choose amongst themselves who will be the next Voivode—" He scratched at his chin, contemplating the possibilities.

They sat and quietly held one another for what felt like a long time within the small chapel. Cyril debated the merits of sneaking out of Triadoara before voting commenced. He couldn't accept the title if he wasn't in town, after all.

Tired of hiding, Cyril decided to brave the halls and hurried with Daumantas back to his room. The chamber offered a welcome respite from the now bustling palace halls. He remained there the rest of the afternoon, evening, and well into the next day, until the bells began to ring, summoning them back to the council chamber.

Two priests stood on either side of the doors, handing tokens to those entering the chamber.

Cyril stood back, observing the crowd. "Is this everyone in the palace?" he wondered aloud.

The crowd entering was much more diverse than the aristocracy and wealthy folk that had attended yesterday's proceedings. Most of the crowd focused on getting their token and casting their votes, but one man rushed through the crowd to greet them.

"Pyotr!" Daumantas smiled and greeted the shaggy-haired guardsman.

"Daumantas and Cyril!" Pyotr laughed and clapped Cyril on the shoulder. "I haven't seen you since we were lads!"

Cyril looked deep into Pyotr's face and smiled. "You became a guardsman!" Cyril laughed and embraced his old friend, then explained to Daumantas, "Pyotr was my guide to Triadoara when I was young. We used to get into so much trouble together!" The two old friends laughed for a moment, before becoming more serious.

"They're allowing anyone who fought in the battle to vote!" Pyotr declared as they began to work their way towards the door once more. "All of the servants who returned to help put the palace back together, too! The boyars seemed to feel it only fair."

Cyril nodded. "Perhaps we can include all citizens the next time we pick a Voivode," he mused aloud.

They stood solemnly in line until it was their turn to cast their votes. The humble room now had a screen within the speaking pit. Behind it were crates with cloth covers. Each canvas cover had the name of the candidate's name written on it and a hole for the voting token. Cyril took a few moments to contemplate his options and tossed his token into a crate for another boyar before limping away with the assistance of a priest.

The rest of the day passed by Cyril in a blur. Friends and family and well-wishers came to find him and talk about the election. Cyril's brother, Symon, begged him to stay in Vodomeria and teach him swordsmanship. He eventually retired to the bedchamber he'd been given to escape all the attention. Daumantas joined him, reading quietly in a corner by himself.

Cyril spent most of the following day resting in his chamber. As much as he loathed to admit it, his body needed it, and the excitement surrounding the election had taken a great deal of his energy. Daumantas dutifully brought him all his meals and more foods besides, encouraging him to eat so his body could more quickly replenish his lost blood. Rapping at the door disturbed their afternoon of quiet reading.

Dan stood at the door a bit awkwardly with Iuliana and Bohden. "I wanted to, ah, give you something before we left."

The trio shuffled in. Dan held out a finely crafted cane.

"You made this?" Cyril stared at it in wonder. The freshly carved wood had been smoothed and wrapped in bands of familiar-looking steel.

"The healing monk we were traveling with—Gavril, I think?—said it would be a while before you'd be able to use your leg like before." Dan shrugged and rubbed the back of his neck as he talked. "I wanted you to be able to keep your father's blade, so I recycled it. It had this nice etching, and it made a fine handle and decorative inlay."

Leaning his weight on it, Cyril used the cane to do a lap around the room. He turned back to Dan with a grin. "Thank you so much!" He clasped one of Dan's big, rough hands. To his surprise, Dan smiled.

Bohden gently laid a bundle on the table. "I kept the hilt. Dan didn't know what to do with it, and I thought you should have it back."

Cyril picked up the remains of his once trusty blade. He shook his head, turning the hilt over in his hands. "If it hadn't broken, I'm not actually sure if I would have won that duel," Cyril said, half to himself.

Iuliana pushed herself forward through her burly companions. "I plan on staying here in Triadoara," she announced, placing her hands on her hips, "If you ever need a sympathetic ear, you can always come calling!"

Cyril turned to reply when Orest let himself in.

"Come on, son!" the old man beckoned. "They're about to announce the results of the election!"

They all hurried together to the council chamber. A large crowd had gathered, and bells rang all over Triadoara. Cyril was grateful for the cane; it allowed him to move much more swiftly through the throngs and into the building.

The Matriarch and Patriarch of the church stood in front of their seats, waiting for the crowd to settle. On either side stood the heads of the priestly orders of all the Saints. The Matriarch held her wrinkled hands aloft, and the room fell silent.

"We have tallied and certified the votes for Vodomeria's new Voivode." The Matriarch pitched her thin voice into the rafters. "All here have observed the tallies and can attest to their accuracy." The rows of attending priests bowed in unison.

The Patriarch stepped forward. "The person to be awarded the most votes…" He took a breath, and the room leaned in. "…is Cyril Valentin, a Keeper of the Peace of Ford Town!"

Applause and cheers erupted in the room. Cyril was practically pushed onto the speaking floor before the Matriarch and Patriarch by the crowd.

"What say you, Cyril Valentin? Do you accept this honor bestowed upon you by your peers?" The old priest's eyes glittered under his heavy vestments.

Cyril took a deep breath. Being voivode would mean acknowledging his heritage, and officially returning as The Steel Rose of Vodomeria. Returning as his father's son. Returning to his family, and to court life and all its tedium. But *he* would get to choose this time. He looked to Daumantas, who smiled and mouthed, *"I love you."*.

Mouthing it back to his lover, he took a deep breath and addressed the waiting crowds. "I do."

Acknowledgments

I took the leap into longform writing during the pandemic, like so many people who discovered new hobbies over the last four years or so. Comics are my first love but making comics by myself proved too burdensome. While the initial drafting was very much a solo process, I realized I'd need a plethora of helpers to get this first book finished.

First, Parker, Karim and Ash stepped up to give vital Alpha and Beta reader feedback. Along with providing quality editing, Gabriel Hargrave has also given a great deal of emotional support. Michael and Michael (Yes, TWO different Micheals!) helped cover some expenses while also giving encouragement, along with Katherine, Bennett, Jason and a plethora of others who stopped to voice encouragement or give advice.

Last but not least, my loving husband Avery has put up with every crisis of confidence and helped keep me on the path to publication. Without him, this book would not be what it is.

I'd also like to give special thanks to Chuck Tingle, whose mantra 'prove love is real everyday' has kept me going these last couple of years. His trot through the timeline has given me a lot of energy and helped me find the courage to prove love is real in my own way. Thank you.

About the Author

T.G. Joye is a man of many faces. Born a little girl who yearned to be an adventurer, he mostly found adventures in books. Now a grown man, (yes, some girls grow up to be men later,) his adventures mostly consist of exploring cities along the United States Eastern Seaboard and attending various conventions. While he's not fond of showing his face, he is fond of talking about animals, manga, and his enduring love for stories about misfits and underdogs. A hunger for protagonists more like himself drove him to start writing books featuring queer and transgender characters. He currently resides in North Carolina with his husband and two cats.